Nina and John checked into the hotel and were taken to a lovely suite of rooms with its own balcony. While John tipped the bellman, Nina had wandered around the room in awe at its luxurious appointments. She opened the doors to the balcony and walked out to see the view. She was transfixed by the beauty she could only glimpse, already fascinated by the sound of the ocean splashing far below. The balmy night air was enthralling her; she shivered a little as she grew more excited about the next few days. John stepped out behind her, wrapping his arms around her to keep her warm. "Are you cold, baby?"

Nina turned so she could see his face before resting on his broad chest. "I'm thrilled, I'm not cold. This place is beautiful, John, it's just wonderful. Thank you so much," she said with a soft sigh.

She cried out in surprise when John suddenly picked her up and looked her right in the eye. "Stop thanking me. This is for me just as much as it is for you. I don't want thanks, I want love," he growled.

Nina showed all of her perfectly straight dazzling white teeth in a smile of delight. Wrapping her legs around John's waist she took his earlobe in her mouth and sucked on it gently, ending in a mock nibble. She continued to lick his ear and whispered, "Mmm, if you want love I know where you can get some, right now."

John tightened his arms around her and returned to the bedroom at once. "Now you're talking, baby." He placed her on the bed and sprawled next to her. "So what's your choice, this great big bed or that great big Jacuzzi?"

A FOOL FOR YOU

MELANIE SCHUSTER

To Stacy
I hope you enjoy!
Stay Blessed,
Love,
Melanie

BET BOOKS

BET Publications, LLC
http://www.bet.com
http://www.arabesquebooks.com

ARABESQUE BOOKS are published by

BET Publications, LLC
c/o BET Books
One BET Plaza
1900 W Place NE
Washington, DC 20018-1211

ISBN: 1-58314-566-4

First Printing: September 2005

10 9 8 7 6 5 4 3 2 1

Printed in the United States of America

Dedicated to Betty Dowdell,
a lovely lady of style, grace, courage and substance.
Everyone should have a friend like Betty.
You're a real blessing in my life.

And to the most wonderful young ladies I know:
My fantastic nieces,
Amariee, Jilleyin and Jasmine.
And to the fabulous Ali girls,
Kaneena, Karima, Tahara,
Riahanah and Amira
You give me hope for the future.

In memory of two amazing women,
Ruby Lee Moore
and
Daisy Williams.

Acknowledgments

To all the delightful readers who have graced my website and my chat group, thanks for all the friendship, laughter, encouragement, and support. You all make me smile every day.

A very special thank-you to Kicheko Driggins for making my book cover so beautiful. And my heartfelt thanks to my patient and thorough editor, Demetria Lucas, for all your hard work; I couldn't have done it without you.

As always, thanks to my wonderful family for putting up with me when I'm working on a deadline.

To all the aspiring writers I've met and tried to encourage, please keep writing because I'm living proof that your aspirations can become realities.

And of course thank you to Jamil, who continues to make me feel like the brightest star of the rarest constellation in a fantastic universe.

Prologue

The intense blue sky created the perfect ambiance for the outdoor wedding reception of Adam Bennett Cochran and his bride, Alicia Fuentes. The guests thronging the infield at Comerica Park, the stadium home of the Detroit Tigers, were alight with anticipation as the wedding party made its entrance to the happy sound of "The Bright Side of the Road" by Van Morrison. Everyone who mattered to Adam and Alicia participated in the wedding; her sister Marielle and her best friend Roxy Fairchild were the matron and maid of honor, and her new sisters-in-law, Renee, Tina and Faye Cochran were bridesmaids, as well as Benita Cochran Deveraux, Adam's only sister. Her newest friend, Nina, was the last bridesmaid. And all Adam's brothers had stood up with him, too. He actually had two best men, his brother Adonis and his newest brother, John Flores.

John was the long unclaimed son of Big Benny Cochran, the son no one knew about until a few months earlier. Now he felt like one of the family. Even though he'd been raised by adoptive parents out in California and had just discovered his true roots, John accepted the people around him to be his new family, especially since Adam had saved his life. John had been suffering from a liver ailment that would have killed him without a transplant from a closely matched donor. And thanks to a minor miracle, he'd gotten that transplant from his new brother.

As the wedding party was seated at the head table, John looked down a few seats to stare at his other special miracle, Miss Parker. Her name was really Nina Whitney; "Miss Parker" was just his crazy nickname for her. She was the ghostwriter his publisher had assigned to him, but during the time they worked together she'd become indispensable to John. She was much more than a writer; she was like his assistant, his confidante and his friend. And she was also the one who really saved his life by daring to ask Adam Cochran to give John part of his liver. John couldn't bring himself to ask, given that he'd just met the family, but Nina wasn't shy at all about going to Adam and asking for his help. Yes, Nina was truly his guardian angel. She'd saved his life and now that life belonged to her, whether she wanted it or not.

Just then, their eyes met. Nina was seated between Alicia's big handsome brothers and was receiving avid attention from both of them. She was laughing at something one of them said when she suddenly looked at John, her long-lashed golden brown eyes flashing with merriment and her fantastic dimples on full display. John felt an odd sensation come over him, a combination of extreme heat coupled with something like an icy finger running down his spine. He couldn't stop looking at her; it was as though everyone else in the huge stadium vanished and he was alone with Nina. The brief enchantment was broken when one of her seat mates whispered something in her ear, something that made her giggle like a little girl.

John's thick eyebrows came together in a look all his brothers recognized at once, the look of a possessive Cochran male. While John reached for a glass of water to cool the sudden rage that overtook him, the most practical of his new brothers started making bets.

"I'm thinking six months or less. Our boy doesn't look like he can hold out too much longer than that," Alan said sagely.

Andre, his identical twin, shook his head and disagreed. "That girl is gonna give him a serious run for his money. If he lands her in twelve months, I'll be surprised."

They looked at John, still glowering from his seat near the bride and groom, to Nina, who was basking in the flirtatious attention of Raphael and Carlos Fuentes. They looked at each other and grinned.

"Put up or shut up, bro. He's going to make a big fool out of himself before he lands that one. She's *tough*," Andre said in a voice full of admiration.

Alan extended his hand to his twin. "Shake on it, man. Double or nothing if they hook up before the six months are up."

"Done."

Their wagers made, they turned their attention to the sumptuous feast being served. Bet or no bet, there wasn't a Cochran man in history who would miss a meal.

Chapter 1

Nina's eyes widened in amazement as she looked from one Fuentes brother to the other. She'd never seen two men eat as much as Alicia's brothers, and playfully she told them so. "I've never seen two heartier appetites in my life," she admitted with a smile. It was true; the meal that consisted of both Southern and Cuban specialties had disappeared off their plates fast. They'd eaten smoked brisket, ribs, grilled chicken, potato salad, greens, *empanadas, arroz con pollo* and *ropa veijo* in less time than it took to talk about it and came up for air smiling. Several times, in fact, as the waiters kept bringing them fresh plates whenever they finished a serving.

Raphael, the younger of the two men, leaned back and smiled at Nina. "We're growing boys, *querida*. We have to keep our strength up so we can keep the very nice salaries we earn in this place." He flexed a massive arm as she remembered that the brothers were members of the Detroit Tigers and they did indeed earn their living playing baseball in Comerica Park.

Carlos leaned forward and agreed. "Athletes have a higher metabolism than most folks, you know that. Food is like fuel to us. It gives us the energy we need for other activities," he said with a suggestive grin.

Nina's customary aplomb wavered a bit as she looked

at the masculine man smiling down at her with unmistakable interest. "Other activities?" she murmured.

Carlos leaned in even closer. "Yes, *chica*. Like dancing. You like to dance, don't you?"

The flush in Nina's face was his only answer as Alicia's Aunt Gigi took the microphone to announce that Adam and Alicia were about to have their first dance as a married couple. All eyes turned to the dance floor as Adam escorted Alicia to its very center. He took both her hands in his and kissed them before sliding his big hands around her small, taut waist. He nodded to the legendary Bump Williams, the world famous jazz pianist who was an old friend of the family. He'd brought his band to play for the wedding as he did for all weddings of the Cochrans and Deverauxes. The song Adam and Alicia had chosen for their first dance was "We Will Find a Way." Performed by the legendary Ceylon Simmons Deveraux and Vera Deveraux, the simple words of the song took on a deeper, more textured meaning. Alicia and Adam looked into each other's eyes with a passion that burned so brightly it touched the hearts of all who saw them. And when he suddenly picked her up and spun her around, holding her as though he could never let her go, all the women in attendance sighed with pleasure.

All except for Nina, who had to exercise extreme control to keep her eyes from rolling and her lips from twisting into a grimace. *These Cochrans are nice, but they're the sappiest people I ever met in my life.* She was instantly ashamed of herself for thinking such a thing but she didn't have time to brood; all the Cochran brothers were now joining the couple on the dance floor with their wives and the sighs and coos from the guests multiplied. *Okay, this looks like a good time to get a drink.* Nina was about to make her move when she was suddenly pulled onto the dance floor, caught up in John's strong arms. Her eyes grew wide and she had to compress her lips to keep a sound of surprise from escaping. Only the look of amusement in John's eyes kept her from showing her shock. It was obvious he'd get a huge kick out of her discomfort, so she turned on the deep freeze, something at which she was very skilled. She refused to look at him; she just allowed him to turn her around the dance floor.

"You're supposed to be dancing with the maid of honor," she said tightly.

"Says who? I'm supposed to be dancing with someone special," John answered.

Nina blinked and looked into John's chest instead of his eyes. "Boy, have you got the wrong person," she said with grim amusement.

John pulled her even closer and put his lips against her ear. "You're more than special to me," he said softly.

Nina was trying her hardest to do what she did best, act aloof and disinterested. Unfortunately for Nina, the smell of John's cologne and the warmth of his body was enough to melt even the coldest of hearts, that being hers. Like an automaton she raised her eyes to his and stopped breathing. He wasn't smiling; he was looking at her with tender, intense eyes that seemed to see straight through to her soul. Without realizing she was doing it, Nina melted against him and allowed the emotions to grow, forgetting everything except how she felt at that very moment. Right then she felt nothing but wonderful, held so close to John she was sure he could feel every beat of her heart.

Suddenly the song was over, with everyone applauding and cheering. The music changed to a lively Latin number perfect for salsa dancing. Nina blessed the band from the very bottom of her heart for the rapid change in tempo because she was immediately claimed for a dance. Carlos Fuentes made good on his earlier comment and whirled her out of John's arms in a flash and they were dancing a spirited salsa with the panache born of long practice. Carlos grinned wickedly as he complimented her on her form. "*Chica*, I can see you've done this before," he teased. "And you're going to do it a lot more before this party's over."

Nina gave him a brilliant smile in return. "I can handle it, *Papi*. The question is, can *you* handle *me?*" The music drowned his laughter as the couple took the center of the dance floor and captured everyone's attention with their footwork.

The dancing continued with jazz and Latin music filling the air and everyone having a wonderful time, with the exception of John. For reasons he didn't want to examine too closely, he wasn't enjoying the reception at all. He simply couldn't take his eyes off Nina as she danced with partner after partner. Her beautiful chestnut skin was moist and dewy, her face was alight with pleasure and she was obviously having the time of her life. For once her hair wasn't confined in a lacquered updo that was her typical style; it was a mass of loose waves that came to her shoulders. Like the rest of the bridesmaids, she'd taken off her elegant champagne colored gown and put on something more suited to dancing. She was now wearing an off-the-shoulder dress in a brilliant shade of purple that would have looked horrible on a lot of women; on her it looked sexy and fun. The dress had a close fitting bodice and a short flaring skirt that showed her long legs to their best advantage, something that made John even glummer. This wasn't the same woman who'd accompanied him to Michigan, not by a long shot.

Both John and Nina were permanent residents of California, John in L.A. and Nina in Oakland. When they met out on the west coast, John had been less than impressed. John was one of the leading psychotherapists in the country, greatly sought after for teaching fellowships, lectures and the like. His innovative techniques and developments in the field were what led to a book offer from a major publisher. John finally agreed with the proviso he would have someone help him turn his theories and case studies into something readable. With his genius-level IQ, he knew perfectly well his writing skills weren't up to the task. Enter Nina Whitney, an extremely talented ghostwriter who could turn a grocery list into a stimulating read. Nina came to him with a long list of impressive qualifications and experience, and the personality of a dyspeptic wolverine. Social skills weren't anywhere on her resume.

John had to laugh to himself as he studied the glass of tonic water in his hand. Leaning back in his chair at one of the deserted tables, he watched Nina step dancing with what seemed to be an army of men, none of whom could stop looking at her legs. *And I thought they were too skinny. I need to have my eyes checked.* He fished the piece of lime out of his glass and chewed on it furiously as he watched her stepping like she'd invented the dance. It was true; his first impression of Nina was distinctly unfavorable.

She'd reported to his office at the UCLA medical center looking like a pipe cleaner in a designer suit. She'd been wearing an obviously expensive and expertly fitted navy blue ensemble, which made her resemble a skeleton dressed for church. She wore glasses too, severely styled designer frames that reminded John of the kind of mask people wore to fancy costume balls. From the sculpted mass of hard, shiny hair on the top of her head to the glistening pointy-toed pumps on her narrow feet, Nina was by far the most unappealing woman John could ever remember encountering. Her demeanor left a lot to be desired too; she seemed to be devoid of all personality and humor. All her utterings were delivered in a dry, deadpan voice that always managed to convey the impression that the recipient of that voice was being measured and found wanting. Nina had mastered the art of verbal intimidation; with a few words she could skewer the unsuspecting leaving them dazed and humbled.

A flash of purple caught John's eye as Nina passed his peripheral vision, doing what looked like the *lambada* or something equally forbidden with one of Alicia's brothers. John swallowed the last bit of the lime he'd been chewing, followed by a long swallow of tonic water. He was still frowning as he set the glass down on the table. He'd only discovered a few months ago that Nina, his Miss Parker, wasn't just an inhumanly efficient assistant, she was a sexy and appealing woman. And for some reason John just assumed that all that delicious femininity was being revealed just for him. The sight of her sharing even a small part of herself with other men was enraging him. The unexpected feelings of jealousy caused him something like pain as he watched her dancing like a siren out of a Snoop Dogg video. He muttered something savage in Spanish under his breath as the hips he once considered nonexistent rotated in a provocative move that earned an enthusiastic response from her partner. An amused voice at his elbow shook John out of his brooding reverie.

"No sense in sitting here grinding your teeth, son. If you want her so bad you'd better go get her."

John looked into the laugh-crinkled eyes of Big Benny Cochran, his biological father. Some people, mainly Nina, couldn't understand why John was so accepting of Big Benny. John hadn't lashed out at the man or denounced him in any way; instead he'd reacted to Benny's overtures with calm acceptance and even gratitude. John had explained to Nina that realizing he had a family gave him something to live for. It put an end to the solitary life he'd lived since his adoptive parents were killed in a car accident and ultimately the announcement gave him life. He was dying of primary sclerosing cholangitis until a perfect donor was found and that donor could have only been a blood relative. Nina tolerated Big Benny for John's sake but she wasn't a big fan of the man. John didn't share her opinion, however. He smiled gamely at his father and tried to pretend he didn't know what Big Benny was talking about.

"Hey, I didn't see you sit down," John apologized. "This was some wedding, wasn't it?"

Big Benny still looked amused. "Yes, it was a beauty. Even more beautiful since I didn't have to pay for the whole thing," he said with a chuckle. "But don't try and change the subject, son. I can tell you don't want your woman out there dancing with those other men so why don't you go get her instead of sitting here looking like you want to hurt somebody?"

John managed a sheepish grin, which was quickly replaced by a look of steely resolve. "Can you excuse me for a moment? I'll be right back, Dad."

He left the table so quickly he didn't see the look of shock that rolled across Big Benny's face, or the look of profound gratitude that followed it. It was the very first time John had referred to the man who'd given him life as "Dad."

Across the crowded dance floor, another couple was watching the festivities with great interest, but for other reasons. "There! He's going to get her right now, just watch and see," Paris Deveraux gloated.

Her table companion helped himself to the rest of her drink with a sound of disgust. "You're supposed to be putting together footage for the interview, not matchmaking. Keep your mind on your job, why don't you? Or better yet, your own social life?" Aidan Sinclair was the only person who could talk to Paris like that and live.

Paris was the first cousin of the Deveraux brothers who owned The Deveraux Group, an international media conglomerate. After finishing her internship, which rotated her through every department of the company, Paris finally had a permanent position. She'd expected to be assigned to one of the many publications of The Deveraux Group, instead her occasional presence as a special correspondent on one of their cable news shows made her a local star. To her own surprise she was now hosting a talk show earning astonishing ratings. The interview, which Aidan, her best friend and art director of the show, referred to, was one with John Flores and the Cochran family. The family saw no reason to try to hide the new relationship since the media had been buzzing about it for months. They decided to have one fully authorized interview and put an end to the speculation, and Paris had the honor of being the one to do it. It was an exclusive which Barbara Walters and other media giants would have killed for and it was all hers. She defended herself immediately to Aidan.

"I'm not matchmaking, for once. It's obvious they have feelings for each other, I'm just observing with the natural interest one takes in these matters," she said in what she hoped was a lofty and disinterested tone of voice. "I'm merely gathering information to make the interview process flow more smoothly."

The rude reply hovering on Aidan's lips was cut off as a shadow fell across their table. A deep voice addressed Paris with warm seduction.

"Excuse the interruption, but I think this is our dance, Paris."

Paris looked up into the smiling eyes of the man who'd

haunted her dreams for too long, Titus Argonne. She didn't hesitate, she put her hand into the one he held out and rose gracefully to her feet. "Yes, Titus, I think it is." They turned onto the dance floor and looked at each other with sincere pleasure as the music took them away in each other's arms.

Aidan flagged down a passing waiter and took a flute as well as an entire bottle of champagne from the tray. "About time," he said as he poured himself a toast.

By now John's long strides brought him to Nina's side, or more correctly, to the side of Raphael Fuentes. Raphael had Nina in his arms and was about to whirl her out on the dance floor again when John deftly pulled Nina away and into his own embrace. Raphael stepped back and took a good look at the expression on John's face, an expression that was lethal in its cool fury. Raphael merely raised an eyebrow and addressed John in Spanish. "Is she yours, man?"

A terse, clipped *"Si"* was John's only answer. Raphael held his hands up and apologized, again in Spanish. "Hey, I didn't know, man. Sorry about that."

A gentleman would have replied *"De nada"*, meaning it's cool, never mind. John was too far gone for more than a curt nod as he tightened his arms around Nina and they began to move to the slow, sexy music. He would have been perfectly content to enjoy the sensation of Nina's slender body pressed close to his, but Nina wasn't about to let him off the hook.

"Do you care to tell me what that was all about?" she asked crisply. "Why in the world did you come stomping over here like a Neanderthal and wrest me out of that man's grasp like a chunk of mastodon meat?"

John didn't answer her. He rubbed his face against her

soft hair and inhaled her delicate fragrance, stroking her back at the same time as he endeavored to bring her even closer. She felt wonderful in his arms, she felt perfect, as a matter of fact. If he'd had any way of knowing how satisfying it was to dance with her he'd have done it a long time ago. Unfortunately, Nina didn't seem to be sharing his reverie.

The hand that was clasped in his moved and her fingers took hold of his little finger, twisting it until she had his full attention. "Don't act like you can't hear me. What did you think you were doing snatching me up like that? If you wanted to dance all you had to do was ask." Her eyes flashed with indignation as she stared up at him.

"I shouldn't have to ask," John told her, amused by the look of incredulity that came over her face. "You shouldn't be dancing with anyone but me, Miss Parker, so let's just enjoy it."

"I can dance with whomever I want," she said hotly. "I'm not your date, or did you forget that little detail?"

John chose to ignore that remark and concentrate on Nina. "Miss Parker, you look absolutely beautiful. You look fantastic in that dress and you smell amazing. What are you wearing?"

Nina narrowed her eyes and stared at John. "Are you drunk? How much have you had to drink? You're not supposed to be drinking and you know it. The medication you're on can't be mixed with alcohol," she said sternly. "If you've been drinking, I'm going to . . ."

Whatever she was about to threaten John with was lost as his lips descended on hers. Their lips met and a mutual caress began, a long, sweet and tender kiss, a kiss that signaled the beginning of something wonderful. When John finally pulled away from her, he smiled in total satisfaction and waited for her response. It wasn't long in coming as Nina raised her right foot in its expensive purple shoe with the T-strap and French heel, which she planted firmly on John's instep.

"You *idiot,*" she snarled before stalking off and leaving him in the middle of the crowd of dancers.

Oddly enough, John was undisturbed by her reaction. *That went pretty well, considering. I should have kissed her way before this,* he thought cheerfully as he followed her from the dance floor.

Chapter 2

"Well, Paris, how have you been?" Titus asked in his deep, sexy voice. He was prepared for an awkward silence since Paris was always so shy with him. More than shy, really; he was used to her blushing like a schoolgirl when he spoke to her and he always found it adorable.

"I've been just wonderful, Titus, and how have you been?" She smiled brilliantly, looking directly into his eyes. This time it was Titus who was almost at a loss for words.

"I've been doing just great, thank you. Even better now that I have you in my arms." He could have kicked himself for that remark. He'd been telling himself to take it easy with Paris because she was so bashful. Every time he saw her, though, she looked more enchanting, more alluring. He liked everything he saw from her long, thick black hair to her creamy complexion with the tiny adorable freckles scattered across the bridge of her sculpted nose to her bountiful figure with its feminine curves. She was wearing a red wrap dress that was molded to her shapely body in such a way he had a sudden urge to take her somewhere and undo the tie securing it in place.

Incredibly, Paris smiled as though she knew what he was thinking. "Well, if you like me in your arms so much I'll just have to stay here, won't I?" she said sweetly.

Titus's bluish gray eyes took on a brilliant deep blue hue

and he smiled delightedly. "Those may be the most words I've ever heard you say at one time," he said, gently teasing her.

Paris gave a throaty laugh and offered to make up for lost time. "I know lots more words, would you like to hear some? I'm actually quite a chatterbox when you get to know me."

Titus pulled her a little closer, and bent his head to make sure she heard every softly spoken word. "Getting to know you is exactly what I have in mind, Paris Deveraux. I think we've wasted enough time, don't you?"

She lowered her long lashes and gave him a look that would have stopped a weaker man's heart. "Yes, Titus, I do. I think we've wasted an incredible amount of time. Let's start making up for it, shall we?"

He answered by rubbing his chin against her cheekbone and brushing his lips against it so softly she wasn't sure he'd actually kissed her. Her long lashes flew up and she looked into his eyes. At that moment all conversation and conscious thought ceased and she was lost in his eyes.

John caught up with Nina inside the stadium in the area that led to the concessions. The reception was taking place in the park infield and the outdoor annex that held several carnival rides and other amusements. If this were a normal game day there would be vendors everywhere selling everything from nachos to the ubiquitous hot dogs, but the long corridors were deserted now. John risked more of Nina's wrath by grabbing her arm and turning her to face him.

"I'm sorry, Nina. I shouldn't have kissed you like that, I guess, but you look so incredible I couldn't resist."

"I look good, so you kissed me and now you're sorry for it? What happened, John, do I suddenly not look so attractive and you wish you'd never touched me?" Nina crossed her arms tightly and glared at John who was trying not to look amused.

"Not at all, Nina, if anything you look even prettier. You really do look beautiful when you're mad, you know."

"So if I look so good why are you sorry you kissed me?" Nina's expression was even more forbidding than usual but all it did was turn up the heat in John.

John put his hands on her shoulders and this time he did smile, a calculated risk as Nina was still quite put out with him. "I'm not sorry I kissed you, not at all. My only regret about the kiss is that it didn't happen sooner. Your lips, Miss Parker, are delicious."

He moved closer to Nina, stroking her shoulders in an effort to soothe her ruffled feelings and also because he just liked the feel of her. It seemed to work because when she spoke again she wasn't quite as snappish.

"So why were you apologizing, John? For a supposedly intelligent man you're making very little sense."

John took one hand off her shoulder and tipped her chin up. He seemed to have lost all common sense because he was determined to kiss her again. He pressed his lips to her forehead, then her temple and her cheekbone. "I apologized," he said between kisses, "because I made you angry and I didn't want to do that. I caught you off guard and I may have embarrassed you and that wasn't my aim, either." He stopped talking long enough to pull her into his arms and kiss her cheek, then her neck.

In a soft voice completely unlike her usual brisk tone, Nina asked him what he did want. "If you didn't want to embarrass me, and you didn't want to make me mad, what did you want, John?"

"I wanted this, Nina. I wanted to hold you in my arms and kiss you, I wanted to taste your lips and see if they could possibly be as sweet as they looked. I wanted . . ."

Suddenly Nina pulled John's lapels so that his head was bent to hers. "You talk too much," she murmured before placing her lips on his.

After dancing with Titus through a slow number and two fast ones, Paris had to reluctantly take her leave of him. "I'm sorry, Titus, but I have to go back to work. My production crew is filming and I need to make sure that we've gotten enough footage. Once we start editing it never seems like there's enough," she said with a smile.

Titus looked down at Paris and stroked her cheek with his index finger. "I understand completely. How about we meet later and maybe have a cup of coffee or something? I don't know about you, but I don't want this night to end," he told her.

Paris blinked her long lashes and smiled. "You don't?"

"Absolutely not. I've been trying to have a conversation with you for way too long and now that you've finally started talking I want to hear everything you have to say." He put his hand at the small of her back and led her away from the dance floor. "Since I'm working too, how about if we meet after all the festivities have wound down?"

The fact that Titus was attending in an official capacity didn't surprise Paris; he was a private investigator who specialized in corporate security. Although he was a good friend of her cousin Martin Deveraux, he was also responsible for the security of both the Cochran and Deveraux families and his well-trained and discreet staff were at this moment deployed strategically throughout the venue.

"That sounds fine, Titus. But where will we meet? This is a huge place and we could easily miss each other," Paris pointed out.

Titus leaned down and put a soft but penetrating kiss right at the corner of her luscious mouth. "You just take care of whatever you need to do, Paris. I'll come to you, sweetheart. I'll always be able to find you, count on it," he said with a quiet laugh.

"There you are! Come on, you two, it's time for Adam and Alicia to get going so we need everyone on the floor."

The voice was that of Marguerite, another of Alicia's aunts who was directing the wedding with frightening precision. Nina felt her face heat up as she realized there was no way the woman had missed the sight of her and John kissing madly. She was profoundly grateful for the woman's polite discretion in not mentioning what was going on until Marguerite said something in Spanish that made John laugh out loud. The heat flared up again, making Nina feel as though her head were about to burst into flames. John didn't seem to see anything wrong with the situation; he had the audacity to bring his head down for yet another lip caress before going to join his family.

"Stop that!" Nina looked anxiously after Marguerite's retreating figure and tried vainly to push John away. They were still in the corridor, with Nina pressed against the wall and John all over her like a lusty teenager on his first date. He had a generous amount of her lipstick on his face and he wore the glazed look of a man swimming in a sea of sexual desire.

"I don't want to stop, *querida*. I want to keep going," he murmured as he slid his hands down her hips and licked her neck.

Nina wriggled away from him and left him kissing air as she smoothed her dress down with trembling hands. She looked at him sternly and tried with all her heart to not let her desire show. "You look like a sleazy magazine ad for condoms," she sniffed. "You have lipstick on your face and your shirt is all undone. Pull yourself together and let's get moving before someone thinks we've been kidnapped."

John pulled a linen handkerchief out of his back pocket and held it out to Nina who looked at it suspiciously. "I don't have a mirror," he told her.

Nina took the folded square from John's hand and stood about two feet away from him as she removed the evidence of their tryst. In the meantime, John buttoned up his band-collared tuxedo shirt, humming as he did so.

She ignored him as best she could, but when a woman is removing her own lipstick from the smoothly bronzed face of a man well over six feet tall with perfect features, devastatingly seductive eyes with thick black eyebrows, a glossy, perfectly groomed moustache and goatee, and a long thick braid of black hair, she can't help but be aware of him. Especially when he'd just kissed her senseless. Her breath caught in her throat as John slipped both his hands around her waist and pulled her against his hard chest.

"Okay, that's enough of that. Cut it out or you'll regret it," she said weakly.

"*Mi corazon,* the only thing I regret is not being able to sweep you away right now," John replied.

Satisfied that all the lipstick was gone, Nina once again disentangled herself from John and slapped the now stained hankie into his hand. "Here. Let's get this over with. And behave yourself. Are you sure you haven't been drinking? Because I swear I'll call your doctor," she said sternly.

"I'm drunk but I haven't been drinking. You intoxicate me, Miss Parker."

Nina gave him a baleful glare. "That's so lame I won't

even honor it with a retort. Now come on before you provoke me into something I might have to do time for." Taking him by the hand, she dragged him back to where the wedding party was supposed to be.

The bridal couple was almost ready to depart and the traditional garter tossing was about to take place. Nina watched in amusement as all the single men made the usual show of trying to avoid the inevitable; none of them wanted to be the next one caught in the marriage trap. The groom, however, had a plan of his own. Adam called John's name and tossed the delicate garter straight at him. John caught it with a grin and had the nerve to look at Nina with a wink. Before she could mentally react to that, it was time for the wedding bouquet to be thrown and she was determined not to be anywhere near it. She tried to remove herself from the shameless horde of squealing single women but the bride had much better aim than Nina could have imagined.

Alicia's natural heritage as the daughter and sister of professional baseball players came to the fore as the bouquet sailed straight to Nina. She had to catch it to keep it from smacking her right in the face, but she didn't hold on to it very long; two buxom sisters collided in midair as they pounced on the floral trophy and snatched it away from her hands. "Don't mind me," Nina said dryly. "Would you like my arm, too?" Left with only a gardenia, Nina glanced at John with no expression whatsoever on her face. Swept into the eddy of the celebrants as Adam and Alicia exchanged a final passionate kiss before getting into the limousine that would take them away to begin their honeymoon, Nina found herself on the edge of a crowd of cheering relatives, friends and colleagues of the couple. She looked around with a little half smile on her face before leaving by a deserted side entrance.

Chapter 3

The next morning, Nina surveyed the empty track before her with satisfaction. It was a perfect morning for a run; at least it was her idea of perfect. As a member of the Ann Arbor Track Club she got to use the facilities at the University of Michigan, something she took advantage of every chance she got. Running was more than exercise with Nina; it was her passion. She rotated her neck slowly, finishing the stretches that prepared her body to move easily across the surface of the track. Moving her shoulders in circles, she took one final stretch before removing her sweat pants and jacket. Clad in running shorts and a midriff athletic top with a racer back, Nina started running on the deserted track.

It was too early in the morning for even the most avid denizens of the sport, and Nina liked it that way. The overcast sky, the clouds and fog that rolled across the U of M would've discouraged most people, as would the cool, damp morning. Nina thrived on it, though; she liked a good long run in just this kind of weather. She knew that in a little while the natural exertions of her body would produce a warmth in all her muscles that would make the temperature seem ideal to her heated skin. She needed the solitude, the cool moisture of the fog, the eerie isolation of running alone; she needed all of them this morning to cool her overheated thoughts as well as to invigorate her body. She hadn't slept at all last night; she was too nerved up, too restless to sleep.

John Flores had stayed with her all night, not in the physical sense, of course, but he might as well have been in the bed with her for all the rest she got. He'd consumed her every thought from the moment he snatched her away from Raphael on the dance floor. If she was going to be honest about it, there was something compelling about John, something that called to her on a level she'd never thought existed. It was hard enough to ignore that pull when they were working together but when he was holding her, touching her, when his lips were caressing hers, when their mouths parted and their tongues met . . . Nina stifled a gasp as the same sensations that had assailed her the night before made a repeat appearance.

The sudden assault on her sensitized nerve endings made her stumble as she recalled the warmth of his body, the strength of his arms and the taste of his lips. Fine goose bumps covered her arms and the moisture that gathered in her erogenous zones had nothing whatsoever to do with the hard pounding rhythm of her run. It had everything to do with her desire for John, a desire that had to be denied. Only a crazy woman would allow herself to embark on a path that would lead directly to heartbreak and Nina Whitney was far from crazy. She was practical to the point of being stoic, she didn't believe in playacting, fantasy or tilting at windmills in search of impossible dreams and John Flores was the most impossible dream she could conceive at the moment. Life, as far as she was concerned, was what it was and there was no reason to pretend like happily-ever-after was in any way attainable.

Nina lost count of how many times she circled the track. She wasn't timing herself, she was just running until she felt right again, until all the aftershocks of John's kisses were gone, until she couldn't remember his scent, his taste or his touch. Her body was pleasantly heated now and covered with perspiration. She felt loose and relaxed, like an animal racing across some African plain. Little did she realize how much she resembled a cheetah, her long legs and perfect form slicing through the lifting fog. She finally began to slow down in preparation for an end to the run. Breathing easily, Nina continued to slow her pace until she was walking, a long, loose-limbed stride that carried her into the stretches she always performed to prevent muscle injury. She gathered her sweats to go inside the building and shower, and then decided to go straight home and have a long hot bubble bath instead. Sniffing her arm, she made a face. *My, that's tangy! I need to get in the tub fast.*

John stared dolefully into the refrigerator, looking for something to eat, anything at all. He was hungry a lot these days, as his full appetite had finally returned. For a long time after the liver disease struck him he had a problem with eating. He had no real desire to eat and often the mere thought of food simply turned his stomach. He lost quite a bit of weight during the onset of the illness and he'd just about returned to his proper size. During his recuperation from the surgery he'd become interested in food again, due in large part to Nina. She made sure he always had something delicious to eat, something other than the tasteless hospital fare. She knew exactly what he liked to eat and brought it to him, everything from omelets and home fries for breakfast to grilled salmon and risotto for dinner. A sudden awareness hit John like a sledgehammer and he abruptly closed the refrigerator door.

He stopped foraging and went into the living room of his temporary university housing to sit down and think about what had just occurred to him. No one, other than his parents, had ever shown John the care and consideration Nina had given him during his convalescence. She'd taken it upon herself to intercede on his behalf with his brother Adam, which led to his getting the partial liver transplant. She made sure he was comfortable and catered to his every whim while he was in the hospital. Even now, while they were finishing the book she'd been hired to ghostwrite, she saw to it that he took his antirejection medication, that he followed a proper diet and got enough rest. The fact that she did it like a drill sergeant notwithstanding, there was real caring in everything she did for him.

John slumped down on the moderately comfortable, boringly neutral couch that came with the apartment and drummed his fingers restlessly on his thighs. It was perfectly natural for him to start seeing Nina in a different light after all the things she'd done for him. It was the Florence Nightingale effect, when patients fell in love with their caregivers out of misplaced gratitude, that's all it was. He was having feelings for Nina because she'd taken care of him, not because he was really attracted to her as a woman. He nodded emphatically. That had to be it. He stood up and walked around the oatmeal colored room with its dull accessories and nodded again. Then he frowned.

The fact that John now found her sexy and beautiful wasn't part of that phenomena; that was something else. He'd never told her this but he once got a look at her while she was running and he'd never gotten it out of his mind. Even now, the memory could make his pulse quicken. He'd been scheduled to meet with her to go over some notes and decided to pick her up from the track where he knew she spent a lot of time. He could see her making her graceful way around the oval clad in what he thought was a bikini at first, until he realized it was the type of track clothes worn by serious runners like Jackie Joyner-Kersee and Gail Devers. The first sight of her made him stop in midstride and stare, totally transfixed by what he beheld.

He'd never imagined the body that lurked under her clothing, but Miss Parker was nothing short of amazing. She had the taut, muscled body of an Olympic runner with a high firm butt, slender taut thighs, a flat stomach with a feminine equivalent of a six pack, and arms that looked like sculpture. They were so firm and toned. She looked like an exquisite carving brought to life and she moved around the track with a sensual grace he wouldn't have believed possible before witnessing her. Her hair was pulled back in a businesslike knot with a scarf on it and her fascinating eyes had been obscured by big shades, but she was undoubtedly the sexiest thing he'd ever seen.

And her appeal continued to grow, especially last night when she'd danced all over the place in that skimpy purple dress. She'd looked so exciting and smelled so delightful he simply had to claim her and he did so without any thought of consequence. Only the fact that she'd slipped away from him while Adam and Alicia were leaving had prevented him from taking his attraction to the next level. He raised one eyebrow as he suddenly realized why he was so restless and out of sorts and decided to do something about it. His new family was having a cookout today, a chance for everyone to relax and relive the beautiful wedding. His brother Adonis, commonly called Donnie, and his bride Angelique were holding it at the old Palmer Park home they now occupied and everyone who'd participated in the wedding was going, along with both sets of families. John was invited, of course, and he intended to go, but he also intended for Nina to accompany him and not disappear the way she had last night. He reached into his pocket to make sure he had his keys and headed for the door. He had a few questions and he knew where to get the answers.

Nina opened her door and looked into John's broad chest. Redirecting her gaze up to his eyes she glared at him. "What do you want?"

Her nasty tone would have made a lesser man cower, but John wasn't listening to her; he was too busy looking at her outfit. She'd apparently just bathed as her skin still glowed with the moisture and sweet fragrance of a languorous bubble bath. John's eyes warmed with appreciation at the short cotton robe she was wearing. It was feminine in a soft peach color trimmed in white. It wrapped around her slender waist and was secured with a white tie belt. Her feet were covered in dainty matching peach slippers and John had a fierce urge to see her toes. *I'll bet they're just as sexy as the rest of her,* he thought with a smile he prudently hid from Nina. He was snapped out of his reverie by a poke of Nina's index finger in his chest.

"I asked what you want," she reminded him tartly.

Rubbing the spot she'd poked with one hand and grasping her finger with the other, John shook off his daydream to answer her.

"I'm here to interrogate you," he answered. "You left me last night and I want to know why."

Nina raised one perfectly arched brow at the look of determination on John's face. He gave every appearance of being totally sincere. "I'm not about to stand here and let you grill me half naked. Sit down," she said as she pulled her hand away and showed him inside. "I'll be back in a minute."

John looked around Nina's accommodations with interest. She'd been living at an extended-stay hotel since they came to Ann Arbor. The generic furnishings weren't any more welcoming than his temporary home. He was going to have to look for a permanent residence soon; he couldn't keep living as a guest in his own world. He was going to be living in Ann Arbor permanently and he needed to buy a house. Nina, on the other hand . . .

"Miss Parker!"

Nina emerged from the bedroom and gave John an assessing look. "You don't seem to be on fire and there's nothing else I can think of to justify your bellowing at me like that. I think we need to have your meds checked."

He almost forgot what he was about to say once he got a good look at Nina, who was wearing a denim skirt and a long-sleeved silk sweater with a deeply scooped neck. The sweater was a warm shade of red that brought out the golden tones of her chestnut complexion and it was tight enough to show what he knew for a fact was her perfect, sexy body. The skirt fit her as if it were custom made and displayed her amazing legs to their best advantage. Her hair was slicked back into a high, medium-length ponytail. Nina had an array of hairpieces, which she employed on many occasions, something John had discovered earlier. He thought they were cute and admired the fact she didn't try to pretend her hair had suddenly grown several inches.

He continued his scrutiny of her appearance. She was wearing her gold hoop earrings and the bracelet he'd given her that spring. Nina had arranged to have breakfast sent to him one morning soon after he'd found out Big Benny was his biological father. She always seemed to know when he needed some extra TLC and she always gave it to him without hesitation. The bracelet was his way of saying thank you. John smiled as he continued his scrutiny of Nina. She smelled wonderful, as always. Her soft feminine perfume was arousing yet subtle and it drove him crazy.

Nina walked closer to him and waved her hand in front of his face. "Have you added catatonia to your other charms? Snap out of it," she advised. "Why were you yelling my name?"

John shook his head to clear the unexpected carnal images that sprang forth when Nina came into the room. "Ahh, um, I forget. You look wonderful, by the way. And you smell fantastic. Are you coming with me?"

Most women look coy or bashful when given a compliment but Nina never changed expression, nor did she acknowledge his tribute. "John, we've got to work on those communication skills. Come with you *where*?" she asked with a frown.

John was so engrossed with looking at her legs and her slender feet he almost missed her question. Her toes were once again hidden from his view in her chic little flats, but he was convinced the hidden digits were adorable. When she repeated her question with increased irritation he made himself answer.

"Are you coming with me to my brother's house? You know there's a cookout this afternoon for both families and the bridal party, and we may as well go together."

Nina's expression did change a little after that remark; she flushed so slightly that even the keenest observer would have missed it. "*You* may as well get going, then, because I'm not attending."

John finally stopped letting his eyes rove all over her delightful prettiness and sat up straight on the uncomfortable loveseat. Nina turned away from him and went over to the table where her laptop computer was set up.

She sat down and started fiddling with the keyboard, and then she moved some papers around. It was obvious she was trying to look busy, but she wasn't fooling John.

"You're not going? Why not, Nina? You're part of the wedding party, or did you forget that? Don't you like my family? They like you, they think you're something else," he said with persuasive charm.

Nina gave a short laugh that held no amusement whatsoever. "I'm sure they do think I'm something else. I cussed your new sister-in-law out when I told her you were sick, I'm sure no one's forgotten that. And as for me being in the wedding, I think it was just a polite gesture of some kind," she said with a sneer.

John looked at her more closely. He could tell at once she was just acting out because she was uncomfortable with a new situation. "Miss Parker, no one knows what you said to Alicia because the only person she discussed it with was Adam and he's the most close-mouthed person I've ever met. What you said and how you said it was perfectly understandable given the situation. I think the only person who finds your actions reprehensible is you and you're going to have to give yourself permission to forgive yourself so you can forget about it." He spoke softly and in a warm, reassuring manner but his words had the opposite effect on Nina.

"I'm going to tell you this once and I expect we won't have to have this conversation again. Don't psychoanalyze me, ever. Don't try to crawl inside my head and tell me what I'm thinking or how I should be feeling because I'm not one of your patients. I'm not one of your case studies and I'm not some freak in a mental sideshow, do I make myself clear?"

John's lips tightened for a second, but he nodded to acknowledge Nina's outburst. "I apologize if I was out of line. It's an occupational hazard, one I try to avoid. I hope you can forgive me," he said quietly.

Nina looked out the window before responding to John's words. She finally opened her mouth and was stunned when her stomach growled long and loud. She covered her mouth with one hand and her cheeks flamed up, just in time for another rumbling signal of hunger.

Relieved, John burst into laughter. "Well that explains it, you're starving, poor child. C'mon, *chica,* you know there's going to be a ton of food, the people are pleasant and it's a beautiful day. Let's go have some fun."

Nina looked out the window again. The last part was true, at least. The morning fog had dissipated when the sun rose and it was a perfect early fall day with a bright blue sky and brilliant sunshine. She just didn't know if she was up to an afternoon of close proximity with John and his teeming mass of loving relatives.

"I have a lot of work to do, John. I'm at a critical part of the writing and I need to concentrate."

"You can't concentrate on an empty stomach," he pointed out. "In fact, I'll take you to that coffee place you like and get you a muffin and a cup of whatever that foamy crap is you like to drink. That'll hold you until we get to Detroit. Just say yes, Miss Parker. Say yes."

"No."

The single word, spoken in a forbidding voice devoid of any feeling, usually made people scurry to get away from her, but John was made of tougher stuff than that. He stood up and walked over to Nina, putting his hand on her shoulder and giving it a slight squeeze. "It's okay, I understand. I'm just not ready for a lot of Paris Deveraux's questions, I guess."

"Excuse me?"

John elaborated. "Paris is going to be there and I guess she's going to be doing some preliminary research for the big interview," he said resignedly. "I like Paris and she seems very professional and all, but, you know . . ." his voice trailed off.

Nina surprised herself when she touched the hand that was still on her shoulder. "Okay, fine, I'll go."

Chapter 4

John looked over at his companion once again as he drove. Although he was very happy she'd decided to come with him to the cookout, he was less pleased with her attire. Her abrupt decision to accompany him was so unexpected he experienced a dizzy rush of happiness that no doubt accounted for the incredibly stupid thing he said next. After Nina rose from her seat at the table to get her purse, John ambushed her with a hug. He loved the way she felt in his arms, especially when she wasn't trying to wriggle away from him. Reluctantly releasing her, he watched her walk across the room for a moment before he put both of his feet into his mouth at once.

"So as soon as you change, we'll be on our way." No sooner had the words escaped than John realized what a huge mistake he'd made. Nina had turned around slowly and looked at him as though he'd just announced he was from another planet.

"I'm sorry, I don't believe I heard you correctly. Care to try again?" she'd said in a dangerously calm tone of voice.

In that moment, the Latin influence of the Puerto Rican heritage with which he'd been raised manifested itself. Instead of backing down, John crossed his arms and looked at Nina intently. "I said once you change your clothes we'd leave. You're not seriously going to wear that skirt outdoors, are you?"

Nina had looked down at the offending garment and back up at John. "What's wrong with this skirt?"

"It's too short, Nina. You can't be walking around like that; it's like swinging fresh meat in front of a cage full of hungry beasts. I don't want anyone looking at those beautiful legs of yours but me. Go put on something else."

Now as they sped along the expressway that led to Detroit, John cast a chagrined glance at the "something else" Nina had changed into. It was another skirt; a pleated one with a fitted yoke in the classic Burberry plaid and it was even shorter than the controversial denim one. She'd also put on delicate loafers with Burberry plaid on the vamp and when she came out of the bedroom she looked so delectably cute it was hard to fault her choice of outfits. Of course, she also looked truculent enough to put John's eye out if he messed with her so he held up his hands in supplication and they left in total silence.

As they neared the city, an overwhelming feeling of utter stupidity seized John. Why in the world had he tried to tell Nina Whitney, of all people, what to wear and how to wear it? What business was it of his if she chose to put those stupendous legs of hers on display? *Why am I tripping? She's not my woman but I'm acting like I own her. What am I getting myself into?* His jumbled thoughts turned his handsome face into a frowning mask, something his companion was happy to point out.

"John, you're looking awfully petulant," Nina said cheerfully. "Anyone would think you hadn't gotten your way, that you hadn't manipulated me into coming to this little shindig. What seems to be the problem?" she teased.

Taking a deep breath, John looked over at Nina and as always the deep dimples that framed her pretty smile knocked him out. Taken feature by feature, she was perfectly ordinary. She had smooth, flawless skin, a small, nicely shaped nose, eyes that were almost too small due to their slight slant, full lips and a slender neck that just missed being too long. There wasn't one thing about her face that screamed for attention, but each feature combined to make her beautiful, at least in his eyes. And not in the tarted-up, overly painted way of a model or actress; hers was a natural beauty that would last forever. When he'd finally come fully awake after the transplant surgery, Nina's was the first face he saw and he could still remember the thrill of relief that coursed through him when her features came into view. He smiled at the memory and earned a poke in the side from Nina.

"Don't ignore me, John. You tricked me into coming and you know it. Have you no shame at all?" she demanded.

John reached for her hand and pulled it up to his lips. Yes, he'd played his trump card with Nina. He knew if he said something about Paris and the interview, Nina would go with him in a heartbeat. She might be as cuddly as a cactus, but she cared about his well being enough to do things she didn't really want to do, as long as it meant he was happy.

"I apologize, Miss Parker. It was a low trick, I admit it," he said solemnly, his thumb stroking the hand he was still holding. "I promise to make it up to you, though. And you have to admit it's too nice a day to be closeted up inside. We'll have a good time, wait and see."

Nina didn't seem to be in a hurry to take her hand back, she allowed John to continue to hold it. She seemed relaxed and content until they arrived in the Palmer Park section of Detroit where Donnie and Angelique Cochran lived. With a slight sigh she took her hand back and smoothed the fabric of the dangerous skirt while John parked the car. She adjusted her chic sunglasses and gave John a quick glance. "Okay, I'm ready."

He touched her cheek and gave her his most lethal smile, the one that could charm the panties off any woman within a fifty-mile radius. "You'll be fine, Miss Parker. This time I'm looking out for you."

Nina smiled in spite of herself. He really was irresistible. There was something about John that made her melt inside, especially when he flirted with her the way he was doing now. She tried to stare him down, abruptly asking him why he still called her Miss Parker. "Isn't it time you stopped doing that? Why do you insist on calling me by that ridiculous name?" she asked crossly.

John helped her out of the car and pulled her into his arms for a hug while he kissed her forehead. He didn't watch much television, but he liked to watch syndicated reruns of *The Pretender* whenever he could. The hard-as-nails character "Miss Parker" reminded him of Nina. The woman on the show was always immaculately groomed and totally intimidating to everyone but she had a tender heart and a deeply wounded soul, something John associated with Nina for some reason. He looked down at her and kissed her again, this time a soft one on the lips. "Sorry, Nina. I try to stop using that name but you just remind me of that character so much," he told her. "You must admit she's a fabulous dresser," he pointed out. "She always looks like a high fashion model and so do you."

Nina gave him a mischievous smile. "Yes, and she wears really short skirts, as I recall. So you can't complain about mine anymore, can you? Let's go," she said, stunning John by taking his hand.

"Why, Miss Parker, if I didn't know better I'd think you were starting to like me a little," John said with that incredibly sexy smile of his.

"Don't be ridiculous," she murmured, but she didn't let go of his hand as they walked to the house.

Despite her initial reluctance, Nina found herself having a good time with John's family. They entered the spacious house by the back door as was customary with friends and family. Donnie and his bride Angelique were in the kitchen with their baby, Lily Rose. She was full of smiles for her new uncle and waved her arms to indicate she wanted to go to him. John held her for a few minutes, talking to her in Spanish and kissing her behind the ear to solicit giggles. Lily then reached for Nina, who held out her arms for the baby and smiled with pleasure as she got used to Lily's warm weight against her body.

Angelique looked at the charming picture they made and said she was going to get a camera. "Nina, you don't mind holding her for a minute, do you? I've got to get some pictures. I love taking pictures of Lily with all the family so I always try to get as many as possible."

"We'll be just fine, won't we?" Nina nuzzled Lily's neck and was rewarded with laughter and a bubbly smile from the happy baby. "Is there something I can do to help?"

The suggestion was met with a chorus of "no's" from the other occupants of the kitchen, John's new sisters-in-law, Tina, Faye and Renee Cochran. Renee reiterated the refusal. "We've got this under control, Nina. Why don't you and John just take it easy? By the time everyone gets here there'll be plenty to do, believe me." Nina did as Renee suggested and went into the living room with John and Lily Rose. Nina sat down at the piano with the baby in her arms and smiled when Lily Rose started wriggling and waving her hands at the keyboard.

"So you're a music lover, hmm? Okay, let's see what we can do," Nina told her. Soon Lily Rose was laughing with pleasure as Nina picked out a tune for her on the piano and sang her a little song. John smiled at the two of them and was about to say something when the newlyweds entered the room.

"Hey, what are you two doing here? I thought you'd be on your way to some exotic locale by now," John said.

Alicia and Adam exchanged a very private look indicative of some very passionate thoughts. "We're leaving tonight," Alicia, said when she could finally tear her eyes away from her husband. "We spent our wedding night at home," she murmured.

Nina relinquished Lily Rose to her Uncle Adam and turned around on the piano bench to face Alicia. "At home? Isn't it more traditional to go to some luxury hotel somewhere?" she teased.

Alicia sat down on the bench next to Nina. "Girl, now you know we're not much for tradition. Our families kind of expect the unexpected with us, but you know that, since you eloped with us!" Alicia laughed merrily, and then gave Nina a big hug. "Thank you again for making both our wedding days so special. It was so wonderful of you to stand up with us, even though you don't know us very well. I really appreciated it, Nina."

Nina and John, together with Alicia's friends Roxy Fairchild and Bryant Porter, had indeed eloped with Adam and Alicia. Alicia had panicked under the weight of all the wedding preparations of her formidable aunts and it was Adam's idea to go to Idlewild and have a simple ceremony before what Alicia referred to as her "Big Fat Cuban Wedding." Nina felt her face turn hot from the unexpected and very sincere thank you. She'd been touched and surprised to be included and Alicia's sincere thanks was rather embarrassing. A sudden influx of Cochrans deflected attention from her and also made it unnecessary for her to respond. An answer was not only superfluous, it would have been impossible to hear as Benita and Clay Deveraux entered the living room, each carrying one of their twin daughters. Their three lively sons followed them and the room was noisy with happy greetings. Trey, the oldest son and the most like his formidably handsome father, kissed his Aunt Alicia and followed suit with Nina. "Miss Nina, you can *really* dance," he said admiringly. "I wanted to dance with you but I couldn't find you. Where did you go last night?"

"Umm, I had a headache and I had to go lie down," Nina offered lamely. She didn't dare meet John's eyes, although she could feel him staring at her intently. She did her level best to avoid another look like that the rest of the day. She conversed with the bride's parents, with John's brothers and admired all the babies and assorted small children. And despite earlier protests, she did end up helping to get everything set up for the buffet. Those Cochran women were absolute dynamos when it came to entertaining. And everything else, apparently, as they all had brilliant careers, too. These women were more than dynamic; they were positively intimidating.

Nina watched Faye putting an olive garnish around the huge bowl of potato salad and said to her, "I don't know how you all do all this."

"What do you mean, hon? All what?"

"I mean, how do you manage your careers, your family and still manage to pull these gigantic feasts out of your back pockets at a moment's notice? With all you do, you still manage to cook like this. I'm amazed, that's all." *And I'm also scared of every one of you.*

"*Cook?* Oh bless, your heart, Nina. I love to cook, we all do. But who has time? This potato salad was made from scratch, and the cornbread. But everything else? Costco, Nino Salvaggio's, Trader Joe's and Farmer Jack's have provided the rest of this bounty. We might know how to cook but we also know how to shop," Faye said with a cheery lack of repentance.

Tina chimed in with the same sentiments. "I almost drove myself crazy for a while trying to be superwoman. I was trying to be the perfect wife, a domestic diva and have a career. When I was finishing law school, it was okay. As long as I was really organized, it worked. But when my babies came along and I was working in the prosecutor's office, it got to be a little too much. Luckily I have a very helpful and understanding husband and he not only pitched in, he had sense enough to insist I hire someone to help out. Our lives have been much better since then. We eat a lot of store bought food, but it's *good* food. At least no one complains," she ended with a shrug.

Once again, Nina was saved from having to make a reply by another arrival. This time it was Paris Deveraux. "Hey, everybody! What smells so delicious?"

While everyone was saying hello to Paris, Nina quietly left the room and went in search of John. When she found him he was outside sitting with his father watching his brothers Alan and Andre deftly grill the meat. John stood as she approached and took her slender wrist in his hand.

"Is everything okay? Are you having a good time?" he asked softly.

Nina gave him one of her rare smiles and was touched when she saw John's genuine concern reflected in his eyes. "I'm fine. I'm just checking on you," she admitted. "Paris just got here," she added in a guarded undertone.

John entwined his fingers with hers and smiled down at her. "It's okay, Miss Parker. She's just going to talk to us a little bit, nothing too intrusive or weird. She just wants to get a feel for things so the actual interview will go well."

Nina looked at their hands with their fingers entwined before looking into John's eyes. He smiled at her again and brought their clasped hands up to his lips, giving the back of her hand a quick kiss. "Nina, I'm fine. I love the fact that you're so concerned about me, but there's nothing to worry about."

Her self-control was slipping fast; for some reason Nina wanted nothing more than to throw her arms around him and kiss him really hard. Instead she shrugged her shoulders as though they'd been discussing nothing more pressing than the weather. "Who's worried about you? You're more than capable of taking care of yourself, I'm not your nanny," she said with a sniff. She pulled her hand away from John and left to go back into the house.

Alan and Andre snickered to each other and shook their heads. "What did I tell you? The woman is tough," said Andre.

"Yeah, but I still think he can do it in less than a year," returned Alan.

"Okay then, let's raise the bet."

"If you're so sure let's *double* the bet, can you handle that, Big Baller?"

The two men continued to bicker while Big Benny took a long, assessing look at his son. John resumed his seat, watching the elegant sway of Nina's body as she walked away from him.

"Looks like you've got your work cut out for you, son. Your woman's gonna give you a hard time every inch of the way. Don't give up on her though, she's a good match for you," Benny said with quiet amusement.

"Oh, look Dad, it's not like that. We're not involved or anything. We're just . . . it's just . . . I," John tried vainly to come up with a coherent sentence and then started laughing. "Am I that transparent?"

Benny assured him it wasn't that. "Just remember I have five other sons and I've watched every one of them go through the same thing. All my boys had sense enough to find smart women with a lot of spirit and that kind never go quietly. Like I said, you've got your work cut out for you."

Inside the house, the women were conducting the same kind of avid speculation as the men, but with more finesse. "I think there's more to this than meets the eye," Tina said to no one in particular.

Alicia agreed wholeheartedly. "I think they really, really care about each other but neither one of them realizes it. Eventually it's going to all come out, but right now I think they're clueless."

Paris's eyes got big and her face took on the familiar matchmaker look, the look she always got when she was contemplating fixing someone up. Angelique recognized it at once and warned her cousin off.

"Paris, you need to stay out of this and attend to your own affairs. Am I imagining things or were you really engaged in conversation with Titus Argonne last night?" Her ploy worked as Paris's face lit up in a dreamy smile.

"Yes, cousin, I actually talked to the man and we danced together, several times. I wasn't goofy and tongue-tied and fumbling for words this time. For once we had a real conversation," Paris reported with a becoming pink flush across her cheekbones. "We went to some little diner after the reception and drank coffee and talked for hours and when I'm back in Atlanta we're having a real date."

Angelique laughed and applauded. "Well honey, it's a date that's long overdue. How long have you had the hots for that man?"

Paris glanced out the big multi-paned window above the kitchen sink and watched John staring at Nina as she walked away from him. "About as long as those two have been heating up, at least. I wonder what's taking them so long to make a move?"

All the women in the kitchen turned on her and in unison said, "Paris, mind your own business!"

"Ya'll don't have to be so mean," Paris said in a fake hurt voice. "I'm just trying to be helpful."

"Well help yourself to Titus Argonne and leave other folks alone," Angelique said emphatically.

The ride back to Ann Arbor was pleasant and uneventful; neither John nor Nina had very much to say. They listened to a jazz station on the radio and once in awhile one of them would say something inconsequential to which the other would make a brief response. After parking the car, John walked Nina to her door and waited until she opened it. He could sense her uncertainty and tried to put her at ease by running his index finger down the nape of her neck. She gasped softly and closed her eyes.

"Aren't you going to invite me in, Miss Parker?"

In a tiny voice she asked, "Do you want to come in?"

"More than anything," he said softly.

In a few minutes they were in the living room of the suite, John leaning back on the boxy looking sofa and Nina curled up on the loveseat. They were trying so hard not to stare at each other they gave up and looked at each other intently, as if they were seeing each other for the first time.

"Would you like something to drink?" she murmured.

"No, thank you, I'm just fine."

Nina cleared her throat and looked around the room, trying to find something new at which to stare. Failing that, she spoke again. "It was a nice party," she said lamely.

"It was great," John agreed. "My family is wonderful.

They think you're exceptional, I had a fantastic time and I don't want this to end."

"'This' what? What *this,* John? What are you talking about?" Nina hated her bitchy tone of voice but she could barely trust herself to speak.

"Why are you sitting way over there, Nina? You look like you're about to run away from me," John teased her.

"I might do just that if you don't make yourself less obtuse. What are you talking about?" Her anxiety made every word sound irritated.

John held out his hand to her and gestured with the other hand. "Come over here, *mi corazon,* and I'll tell you."

Nina made him wait for almost a minute before she put her hand in his and gracefully undid her long legs. She sat down next to John and allowed him to put his arm around her so she was nestled against him.

"That's better. You feel very nice next to me, *querida.*" John kissed her hair, then her face as he inhaled her fragrance. "You also smell very nice."

By now Nina's nerves were shot and she wasn't in the mood for any more foolish small talk. Unaware that her voice was trembling as much as her hands, she snapped at John. "If you wanted to conduct an inventory you could have made a checklist and slipped it under my door. What do you want with me, John?"

John smiled into Nina's neck and felt her trembling. Before she could protest he shifted her so she was sitting in his lap. Holding her close to his heart, he tilted her chin up so she had to look at him. "What I want is for us to be closer, Nina. I was watching you play the piano today and I suddenly realized I know almost nothing about you, and I want to know everything. I want to know all about you, where you came from, what you like and don't like, what you want out of life. I was thinking about finding a permanent place to live today and it dawned on me that I have no idea what your plans for the future are. I don't know if you're going back to California or what. I don't like that uncertainty, Nina."

As he spoke, he was massaging her back with his free hand, bringing her closer to his body until they were a kiss away from each other. He looked into her eyes with great tenderness and was awed by the soft, yielding look on her enchanting face.

"I want to spend more time with you, Nina, and I don't want you dancing with anyone but me," he whispered.

Nina laughed when he said that, a soft, throaty chuckle he'd never heard before, not ever. When she began to speak, he caught his breath, not sure of what she'd say.

"So is this your way of saying we should date? Are you asking me to go steady or something?" she asked in a gentle tone John never expected to hear from her.

"Yes I am, Miss Parker." His lips were almost on hers, but he had to hear her answer.

"Okay," she whispered, just before their mouths touched. The hot, sweet explosion that followed was much better than the night before. This time it was deliberate and prolonged, an exploration of passion and tenderness. John traced the outline of Nina's lips with his tongue, urging her to part her luscious lips for him. She sighed softly and opened her mouth to find John waiting for her, his tongue eagerly merging with hers in a burst of unexpected pleasure. Nina's arms went around John's neck and she clung to him, her desire for him growing with every stroke of his tongue, every motion of his wonderfully sensual mouth. John kissed and sucked and nibbled on her lips until she thought she would faint. She captured his lower lip and pulled it into her mouth, sucking on it gently until he moaned aloud. When they finally broke apart they stared at each other with equally dazed expressions.

John wanted to say something clever, something sexy to further bind Nina to him but his mind was a complete blank. All he could think about was how incredibly sensual Nina looked with her dreamy eyes, her juicy lips and her now-erect nipples pushing through the thin silk of her sweater. He had no idea there was so much passion contained under the smooth veneer of his Miss Parker but it was there, a veritable volcano of it. She wasn't exactly immune to him, either.

Nina was doing everything she could to let him know how much she craved him. She stroked his face, making a soft little purring sound. She leaned forward, arching her back as she did so, pushing her body against his so there was no mistaking her desire. She kissed his neck, tasting him, committing his unique personal fragrance to her memory, abandoning herself to the sensations created by his touch. Finally she lay her head on his shoulder with a ragged sigh.

John breathed her name reverently and pressed his lips to her hair. "I think we made the right choice," he whispered.

Nina lifted her face for one more taste of John's very talented lips. After another shuddering sigh, she placed one slender hand on either side of his face. "So what do we do now?"

John looked at her serious face, relishing the feel of her in his arms, the aftertaste of her kisses in his mouth and smiled as he kissed the tip of her nose. "We do everything, Miss Parker. Everything."

Chapter 5

All it took was another sleepless night to convince Nina that she'd done something incredibly stupid. *Why did I do that? Why?* She stared at her reflection in the mirror and thought seriously about bursting into tears, something she hadn't done since she was a little girl. Her eyes looked puffy, her hair was a mess and her lips were still tender she realized, as she touched her lower one gently. She frowned at the mirror one more time, and abruptly left the room. It was time for a run. A good long run would clear her head and maybe she could think of a way out of the whole mess.

A short time later she was pounding along at her usual pace, looking way more composed than she felt. Her thoughts seemed to be running in a continual loop matching the measured cadence of her footfalls: *Why did I do that? Why did I do that? Why did I do that?*

A little voice in her head spoke up and asked, *why* not? *Why shouldn't you have some fun with a good-looking man? He's smart, he's kind and gentle, he likes you, he doesn't have any diseases and he has a good job. End of story. If you want to kiss a pretty man like that, more power to you.*

But I agreed to date him, not just kiss him, Nina fretted.

The voice came back again, this time more insistently: *Girl, what is your problem? Women all over the world are dying to have dates with men who don't have half of what the doc has and here you are acting a fool. If the man wants to date you, go for it. Don't be stupid.*

Nina tried to outrun the words but they trailed after her, right into the parking lot of the track club. She actually cut her run short, an unprecedented move but a necessary one. She couldn't concentrate on what she was doing with all that racket in her head. After the briefest of cool downs, she was headed to her car when a voice stopped her.

"Excuse me for intruding, but I've been wanting to say hello to you for a long time. My name is Marlon Reynolds and I see you running out here a lot. You have great form, I must say."

The man who stopped Nina was about six feet tall and very attractive with smooth, chocolate brown skin and a winning smile. The smile slipped a little when Nina didn't answer right away. Finally she spoke.

"Thank you for noticing. You have a great day," she said crisply. With a brief nod, she continued to her car, only to be followed by the young man.

"Since you and I both like to run, I was thinking that maybe we could run together sometime. Maybe grab something to eat afterwards, how does that sound?"

By now Nina had reached the rented Ford Focus she'd been driving and carefully unlocked the door, stowing her belongings in the back seat before addressing her admirer. She adjusted her sunglasses and turned around with a tight little smile on her face. "Look, Marvin . . ."

"Marlon," he corrected her.

"Okay, *Marlon*. Thanks for the offer, but I'm not interested. Now you have a nice day, okay?"

She was about to enter the car when Marlon stopped her. "Come on, now, you just gonna blow me off, is that it? You're not even gonna give a brother a chance?" he said with a note of playful pleading.

If he hadn't touched her he might have gotten off light but once his hand touched her arm it was *on.* She shook it off viciously and snarled, "Look here, Marlon, Jackie, Tito, whatever your name is, you're old enough to take no for an answer and keep going. I come here to run, period. I'm not interested in socializing while I'm here, thank you, so you go your way and I'll go mine and we'll forget this ever happened, okay?"

"So you got a man or something?"

"Yes, she does. And he's not nearly as polite as she is so I suggest you move along while you still can."

There stood John, looking murderously angry. Before Nina could react, Marlon was skittering out of the parking lot in a cloud of dust and she was left alone with John, who was towering over her with a menacing frown on his face.

"Where did you come from?" Nina asked.

"I came over here to see if you wanted to have breakfast with me, and look what I find. Some jackass trying to push up on you! Is this the first time he's said anything to you?" John demanded.

"John, don't tell me you're the jealous type," Nina said incredulously.

"It has nothing to do with being jealous, it has everything to do with your safety. What did I tell you about letting other men see your body? Look at you, you might as well be wearing underwear," he said hotly, gesturing at her usual running attire.

Nina raised one eyebrow and gave him an amused smile. "Not really, my underwear covers a lot less than this."

"It does?" John's expression changed and he was clearly picturing Nina in some provocative ensemble. That didn't deter Nina, however. She poked him in the stomach and spoke sternly.

"You and I need to have a little talk, friend. A serious one."

A few hours later, John and Nina were seated in a small restaurant on campus, sharing lunch. She was dressed in an immaculately pressed pair of jeans and a crisp white shirt with the sleeves rolled back to reveal her taut forearms. A cherry red sweater was thrown over her shoulders and expensive-looking black loafers completed the chic but casual ensemble. John was wearing the same outfit he'd had on earlier, a pair of khaki slacks with a blue oxford dress shirt bearing the unmistakable Ralph Lauren polo rider crest. The shirt was open at the collar and he'd left his sport coat at the office. He looked wonderful with the bright sunlight streaming over him through the window of the restaurant, but there was still a certain tension about his face. It was plain he was still not over the incident in the parking lot. Nina, on the other hand, looked relaxed and quite in control.

John watched the light playing along her fabulous face and the knot in his stomach lessened slightly. She didn't seem angry, she was perusing the menu with avid interest and she appeared to be in a good mood, despite the fact he'd acted like a barbarian back at the track.

Their waitress approached the table and Nina placed her order. "I'd like a cheeseburger, well done, with lettuce, tomato and mayo on the side, please. Are your fries frozen or do you make them here?" When told they were made on the premises, Nina beamed and said she'd like an order. "And a chocolate malt, please, if it's a real malt."

"It's as real as my hips, honey," the buxom server assured her.

John said he'd have the same. The waitress tucked her pencil behind her ear and ambled off in the direction of the kitchen. John watched as Nina daintily sipped water, bracing himself for whatever was coming. He didn't have to wait long as Nina started talking as soon as she put the glass of water down.

"John, this is not going to work. I think we were both caught up in the romance of the wedding, it happens all the time. All that kissing and hugging and flowers and whatnot, it makes people a little crazy," she said in a measured, neutral voice that was somehow more piercing than a scream. "I don't think we're suited to one another at all and we need to put this whole dating thing out of our heads before it goes too far."

She sat back in her chair and put her clasped hands on the table, looking at John expectantly. John's reaction to her statement was immediate.

"Nina, you couldn't be more wrong. I admit, I might have been a little out of line this morning, but that's no reason to put an end to our relationship before it even gets off the ground."

"A *little* out of line? John, you came up out of nowhere like some kind of ninja warrior or something. That poor man will probably never speak to another woman again in this life. I had no idea you were the jealous type," she said with a smile of genuine amusement.

"You know what? I didn't realize that either," John said ruefully. It was true, John had a rich and varied dating history but he couldn't remember ever losing control over a woman. He'd done it with Nina twice in less than a week. Something was happening to him that he didn't understand, but he didn't want it to end. Nina seemed determined to derail the love train before it left the station and he wasn't going to allow that.

"Okay, we can blame it on my rich Latin heritage," he said with a wry twist of his mouth. It was true in a way; his adoptive parents were Puerto Rican and John had grown up believing he was, too. His father, uncles and cousins had quite naturally influenced his ideals and impressions of life and there was indeed a streak of Latin machismo running deep in his veins. He couldn't think of anyone less likely to tolerate it than Nina Whitney. "I don't think of myself as some macho man and I've never tried to tell a woman how to dress or how to act in public, but I've done it to you twice in as many days. I can only tell you it won't happen again," he said sincerely.

"Actually, John, it was three times in three days or do you not remember snatching me away from Alicia's brother at the wedding reception. I think you'd better confine your promises to things you can control. I think there's a big untapped streak of he-man running through your veins," she said, again with a smile.

John felt a pain deep in his gut. "So is that why you're saying this won't work? Because you think I'm some big chest-thumping caveman who's going to try to subjugate you and control you at every turn?"

Nina looked serious for the first time and slowly shook her head. "If I'm going to be completely honest I have to tell you I actually thought it was kind of sweet. You were really cute when you went all primitive and territorial," she said with a slight blush. "That's not why this won't work, John. It's because you and I could never make it. I'm not the woman for you, not at all. This could never, *ever* work and the sooner we get back to being colleagues the better."

"What do you mean, you're not the woman for me? It seems to me I should be the one who decides that and from where I sit, you're just perfect." He leaned across the table and lowered his voice several octaves. "Think about last night, Nina, you can't tell me that wasn't perfect," he murmured.

Nina's face flushed and her long lashes lowered. "I admit it was nice," she said demurely. "But let's face it,

John, any healthy man and woman can generate the same kind of heat given the right circumstances. We don't have a patent on sexual chemistry, you know."

The waitress returned at that moment, and all conversation stopped as the food was arranged in front of them. Nina looked at her order hungrily and remarked that she'd missed breakfast. "I love a good burger, I really do." She cut hers in half neatly and took her first bite, sighing in satisfaction. "This is a really great cheeseburger, John, aren't you going to eat yours?"

"Not until you stop all the double-talk and tell me what's going on in that magnificently complex head of yours. Talk to me, Nina, and try to make me understand why you think we can't be a couple."

Nina put down the fry she'd just picked up and wiped her hands on her napkin. "Okay, John, if you want to know why it won't work, here's your answer in one word: *me*. I'm all wrong for you. I'm not adorable, I'm not accomplished, I don't have clever, wonderful girlfriends and I can't pull gourmet feasts off at a moment's notice. I'm not terribly sociable and I don't do well with crowds. This relationship is doomed, so there's no real reason to prolong it. We kissed, it was a mistake, life goes on. End of story," she said firmly.

John felt a warm flood of relief at her words, even more so when he noticed her hand shaking as she picked up her malt. As long as she didn't find him repulsive or ridiculous, it would be okay. So her issues were with how she perceived herself, not with him; that was something he could handle. Giving her a rakish grin, he finally picked up his sandwich and took a huge bite. After he swallowed it, he nodded to Nina.

"You're absolutely correct, Nina." He was pleased to see a look of panic flash into her eyes at his words. "You were right, this is a great burger." *And I'm right about us and I'll have to prove it to you.*

True to his word, John simply refused to heed Nina's concerns. He understood to an extent where she was coming from; she was comparing herself with his brother's wives and somehow decided she was lacking in some way. He decided the best way to handle the situation was to let her know as often as possible she was the only woman who held his interest and he liked her just the way she was. So despite her misgivings, the dating began. As far as John was concerned, it started right there in the little campus restaurant. After finishing their lunch, John drove Nina back to his office where she'd left her car. He opened her door for her and handed her the keys. Before she could slide under the steering wheel, John caught her up in a close embrace and planted a big kiss on her, right in front of God and everybody.

"Thanks for having lunch with me. Now what time is dinner?"

Nina's slender hands tensed and relaxed on John's big biceps and she answered him so softly he almost didn't hear it. "Seven," she whispered.

And so it started, innocently enough, with lunch together, then dinner. Sometimes breakfast, if Nina needed to go over something with John pertaining to the book. They worked well together, although Nina did the majority of the work in her suite. On occasion they worked in his office, but those times weren't as productive as Nina would have liked. Instead of getting right down to work, she and John would spend long hours talking about nothing in particular and trying to keep their hands off each other. It wasn't easy because despite what Nina had blithely told

John, they had a remarkably potent chemistry that got stronger with every kiss.

Nina was thinking about John's kisses at that very moment. She was sitting at the table she used for a desk, staring out the window at the steady rain. The rain was soothing to her easily rattled nerves and it was also arousing in a way. The clean scent of it drifted in the slightly open window and the elusive fragrance reminded her of John's aftershave. She sighed deeply and tried to get her mind back on her work, but it wasn't possible. All she could think about was John. They'd had a lot of fun in the past couple of weeks. So much it was like torture to try and remember it all, but it was the sweetest kind of torture.

They had been to a few art galleries, to a play, to a U of M football game, and they shared almost every meal. On a few occasions they'd been entertained by Adam's brothers and their families, which was quite nice and not as strained as Nina would have imagined. Once you got past the sappiness, the Cochrans were intelligent, friendly people who went out of their way to make her feel welcome. Yes, she and John had shared a lot of fun lately, even when they weren't doing anything but playing Scrabble or watching a movie. And every single date ended in John's arms with his lips on hers. She'd had no idea that merely kissing a man could be so satisfying, so sensual. The way John touched her, tasted her, the feel of his arms around her . . .

A knock at the door roused her from her thoughts of John and she welcomed the interruption. Fanning herself lightly, she jumped up from the table and went to answer the door. She guessed it was the florist and she was right. There was the same nice little man, delivering what had become regular floral tributes from John. The sight of the beautiful bouquet of exotic flowers in sultry pink hues brought a smile to her face as always, but a sense of melancholy also pervaded her very being. She looked around for a surface on which to put the flowers and took them into the bedroom so they would be the last thing she saw at night and the first thing she saw in the morning. John was so thoughtful, so determined to delight her each and every day. She'd always suspected John would be an ardent and attentive suitor and she was right. He was warm, loving, charming and affectionate and to think she'd have to let him go was heartbreaking.

A single tear trickled down her cheek as she contemplated going back to her normal life, the life she had before there was John. The book was almost finished; she couldn't drag the project out forever. And when the book was done, her contract was up and back she'd go to California to get another assignment from her publisher and that would be that. Life would go on almost like it had before. Almost, but not quite. Her life would be bleak and empty for a while because she wouldn't have John in it anymore, but loneliness was something she knew well. She'd had a lifetime of it. The tears were falling freely now, and Nina was disgusted with herself for being such a wimp. It was true though, that old saying about "you can't miss what you never had." But she *would* know what wasn't there because she'd had a little taste of John and she knew very well what she'd be missing. It was what she'd missed for most of her life and would never have again.

Just before she abandoned herself to a torrent of tears, her cell phone rang. She knew it was John because she'd programmed the phone to a certain ring when he called. Hastily she wiped her eyes and cleared her throat so she'd sound normal when she answered. "Yes, what is it?" she said in her usual deadpan voice. Despite her angst she smiled upon hearing his voice. "I'm working, of course. What are you doing that you have the leisure to call me during a work day?"

John laughed. "What if I told you I was in the middle of a lecture and I was overwhelmed with the urge to hear your voice?"

"I'd say you were lying because you're not in a lecture right now. You don't have another class until two," she said dryly.

"Miss Parker, my highly efficient superhuman colleague, you need to check your watch. Not only is it three o'clock, but I just gave them a five-minute break so I could hear your voice. Now you have to eat your words, woman."

Nina gasped and looked at her wristwatch as well as the digital clock on the bedside table. John was right; somehow the time had slipped away from her. For once she was at a loss for words. A soft "Ohh" was all she could say.

John loved her reaction. "Ha! I seem to have rendered you speechless! I'd say that calls for a celebration. How about dinner at Paoli's tonight?"

"That sounds wonderful. What time should I be ready?"

"I'll pick you up at seven, so you might want to reset your watch now. Don't be late or I'll leave without you."

"And who's going to laugh at your lame jokes and admire your manly beauty if not me?" She could have cheerfully bitten her tongue off for that comment about his beauty but John apparently didn't hear it.

"Listen, *chica,* my class is coming back. I'll see you tonight. Take care, baby."

Nina ended the call and once again her eyes filled with tears. In a ridiculously short period of time John had become as essential to her as breathing but he wasn't hers to keep, he never could be. *If he knew the truth about me, he'd drop me like a bad habit. He'd never get involved with someone like me, never in this world.*

Chapter 6

John was in the middle of getting dressed when his cell phone rang. He depressed the talk button impatiently and said hello, then smiled widely as he recognized the voice on the other end. It was his old friend Abe Gold, checking up on him from L.A. "Abe! It's good to hear your voice. How's the family?" John asked.

"Everyone's fine and sends their love. I hadn't heard from you in a while and thought I'd better make sure you were staying out of trouble," Abe answered with his usual dry humor.

"Abe, life couldn't be any better," John said honestly. "I feel great, the medication is doing its job, I'm enjoying getting to know my new family and the job is working out well." He took a deep breath and smiled again. "And I'm falling in love." He braced himself for Abe's reaction.

"Don't tell me, let me guess. I'm assuming you're smitten with your Miss Parker, right?" Abe knew who Nina was, having met her when he came to Michigan to attend John's liver transplant. "She's a lovely woman, but are you sure you're not confusing gratitude with affection, John?" Abe's concern for John was evident in his voice and was indicative of their long friendship.

"I thought about that, Abe, but I'm afraid this is the real thing," John said with a short laugh. "This isn't some crush on an angelic caretaker because Nina is the total opposite of angelic in behavior. She's stubborn, sarcastic, and bossy," he admitted. He checked his goatee in the mirror as he spoke. Conversation with an old friend notwithstanding, he had to make sure he looked his best for Nina.

Abe's voice was full of doubt when he asked the inevitable question. "You're sure this isn't some misplaced devotion? You're not making her sound very, um, *appealing*."

John cradled the small flip phone under his chin and laughed again while he buttoned his shirt. "Appealing doesn't begin to describe her, Abe. She's sweet and funny and underneath all the bricks and mortar of her carefully constructed façade, she's the most adorable and loving woman in the world. She may fool a lot of people with that act, but she's not fooling me," he said confidently.

"I hope you know what you're doing, John."

He got serious as he answered his friend. "I know exactly what I'm doing, Abe. I'm falling in love with a beautiful, complicated woman who exhibits the classic symptoms of a woman who's hiding something. There's something in her past she doesn't want anyone to know, I'd bet my medical license on it." John was silent for a moment as he tried to apply cologne while balancing the phone. Giving up, he added, "All I have to do is get her to trust me enough to tell me what it is and we can live happily ever after."

"Is that all? Sounds easy enough," Abe said dryly. "Just watch your back, John, I wouldn't want to see you get hurt."

John smiled as he buckled his belt and stepped into his Cole-Haan loafers. "Then you have nothing to worry about, Abe. I don't know much, yet, but I know Nina would never hurt me. Not for anything in this world."

* * *

Despite his cavalier and confident words to Abe, John wasn't completely devoid of anticipation. He was trying hard not to let it show, but he was as nervous as a sixteen-year-old on his first date. Dating Nina was everything he knew it would be. She was a constant delight to him; her sharp acerbic wit combined with a feminine charm very few people got to see. She was smart, engaging and hilarious and he knew for a fact she had his back come hell or high water. That alone made Nina different. He'd dated a lot of women in his life, but there was no one who had gone or would go to the lengths Nina had for him. There was nothing she wouldn't do for him and he knew it. In the relatively brief time they'd known each other she'd become a part of him. He couldn't read an article or hear a news report without wondering what Nina's take on it would be. If he saw a preview for a new movie he thought she'd like, he'd automatically make a note to get tickets. It delighted him to think up ways to please her; he was sickeningly eager to see that lovely dimpled smile of hers. And when he could make her laugh, his day was made. Nina was by far the most satisfying woman he'd ever been involved with.

In addition to being lively and interesting, she was passionate beyond belief. When he first met her, John thought she was dry and asexual and he'd never enjoyed being so very wrong about something. It had never occurred to him that Nina would be affectionate, but she was, enticingly so. They seemed to always be touching each other, either holding hands or hugging or kissing like their hope of salvation depended on each other's lips. The nights they stayed in and watched television were like sweet torture. She would be curled up next to him, or they would be reclined on the sofa with her resting on his chest and their legs entwined. And the way she kissed him . . .

Madre de Dios, there was nothing in the world to compare to it.

John took a deep breath as he maneuvered the car through the streets of Ann Arbor to pick up Nina for their date. He was feeling the familiar stirring in his loins that never went away when he thought about her. Right now he wanted nothing more than to unite with her completely, to make exquisitely passionate love to her until she knew how much he loved her. *Whoa. Where did that come from? What am I thinking, I can't tell her that, not yet.* He laughed at the futility of his protest; anytime you tried that hard to conceal your feelings from someone it was a foregone conclusion they would become glaringly obvious. Sooner or later he was going to spill everything to Nina. How she'd react to it was another story entirely, but he knew a declaration of passion was on its way.

The mere thought of her consumed him and turned him into a mass of unfulfilled desire. He wanted to make love to her so badly it was a physical ache, but one he didn't know if he could relieve. It had been almost two years since John had been physically intimate with a woman. When his illness first manifested itself, before it had been properly diagnosed, John had a gradual lessening of physical desire combined with a general listlessness and lack of energy. As the disease ran its course, sex was driven completely from his mind. Daily living was challenging enough; the very notion of intimacy was out of the question. After the surgery, though, as he recovered and regained his strength, his normal stamina returned and with it his normal male desires. And each moment he spent with Nina served to increase those desires into a longing so keen it was like a knife piercing his soul.

When Nina opened her door, John got a head rush just from looking at her. She looked incredibly lovely in a chocolate brown dress made of some kind of soft knit material. It had a high neckline and long sleeves, and it was rather long, stopping below her knees. Her hair was different; it was loose around her pretty face in an artlessly styled coif that served to emphasize her features. Her only jewelry, besides the thick gold bracelet he'd given her earlier in the year, was a pair of earrings that consisted of smoky topaz set in yellow gold, five delicately graduated stones that swayed with every movement of her head. Her legs looked fantastic as always, especially since she was wearing high heels for change, a pair of strappy mules made of leather embossed to look like snakeskin.

John took a deep breath as he beheld Nina looking like something delicious to eat. "Miss Parker, you look nothing short of amazing. Turn around and let me see the whole effect."

Nina didn't move, she just smiled and said John looked equally handsome. "I like that suit, John. And I like you in those band-collared shirts. You look very debonair," she said softly. "What's that in your hand?"

John presented her with a box of Godiva truffles. He knew chocolate was a favorite of hers and he'd yet to meet a woman who could resist a truffle. Sure enough, Nina's eyes glittered like the topazes in her ears when she saw the box. "John, I know it'll spoil my appetite, but I must have a piece," she confessed. She took the box from him and turned to put it on the table so she could inspect its bounty.

"Nina! I know you weren't planning to go out of here in that! John's voice boomed so loudly it made Nina drop the box, which luckily landed on the table.

She tried to look guileless, as though she didn't know what he meant, but when John's expression didn't change, she put her back to him so he could see the dress in its entire splendor. The front of the dress was demure, but the back was nonexistent. It was obvious that she wasn't wearing a bra or anything close to it because the fit of the dress wouldn't allow it. Nina tried not to laugh but she couldn't help a kittenish smile, the look on John's face was too priceless.

"Now, sweetie, don't look like that." She removed a truffle and held the box out to John. "Want one?" she asked provocatively before putting the piece in her mouth. John still hadn't spoken; he was watching her intently as she tasted the chocolate. He could tell from the look of bliss on her face exactly when her tongue pushed through the creamy shell to find the even creamier ganache filling that awaited her. At that moment he pulled her into his arms and covered her mouth with his. The surprise made her lips part just enough to allow him access and he seized the opportunity, sliding his tongue in to join hers in an orgy of sensation, their tongues mating in a molten chocolate bliss. They shared the candy and the kiss while John took advantage of the low back of the dress. His hands stroked and fondled Nina's willing flesh until she was weak from the dual assault.

When it was finally over, John was the first to speak. He didn't release Nina from his embrace, he continued to stroke her and murmured into her hair, "I think I've lost my appetite for food."

Nina stretched against John's body, wrapping her arms around his neck as she planted one more luscious kiss on his lips. "Is that your charmingly discreet way of saying we should go to bed?"

"Yes, it is, Miss Parker."

"Then let's go. Bring the candy," Nina whispered.

Holding hands like childhood sweethearts, John and Nina went into the bedroom. It was pretty standard hotel room fare, with a generic looking bedspread that matched the curtains and carpet, and the ubiquitous quasi-oil painting over the bed. Bedside tables flanked the head of the bed, and Nina had left one lamp lit, as was her custom. The only personal, inviting note in the room was the beautiful vase of flowers sent by John. They looked at the bed and each other and it was then Nina's knees began shaking.

John, however, showed no signs of nervousness. He set the infamous box of truffles on the bed, and turned Nina so that she was in front of him. Wrapping his arms around her, he kissed her cheek, her ear and the tempting nape of her neck. "Are you sure you want to do this, *querida?*" Nina pressed her body against John's warmth and slid her hands around so they were grasping John's hips.

"Yes, John, I am."

They were facing the mirror over the dresser and even to her critical eye they looked incredibly sexy. She stifled a giggle, which made John raise his eyes to hers in the mirror. "What's so funny? This isn't a good time to start laughing, trust me," he growled and traced the outline of her ear with his tongue.

"Look at us, we look pretty hot," Nina told him.

They looked beautiful together, both of them radiating sensuality and desire, John's eyes heavy with lust and Nina's blossoming nipples standing in sharp relief against the supple knit of the dress. John said something in Spanish and cupped Nina's breasts in his big warm hands while he started kissing down her back.

Nina gasped and started to tremble as John parted the opening of the dress and began to slide it down her shoulders to gain more access to her warm, taut skin. "John," she breathed, "oh, John . . ."

John slid the dress off her body and made a sound of pleasure as it puddled around her feet to reveal her fantastic form, wearing nothing but a leopard print thong.

He put his hands on her trembling shoulders and slid them down her arms, then scooped her up and put her in the center of the bed. It was his turn to undress, and he kicked off his shoes while he stripped off his sport coat, then his shirt. He reached into the pocket of his pants to retrieve the condoms he carried with him, then unbuckled his belt and began removing his slacks. When he was completely naked, he joined Nina on the bed.

"*Dios,* you're beautiful," he breathed as he reached for her. Their lips met and tongues mingled until John uttered a loud "ouch." Nina's stiletto heel had poked him in the calf.

"Sorry," Nina mumbled and John gave a brief laugh.

"My fault, baby, I should have taken them off but they look so hot on you, I just forgot."

The lethal shoes cast aside, John began to explore Nina's body with his lips as his hands began to remove the delicate thong encasing her femininity. He captured a nipple in his mouth and the hot sensation that coursed through his body made him respond with mindless excitement.

"Ouch! Hey, that's attached to me," Nina protested.

"Sorry, baby, I'm just a little too overwhelmed to take it slow, but I'll try," he promised. The thong successfully removed, they lay in a warm embrace and kissed softly and slowly to allow the loving to begin in earnest. Now John took his time and stroked Nina's breasts, following each stroke with a moist caress of his tongue, gently pulling the nipple into his mouth and feasting on its ripe bud until Nina cried out again, this time with satisfaction. While he was paying tribute to her small, perfect breasts, his fingers were fondling the center of her womanhood, preparing her for what was to come next.

His long fingers sought and found her vaginal opening, moist with the response to his loving. He slipped one finger in, then two, while his thumb massaged her hot, juicy pearl, finding it throbbing and ready. He continued to apply his mouth to her breast, sucking and gently nipping the hard, aroused nipple while he increased the erotic pressure to her clitoris, massaging her until the sudden spurt of warm liquid told him she was about to explode in an orgasm.

Nina was crying John's name over and over, one hand clenching his broad shoulder while the other hand hung on to his thick braid for dear life. She was feeling things she never knew existed; she was being taken to paradise in John's arms. Just when she thought the trip was over, John moved over her body and took control of it in a way she'd only read about in *Cosmo* and *Essence.* When he was finally able to stop ministering to her breasts, John began kissing his way down her body. He stopped at her navel and she learned for the very first time it wasn't just a punctuation mark in the middle of her tummy; it was a full-fledged erogenous zone.

"John," she moaned, "John, what are you doing to me?" At least that's what she meant to say. The sound that actually came out was a low, moaning purr. Her eyes flew open when she realized his ultimate destination. She'd read about "it" but she'd never experienced the art of love in this manner. She had no idea there were so many nerve endings there and no idea how John's talented tongue was finding them all, but she felt as though she were splintering into billions of tiny planets each in orbit around a great pulsing sun called John. The sensation built in her until she could feel herself levitating off the bed into a spiral of passion that would surely drive her mad if it didn't stop.

"JOHN!"

This time her voice seemed to work because John finally began kissing his way back up her body, soothing her trembling with his every touch. He finally ended at her lips, kissing her mouth with the same intensity he'd applied to her clitoris and she was shocked by how erotic it was to taste her essence on his tongue, to smell her own intimate fragrance in his thick moustache. If she'd been thinking clearly, she would have thought it was repulsive but it was so sensuous and sweet all it did was arouse her more.

"John, I want you," she breathed.

"I want you, too, *mi corazon.* You are my heart, you know that, right?"

And you are mine, she thought, but the words didn't leave her lips. Instead, she shivered delicately and snuggled closer to John, nestling next to his heart. They'd finally managed to get under the covers while still remaining entwined in each other.

"Are you cold? Do you want to take a shower to get warm?"

"I think I know another way to get warm." Nina gave John a smile of three parts mischief and one part pure joy as she turned so she was on her back looking up at his handsome face smiling down at her.

"Oh, you do?" John's words turned into a moan of pleasure as Nina's hands found his sex, by now hard as steel and engorged with the proof of his longing for her. "Nina, baby, sweetheart, don't do that," he pleaded.

"I think turnabout is fair play, John. You had your way with me," she murmured as she fondled the turgid flesh, delighting in the incredible softness masking the steely pole within. "Now it's time for me to have my way with you, sweetheart."

"No! Not yet, Nina, not yet. Please baby, you're playing with fire. There's plenty of time for that, but let me get this on right now," John said firmly as he gently removed himself from Nina's agile fingers.

While he was applying the condom Nina got her first

really good look at his massive member and her eyes grew enormous.

"Umm, John, I don't think that's going to fit," she said hoarsely.

John gave her a beautiful loving smile and kissed her softly. "Oh that's where you're wrong, *querida.* Come let me show you how well we fit together."

A couple of hours later, Nina was ready to concede that they fit together just perfectly. John had turned over on his back and lifted Nina onto his body, holding her hips until he was sure she could handle the girth and length of him. As her sighs of enjoyment turned into moans of ecstasy, John began moving his own hips to establish a rhythm for them, one that would bring them both to complete bliss. But as John feared, his long period of abstinence took its toll, and even though he quickly rolled Nina over on her back to better control the sensation, she was simply too much for him. She was so incredibly hot and tight he felt his control slipping and in mere minutes it was over.

"Oh damn, my bad, baby," John moaned. Nina just wrapped her arms and legs around him and held him tightly.

"It's kind of flattering, really," she said sweetly. "You must think I'm a real hot mama."

John rose up on his elbows and looked down at the woman he'd come to love so dearly. "You have no idea, Nina. You're amazing, you really are. You're funny, and beautiful and kind and you're so sweet it makes my heart hurt when I think about all the wonderful things you've done for me. And the passion is so incredibly hot, baby." At her look of disbelief he kissed her softly and kept talking to her in a low voice full of tenderness.

"Your mouth is a treasure all by itself, Nina, it makes me dizzy to think about kissing those lips, and the things you can do with that tongue just drive me crazy. Your skin is so soft and sexy, and the way you move your body makes me want to kidnap you and take you somewhere far way from here so we can make love around the clock. And the way I feel when I'm inside you . . ."

His erection had returned, harder and even more engorged and this time he was ready for the volcanic response his body had to Nina's. This time he entered her swiftly and with assurance, driving his sex into her moist, welcoming opening over and over, piloting them both to the edge of blinding ecstasy. He reached for her hands and they entwined their fingers, preparing to drown together in the eddying abyss of ultimate fulfillment. This time he was in total control and using every bit of his skill to make sure Nina was fulfilled. When her wet canal clenched on him and she cried out, he knew it was time to let go and join her in the *pue de mort* that signaled the birth of their love.

Nina, my love, Dios, I love you so. For the life of him he didn't know if he'd spoken the words aloud or not.

Now, in the bathroom after a long hot shower, Nina knew for a fact that John was a very wise man about some things. There were a few other things, however, he still needed to learn.

"You simply cannot be my boyfriend. I can't have a man who has prettier hair than I do," Nina pouted.

John's thick, wavy black hair looked no worse for having romped around in the throes of passion, but Nina's looked, as she put it, "right witchy." She'd insisted on wearing a cap as they showered, something that amused John even as it further endeared her to him.

"Look, I don't have blow hair, okay? Lots of chemicals and potions are needed to keep my hair looking even this raggedy so you can imagine what it looks like impromptu. I told you I was the wrong woman for you, you need one of those Cochran-type women with the good hair," she said with a frown.

He squeezed the excess water out of his long braid and leaned over to kiss Nina. "Baby, I love your hair. Lots of sisters relax their hair so why should that be a big deal? My *Mami* relaxed her hair all the time. I used to go to the beauty shop with her when I was little. It was fun to me, I loved watching the ladies get hooked up and they always gave me candy and lots of hugs. Especially the older ladies with the big bosoms, that was the best. Can I come to the beauty shop with you, *chica*?" he asked hopefully.

Nina assured him that he could not. "In the first place, I do my own hair. It costs too much to go to the salon. In the second place, I have my girls. They eliminate the need for going to the hairdresser because they always have my back when my hair goes back to Africa on me."

John burst out laughing at her comment. Nina did indeed have several ponytails, both human and synthetic, with which she augmented her hair as the whim took her. John had found that tidbit out earlier in the year. Nina's hair had been scooped up in a high ponytail that hung past her shoulders and he'd stupidly asked if it was all her hair. Instead of slitting his throat with a nail file, Nina had said, "What are you, the hair police? Of course it's mine, want to see the receipt?" While he was recuperating from surgery Nina had amused him by revealing that her pieces had names; Jeannie was the high one, after *I Dream of Jeannie*. And there was a Beyonce, a Barbie and a Sophia as well.

Nina had to get the last word on the hair thing, though.

She looked at him over her shoulder as she removed the shower cap and fluffed her hair out.

"And in the third place, if you think I'm going to sit around and watch a bunch of women make fools out of themselves over you, you've got another thing coming. That's my job," she said smugly.

John looked at the adorable picture she made in her pink terry cloth wrap and picked her up to carry her off to bed. "Well *my* job is to make you happy. Let's make love again, baby. I told you I couldn't get enough of you."

"I seem to be pretty insatiable myself. And I seem to have a really strong craving for chocolate, too. What do you think we should do about that?"

John gave her a wicked smile as he deposited his treasure on the bed. Picking up the box of truffles he said, "I think I have a really good idea about that. Have a piece?"

Chapter 7

Nina lay perfectly still, facing the ceiling with her eyes closed. She was playing the "if" game, something she hadn't done since she was very small. If I go to sleep right now, Santa Claus will come. If I eat all my beets my hair will be long and pretty. If I don't make any noise they won't beat me anymore. *If I don't open my eyes, I'll never wake up and this will all be true. If I keep my eyes closed forever, last night will be real and not just a dream.* She took a deep cleansing breath that ended with a shaky groan. Sitting straight up in the bed she opened her eyes and tried hard to smile, but it was impossible, the corners of her mouth refused to cooperate. They felt, in fact, like little anchors were weighing them down. The harder she tried to bring the corners up, the more hangdog her expression became.

She tossed the covers aside and threw her legs over the side of the bed. She looked around for something to cover her nude body and finally saw her pink terry wrap on the dresser where it had landed after John tossed it across the room. The sight of it made her mood even worse as she recalled the exact circumstance that led to its new position. She stood up so quickly she almost lost her balance and stomped across the room to retrieve it. The little voice in her head had a comment about her attitude. *Look at you. Got the first decent loving you've had in your life and you're acting like a big fool, aren't you. You really need to* chill, *girl.*

"And you need to mind your own business," Nina muttered as she went to tend to her morning needs.

Fifteen minutes later she emerged from the bathroom after a hot and efficient shower, dressed in her peach and white robe. She was looking anything but radiant and rested after her ablutions; her mood hadn't lifted one little bit. She stared at the rumpled bed for a moment and her stomach clenched like a fist. How could she have done it? How in the world could she have succumbed to the desire she'd felt for John from the first moment they met? And more importantly, how was she ever going to face him again? She couldn't stand looking at the bed another second, she removed all the linens and folded the coverlet and blanket and put them on the chair in the corner of the room.

By now her electric curlers had heated sufficiently and she put them in her hair, managing to stab her scalp viciously each time she tried to secure a roller. Maybe if she hadn't awakened by herself, maybe if John had stayed instead of sneaking off like a thief in the night, maybe then she wouldn't feel like such a prize fool. But the fact was he'd gotten what he came for and left. *No big surprise there,* she thought derisively. *Just par for the freakin' course. The only surprise here is me, letting myself get taken in like a yokel.* She made a horrible face in the mirror and dared herself to cry. *You're not too big to beat, heifer, let a drop fall from yo' eye and see don't you get your ass beat.*

She didn't realize she was speaking aloud until the ugliness of the words brought up a past she kept locked up so tightly she refused to ever speak of it to anyone. The shock of memory made her start shaking with repressed anger and sorrow and she had to get out of the bathroom. She couldn't breathe. She left hastily, going straight through the bedroom and into the living room, intending to open the door for just a breath of non-conditioned air. She fumbled at the doorknob and pulled the door open hastily, then let out a shrill noise like a steam engine when she saw John's tall frame filling the doorway with a newspaper under his arm, a rose between his teeth and a large takeout bag from a local restaurant in his hand. He looked more startled than Nina felt as he entered the suite while taking the rose out of his mouth.

"Baby, what's the matter? Is something after you, what is it?" John looked all around the room and saw nothing amiss as he put the bag and newspaper on the table. He turned to face Nina, grasping her shoulders so he could get a good look at her. "What's wrong, baby, why did you look so scared?" he asked her gently.

"What's wrong with *you,* don't you know how to use a phone or knock or something? You scared ten years off my life, you dolt. I wasn't expecting you on the other side of the door, that's all." Nina sounded like a total shrew and she knew it but it was better than bursting into the soap opera-ish tears of joy she was trying desperately to stifle.

John tilted her chin up and put an endearing little kiss on her pouting lips. "Aww, Miss Parker, I had to go shower and change and bring you breakfast. It was supposed to be a surprise, a pleasant and romantic surprise. I wasn't trying to scare you," he crooned. "So why don't you sit down and I'll serve you, my lady. My Martian lady," he added with a grin.

"Martian lady?" Just then the unpleasant warmth of the rollers reminded her of how her hair was arranged. "Oh, crap!" She put her hands up to cover the horrible rollers and like many a surprised woman before her, flew out of the room in her bare feet.

"Why are you running off? I already saw the worst and

you look cute to me, honey." John shook his head. *Why do women get so bent about things like that? Papi saw Mami looking much worse than that from time to time and he was still hot for her until the day they died.* He frowned at the feeling of melancholy that claimed him momentarily. His parents had truly adored each other and kept their marriage full of passion until the day they died as the result of a horrific car crash. They never stopped showing each other how much they cared and the sexual energy had never flagged; John knew this to be fact from the few times he'd come home unannounced after he was living on his own. He smiled at the memory and the smile got broader when he thought about sharing that kind of passion with Nina.

He was still smiling as he arranged Nina's breakfast on the bar that separated the living room from the tiny kitchenette with a mini refrigerator, microwave and sink. The Martian queen finally came back to the living room, this time fully dressed in jeans and a long-sleeved peach colored T-shirt with a dangerously deep V-neck. Her hair was becomingly styled in loose curls and there was a tiny bit of makeup on her flawless skin, just enough to make her lashes stand out and her lips gleam enticingly. She gave John a mildly hostile look and asked, "What are you grinning about?"

John raised an eyebrow as he walked over to stand next to her. "I'm *smiling*, Nina. Grinning implies a stupid look of inane glee. Smiling is a refined show of happiness, like the happiness I feel at serving breakfast to my *querida* on the morning after our first . . ."

Nina held up her hand. "Don't go there, John. Just stop it," she said crossly.

John laughed at her and put his hands on her waist. "Oh,

I'm going there, baby. I'm going there," he murmured as he kissed her lips, "and there," he promised as he looked down her cleavage, "and you know I'm going *there,*" he said as he pulled her flush to his body and thrust his pelvis into hers for a long slow gyration that took Nina's breath away. "So sit down, eat the food I've already had to nuke once to keep warm, and try to be pleasant if not happy. Please?"

Nina was torn between continuing her tough-girl act and succumbing to John's infectiously happy mood. She looked up at him, so handsome and appealing in his well-worn jeans and faded Polo shirt, and shocked him by wrapping her arms around him for a hug she was loathe to end. She turned her face up to his and kissed him with great sweetness and tenderness while murmuring, "Thank you, John, it was wonderful for you to do this for me."

They finally sat down to eat and the food was still warm and still delicious. John had brought her scrambled eggs with turkey sausage, hash browns with onions and peppers and a huge cheese Danish. And there was fresh orange juice and coffee as well. Nina ate neatly and daintily but she cleaned her plate. John was always impressed with the prodigious amounts Nina could put away; she could easily eat as much as he did.

"John that was really wonderful. Thank you again. Of course, I'm going to have to run a few extra miles to metabolize it, but that's okay. Yum," she sighed, licking her lips. She got up from the breakfast bar, started clearing away the remnants of the meal, and John stopped her.

"I'll get this, baby. There's something interesting in the newspaper, though, why don't you take a look?"

With an expression of curiosity, Nina went into the living room and picked up the newspaper off the coffee table. Something fell out of its folds and hit her foot. She bent over to pick it up, completely missing the look of lust and adoration John gave her as she unwittingly pointed her butt in his direction.

"John, these look like tickets," Nina said.

"They are tickets, Nina."

"Oh." She placed the tickets on the table and refused to look at John. "So where are you going?" she asked dully.

"*I'm* not going anywhere, beloved. *We're* going somewhere together," he said gently. "How'd you like to come to the old country with me?"

Nina didn't even try to disguise the look of pleased excitement on her face; she ran to John and threw her arms around his neck, kissing him soundly. "I'd love to," she said between kisses. "When do we leave?"

Their getaway was scheduled for the next weekend. John's classes were on Tuesday, Wednesday and Thursday and there was a two-day study break scheduled before midterms, so he didn't have to be back on campus until the following Wednesday. Nina was still dazed by John's thoughtfulness and told him so as they made plans. They were on the sofa, John lying down with Nina resting on top of him, her long legs twined with his. "What made you decide to go to Puerto Rico, John? Not that I'm complaining, you understand, I'm very pleased you asked me to go, I'm simply curious," she said softly as she stroked his chest, running her hand in a slow, steady circle. She just enjoyed touching him; there was something so comforting about feeling the warmth of his body next to hers.

John shifted her so he could kiss her forehead. "I wanted to take you somewhere warm and sunny and it was the first place I thought of. I have many fond memories of the place from growing up. It's where my mother and father met and fell in love so it's always seemed like a romantic place to me." He paused while he put his hand on top of the one that was still tracing circles on his chest. He brought her hand up to his lips and caressed it gently. "I wanted to take you someplace exotic so we would have beautiful surroundings, someplace where we could really get to know each other."

Nina raised her head and looked around the totally unremarkable room. "You mean this ambiance doesn't suit you? But it's so warm, so personal," she laughed.

"Cold and generic, I think you mean. I want to go someplace with a really big bed and a great big Jacuzzi tub and room service so we can wallow in luxury for a few days. Doesn't that sound wonderful?"

Nina agreed that it did. "What should I pack? I've never been anywhere tropical. I probably don't have anything to wear," she mused.

"Just bring casual things, nothing too dressy. We're going to be relaxing on the beach, eating in some places that have really good food, but nothing too fancy, it's not like you'll need a formal gown or anything," John said sleepily.

"How about a swimsuit?" Nina asked innocently.

"Oh, sure. The beaches there are amazing," John yawned.

"Good, because I have a great bikini. It's red with a thong bottom," she said mischievously.

John was instantly wide awake. "You can burn it now, Nina, because there's no way you're wearing it. Don't you have something that's one piece? Maybe with long sleeves and a skirt or something?"

Nina laughed. "You just described an ice-skating costume, John. Don't worry about it; I don't think I even brought a suit with me. I didn't come to Michigan to swim."

"We'll get you one at the hotel. You have to go in the water down there, you'll love it. Of course, I get to pick it out," he said sternly.

"In your dreams, buddy." Nina slid her body so she was completely on top of John, issuing a little sigh of contentment as she enjoyed the sensation of being so close to him. He continued to hold her hand, his thumb stroking the inside of her wrist. She smiled sleepily. "When I was really little I had a charm bracelet and there was one special charm on it from Puerto Rico," she murmured. "It was shaped like the island and it was silver with pretty colors enameled on it. It really came from Puerto Rico, too. My mommy brought it to me because she missed me so much when she was there."

"That's sweet, baby. Where's your bracelet now?"

Nina rolled off John's body so quickly he didn't have time to react. "It's gone. I don't have it anymore."

She went into the bedroom and sat down on the still-bare bed, looking down at her feet. John followed her at once, looking concerned. "What's wrong, Nina? That obviously triggered a painful memory for you, do you want to talk about it?"

Nina looked at John angrily and pointed her finger at him, mindless of its shaking. "I told you to stay out of my head," she said angrily. "I'm not one of your patients, John. I don't need your psychobabble, do you understand? I don't need you trying to interpret my every thought and emotion and trying to make me over, okay?"

"Good, because that's the last thing I want to do," John said calmly. He sat down on the bed next to her and gave her a long, serious look. "I don't know how to tell you this without seeming like a total jackass, but there are times when I wish I had any kind of job except mine. Not all the time, of course, but there are those moments when I wish I was a pediatrician, a butcher, a steelworker, anything but what I am.

"There are many times when it's tremendously gratifying to be able to help someone come out of the darkness and misery of an emotional or mental illness, times when I see a patient able to break away from their demons and begin to live fully and without fear. That's when I'm absolutely sure I'm doing the right thing with my life." He laughed with no mirth before he continued. "Then there are the times when I want to tell people to just get a life. If your husband is a louse, leave him. If you hate your job so much, quit. You dream about food because you're hungry, go eat something."

He stood up and pinched the bridge of his nose. "The people who really get to me are the ones who can't even articulate their pain, they don't know how or when or where, but somewhere along the line their life has gone so wrong they can't even remember when things were right. And I'm the magician who's supposed to make it all right again."

He walked back and forth a few times before looking at Nina with a bleak expression, not bothering to hide his conflicted emotions. "I'm not going to pretend like I can automatically turn off years of training but I promise you I'll do my best to not treat you like a case study or a patient. I can't swear I'll be one hundred percent effective at it because I care about you so much and I want you to be happy. So if I say something that ticks you off, I hope you'll let me know."

Nina was shocked and humbled by John's words. And she also felt a little guilt; she didn't mean to put John in an awkward position. Yet, she felt closer to John, closer than she'd ever imagined she could feel to anyone. "John I don't know what to say. I thought you loved your work," she said softly.

John stopped his pacing and threw himself across the bed. "Don't get me wrong, *querida,* I can't imagine not being a doctor. I just wonder what would have happened if I'd picked another specialty. That's the problem with deciding on a career early in life, I guess. I let a twelve-year-old boy decide what I'm going to do for the rest of my life and somehow there's something wrong with that."

"What do you mean, John?" Nina asked curiously.

John sighed and reached for Nina. "When I was a kid there was a man in the neighborhood who we all called Uncle Buddy. He lived in a nice little house with flowers in the yard and fruit trees and he and his wife, Sarah, were wonderful people. Then Sarah got sick and died and left Uncle Buddy alone, because his children were grown and far away. Uncle Buddy started going downhill fast after that. He started looking disheveled, he would wander the neighborhood for hours and hours, and his lawn went wild and the house started going to seed. My parents tried to help him keep it together but he got worse and worse despite their help. Then he was accused of attacking some woman and even though it was later proved to not be true, some of the neighbors got to be afraid of him," John said solemnly.

"Eventually his children came and got him but I heard they put him in a home, they couldn't take care of him. That really bothered me, the idea that he was old and lonely and going crazy from grief and there was nothing that could be done for him. My parents tried to explain it to me, but nothing they could say made it any better. One time I took a bus out to the home where Uncle Buddy was and he looked terrible, he was so frail and old he couldn't move around and he was totally lost in the past. He thought I was one of his sons and he kept asking me if I had mowed the lawn. Nina, I was heartbroken for that old man. That's when I decided I was going to be a shrink. I was going to help everyone who had those kinds of problems; I was going to make it all better. And sometimes I do, sometimes I don't."

Nina's eyes were full of tears when John finished

speaking. They held each other for a long time after that. John finally kissed her on the forehead and looked at the bed with a fierce expression.

"How are we supposed to make mad, passionate love with no sheets?" he growled.

Nina laughed at the look on John's face. "Housekeeping hasn't been in here yet. And besides, it's broad open daylight or hadn't you noticed?"

"And what has the time got to do with anything? Lovemaking doesn't have a watch, *chica.* I can't believe you're shy, Nina. Don't you know we can do whatever we want, whenever we want, for as long as we want to do it?"

Nina stared at John, sprawled across the bed looking like her idea of the perfect centerfold. He was so beautiful it actually made her throat ache a little to look at him, not to mention what it did to other parts of her body. Now she knew first hand what his long limbs, his sexy chiseled lips and his long artistic hands could do to bring her pleasure and she was eager to join him, but in the middle of the day? She could feel a warm sensation slowly snaking its way through her most intimate regions and the sensation increased the longer John's eyes held hers. She wanted him, no question, but surely there was something decadent about just laying around in the bed all day. Unconsciously, she bit her lower lip, having no idea how adorably vulnerable it made her look.

Nina's doubtful expression was all it took to spur John into action. Moving with the quickness of a jungle cat, he rolled off the bed into a standing position and picked Nina up. Ignoring her cries of laughter, he headed for the front door. "I can see you're going to take some convincing, Miss Parker. And I can show you better than I can tell you."

Chapter 8

Despite Nina's repeated attempts to escape him, John prevailed and in a short time they were in his apartment. He'd distracted her with conversation on the ride over and she'd almost forgotten why they were here until John gave her "that" smile, the one she was beginning to recognize. "What are you up to?" she asked, suspicion heavy in her tone.

John laughed gently and took her by the hand.

"Come sit down, Nina. I'm not going to do anything you don't want me to do. Let's just sit down and listen to some nice music," he said, drawing her over to the sofa and picking up the little remote for his stereo system. Bebel Gilberto's melodic voice filled the room while John and Nina got comfortable on the couch. It took a couple of minutes because Nina was anything but relaxed. Every time John tried to touch her, she alternated between awkward stiffness and limber evasion. John made an exaggerated show of exhaustion by the time she finally yielded against him.

"*Madre de Dios,* Nina, are you related to Houdini? You could get work as an escape artist, girl."

"Hey, I have to be able to take care of myself. I'm a fragile little woman all alone in a big scary world," she said demurely. She wasn't really listening to John; she was too overloaded by the sensation of his nearness. He smelled better than anyone else in the world. It wasn't his aftershave or cologne; there was a clean warmth to the scent of his smooth skin that drove her crazy.

"I take issue with that fragile part, you may be the toughest woman I've ever met," John murmured into her neck. "But you don't have to worry about the big scary world. As long as I'm in it, nothing's going to bother you."

Nina moved in John's arms but he held her even closer. "Don't start wiggling again, woman."

"Don't start talking a bunch of trash you don't mean," Nina countered. She gasped as John swung her up onto his body so she was straddling him. He anchored his arms around her and put a finger under her chin so she'd have to look directly in his eyes. She was so surprised she forgot about telling him off, she just sighed with admiration. "You really are strong, aren't you?"

"Yes, I really am. And I mean every word of what I say to you. I may play around because that's my nature, but nobody's going to bother you or make you unhappy in any way. Don't you trust me, baby?"

Nina looked into his black eyes shadowed by his long straight lashes and she wanted to believe him, she wanted it with all her being. "Yes, John, but . . ." she stopped speaking because John had taken possession of her lips. His mouth was fierce with passion, his hot lips taking control of hers and giving her a glimpse of the depths of his ardor. She responded in ways she didn't know she was capable of, holding his face in both of her hands; she opened to him, finding his sweet tongue waiting for hers. The wild mating of their mouths didn't quiet the stirrings of passion; it ignited them, taking Nina out of herself and into a questing need to be one with John. She began to move again, but this time it was her hips, moving against John in the unmistakable siren dance that told him all he needed to know.

He slipped his hands under Nina's T-shirt and stroked her smooth skin, murmuring endearments to her in Spanish until she pulled away from his embrace long enough to pull the shirt over her head. Pleased by her boldness, John began to remove his own shirt but Nina wouldn't let him. "John, I'm going to explode," she whispered urgently. He answered the yearning in her voice at once, cupping his hands under her hot bottom and standing up with her arms locked around his neck. She wrapped her long legs around his waist while he carried her into his bedroom where they fell, none too gracefully, onto the bed.

While John was taking off his shirt, Nina kicked off her flats and peeled her jeans off hastily. She looked up to see John unbuckling his belt and he looked so masculine, so incredibly sexy she forgot how to breathe for a moment. She touched his arm and murmured his name. "John."

"Yes, sweetie?"

"You're beautiful," she said shyly. At his look of amazed disbelief, Nina moved closer to him and touched his broad chest. "You really are, inside and out. I've never known anyone like you in my entire life," she confessed.

John looked at her tenderly. She looked both wanton and pure, wearing an enticing half-cup bra made of sheer rose-colored lace with a matching thong. Her hair was tousled and her lips were love-swollen from their kisses. He swiftly removed his jeans and briefs and reached for her. "Come here, baby. You talk too much," he murmured as he undid the front fastener of her bra. As her tantalizing breasts came into view John smiled. "You're the beautiful one, Nina. Have I told you how much I like these?" He circled them with his broad warm palms before taking an erect and yearning nipple into his mouth. While he applied a sensual pressure to its throbbing tip with his lips and tongue, his fingers kneaded the other one until Nina moaned with passion and pleasure.

It was John's turn to be delighted when Nina shrugged out of her bra and made short work of the delicate thong. "I want to feel you inside me," she whispered. "I want to be a part of you."

Touched to his heart and aroused like never before, John covered her body with his while he reached for the condoms in the bedside table. "I want you too, more than you can imagine. You're like a fire in me, Nina," he said softly.

They managed to get the condom on John's pulsing, huge erection and Nina cried out when John entered her. The sensation of being filled so completely was overwhelming, it was terrifying, it was indescribably fulfilling; Nina thought she would faint from sheer pleasure. She clung to John's shoulders as he pumped in and out of her body, each stroke bringing them closer and closer to the inevitable explosion that would make them one.

"Look at me, baby, look in my eyes," John moaned. Nina's lashes fluttered up and she was instantly adrift in love. The expression on John's face as his body gave hers the most intimate gift possible was too much for her. He suddenly changed the angle of their bodies just a little, just enough to create a slightly different tension that rocked Nina into a place she'd never imagined before, a place where there was nothing but John and the wild, pulsing sensations he created in her. She tried to keep her eyes locked on John's but her body was no longer hers to control. As John drove deeper into her willing flesh her eyes closed and she breathed his name, over and over until the seismic tremors began to slow down and she was able to breathe again.

John turned so he was on his back and gathered Nina to him, holding her close as she slowly, very slowly came back to earth. He brushed her hair away from her face and kissed her forehead while he murmured to her in Spanish. Suddenly, he uttered a soft burst of joyous laughter.

"What's so funny?" Nina whispered. "You'd better not be laughing at me," she said in a sleepy voice.

"Too late, I am. I was just thinking that you're a quick study. You learned to make love in the daytime really fast, didn't you, *chica?*"

Nina gave him a dazzling smile. "I had a good teacher," she replied as she brought her lips to his for a kiss.

She discovered a hidden benefit of making love early in the day; you still had a lot of the day left to do things and on top of it, you were in a really swell mood. At least Nina was, she couldn't remember ever being so happy. Even the little voice in her head had nothing to say about her mood. She was, in a word, blissful. She was curled up on the sofa in the living room, waiting for John to return with food. They had decided, after much more love-making and a long, soapy shower together, that they were starving.

"We could make something here," John said.

"I don't cook," Nina said at once.

"Well I do, so this is your lucky day. I'll go get us something and you just relax while I'm gone. Are you sure you don't want me to go to your place and get some clothes for you?"

Nina demurred, saying she could put on the same ones, once her underwear dried. She'd washed it out by hand, the way she always did and she assured him it would dry very quickly. In the meantime, he'd dressed her in one of his shirts and she looked charming with the sleeves rolled up and the hem halfway up her thigh. With him kissing Nina and fondling every part of her he could get to under the wholly inadequate cover of his shirt, it took quite a while for John to leave. Nina had to convince him she was starving before he'd go. As soon as the door closed behind him, Nina put the bedroom back in order. She changed the sheets with the linens she found in the bathroom cupboard and made everything tidy. Tidier, actually, than it had been to begin with, as John wasn't a slave to order.

She finally dozed off on the sofa, lulled by the lilting Brazilian music created by Bebel Gilberto and also by the total contentment she felt. She had her arms wrapped around a throw pillow and she looked like a sweet child sleeping peacefully. John found her that way when he returned with the food. He liked looking at her any time but he found this particularly appealing because she was so vulnerable. And he finally had an opportunity to get a good look at her elusive toes. They were, as he suspected, perfect. They were just long enough and completely free of any blemish with the nails done in a sexy French manicure. John smiled broadly. Even though she'd been barefoot that morning she'd been moving so fast he hadn't been able to really look at her feet and he didn't think she'd just show them to him if he asked.

Nina opened her eyes to find John smiling down at her with a goofy look on his face. "You look quite silly up there," she said sleepily. "Did you bring me something to eat?"

"Yes, I did. I'll cook dinner for you later, but I thought you might need some sustenance now. And while we eat we can talk about going away."

Even though her underwear had dried, Nina was in no rush to get dressed. She kept on the shirt while they ate the chicken and pasta salads he'd purchased. It was a pleasant meal, they talked the whole time, touching each other occasionally and smiling for no particular reason. Their good mood continued as Nina tidied up the kitchen. John tried to make himself useful but all he was really doing was ogling Nina's legs and kissing her on the neck and ear while she was trying to wash the few dishes they'd used. She'd make a feeble protest every so often, but in truth she was enjoying their playful interlude.

John was standing behind her, licking the sensitive area right under her ear when she finally managed to escape from him, leaving him standing in front of the sink with the water running. She laughed at the look of surprise on his face, and then squeaked as he wet his fingers and flicked the water in her face.

"Oh no you don't," she warned. "Don't start that or I'll be forced to retaliate."

John flicked more water at her and she popped him with the dish towel. "Stop that! My brothers used to do that to me and it drove me crazy," she blurted out. Dead silence filled the room as she realized what she just said.

"You have brothers, Nina?" John asked gently.

Nina looked stricken for a moment, then nodded. "Yes, I do. I have two brothers." She took a deep breath before meeting John's gaze. Just saying the words was like lifting a weight off her soul.

The jet cut through the night sky as it headed southward to San Juan, Puerto Rico. Everyone in the first class section was quiet, most people, like Nina, were sound asleep. John had raised the armrest between their seats and Nina was snuggled into John's side as naturally as though they'd been a couple for a long time. Every so often she would issue a soft sigh and her lips would curl into a little smile as she moved against the warmth of his body. John kissed the top of her head and held her even closer, making sure she was covered with the cashmere throw he'd insisted on purchasing for her before they left.

It was often chilly on long flights and John wanted her to be comfortable.

Normally her even breathing would have lulled him to sleep too, but he had too much on his mind. Getting to know Nina was the most difficult thing he'd ever done, and that included graduating med school. There was so much about her he still didn't know and he knew if he tried to solicit the information from her it would be futile. She'd resent the intrusion, she'd accuse him of trying to analyze her and she wouldn't be completely wrong. All he knew for sure was there was a lot more to Nina than she revealed. There were secrets in her past and he knew it as well as he knew his own name. Whether she would ever confide in him was another question entirely.

She'd told him she had brothers, but she'd revealed that information by accident. The words just popped out of her mouth and it was obvious she regretted saying anything. John replayed the incident in his mind. As soon as Nina told him she had two brothers, she turned and left the room, saying she was going to get dressed. John stood there for a few minutes, and then went after her, all his instincts for self-preservation gone in the face of her distress. She might tear him a new one but she needed him and he was going to ask her a few things regardless of her reaction. By the time he reached the bedroom, Nina was already dressed in her jeans and T-shirt, sitting cross-legged on the bed looking pensive.

Not looking at John, Nina began to speak. "I had two brothers, two older brothers. I loved them very much and they loved me. When my mother died we were split up and I haven't seen them since. I never talk about them because I still miss them," she said in a voice so small and quiet John almost couldn't hear her. "And that's all," she said.

John felt like something was tearing away a piece of his heart. He sat down beside her and wrapped her in his arms. She in turn put her arms around him and they stayed that way for a long time, not speaking but communicating all the same. Nina finally pulled away from John and gave him a shaky smile.

"Thank you," she whispered and put a slender hand on either side of his face for a soft little kiss.

"I meant it, baby. I'm here for you always Nina, don't ever doubt that." Her answer was a poignantly sweet smile that was sadder than anything he'd ever seen.

John was still haunted by that smile, even now with Nina safely in his arms. There was much more to the story than Nina was telling him and the only way he could find out what really happened was if she confided in him because he couldn't ask. He wanted to laugh at the irony of it; he was probably the best person in the world for Nina to bring her problems to but their relationship made that impossible. Even if they weren't involved, he'd be the last person on earth she'd bring into her confidence. John frowned, wondering if there was anyone in Nina's life for her to turn to. *Dios, no wonder she was always so reserved and standoffish. She probably feels like it's the only way she can survive.*

Nina stirred in his arms and he placed his lips against her hair again, making a vow that come what may, he would be with her until every single mystery was revealed and she was free from her past, whatever it was. *I take care of what's mine and like it or not, you belong to me.*

Chapter 9

Nina's eyes opened slowly. She wasn't sure where she was at first but once she felt the warmth and protection of John's body spooned next to hers, she remembered. She was in Puerto Rico, in the beautiful hotel John had picked out. They arrived in San Juan very late the night before and thanks to John's efficiency, a rental car was waiting for them. It only took about fifteen minutes to drive to the Wyndham Condado Plaza Hotel and Casino, in which time Nina tried to orient herself to her new environment, but failed because it was dark outside. She'd settled back in her seat and smiled. It didn't matter what the countryside looked like, she was with John and she'd have been happy to be with him anywhere.

Nina and John checked into the hotel and were taken to a lovely suite of rooms with its own balcony. While John tipped the bellman, Nina had wandered around the room in awe at its luxurious appointments. She opened the doors to the balcony and walked out to see the view. She was transfixed by the beauty she could only glimpse, already fascinated by the sound of the ocean splashing far below. The balmy night air was enthralling; she shivered a little as she grew more excited about the next few days. John stepped out behind her, wrapping his arms around her to keep her warm. "Are you cold, baby?"

Nina turned so she could see his face before resting on his broad chest. "I'm thrilled, I'm not cold. This place is beautiful, John, it's just wonderful. Thank you so much," she said with a soft sigh.

She cried out in surprise when John suddenly picked her up and looked her right in the eye. "Stop thanking me. This is for me just as much as it is for you. I don't want thanks, I want love," he growled.

Nina showed all of her perfectly straight, dazzling white teeth in a smile of delight. Wrapping her legs around John's waist she took his earlobe in her mouth and sucked on it gently, ending in a mock nibble. She continued to lick his ear and whispered, "Mmm, if you want love I know where you can get some, right now."

John tightened his arms around her and returned to the bedroom at once. "Now you're talking, baby." He placed her on the bed and sprawled next to her. "So what's your choice, this great big bed or that great big Jacuzzi?"

In the broad light of day, Nina smiled to herself as she recalled how they'd made use of both before they finally went to sleep in each other's arms. The smile faded as she made herself remember that this relationship was only temporary. As much as she wished it could be otherwise, she and John had no chance whatsoever for a future. She had to bite her lower lip very hard to keep the gathering tears from falling, but with a resolve forged in the flames of her hellish past, she made it. She started to get out of the bed when John's long arm tightened around her.

"Where are you going, woman? I know you're not thinking about leaving me all alone, are you? You couldn't be that cruel," he drawled.

Despite her anguish of a moment before, Nina giggled madly. She put her hand up to stroke John's face, loving the rough feel of his unshaven chin. "I have some things to attend to, some first-thing-in-the-morning necessities, if you get my drift. Keep holding me down and you'll find out what they are," she threatened. "And if you don't let me go now you'll meet the beast that lives in my mouth first thing in the morning. I need to brush my teeth and get ready for my run."

John kissed the back of her neck and released her at once. She dashed off to the bathroom and took care of all her needs, including brushing her teeth twice, flossing in between brushings. She looked longingly at the shower, but decided to wait until she'd had a good run on the beach. There was something wonderful about a pounding run with the water lapping alongside; it was energizing and soothing at the same time.

Dressed in her running gear, she left the bathroom and felt her mouth fall open as she saw John, fully dressed for a run right down to his Nikes.

"Before you ask, I'm going with you. If you think you're going out in that skimpy outfit without me you're crazy. It's bad enough you do it at home, but down here it's out of the question. So I run with you or there's no running at all, at least not in that little getup." John crossed his arms as if to dare her to say something.

Nina finished twisting her hair up and secured it with a couple of pins. She went to the drawer where she'd stored her things and took out a scarf with which to cover her hair. She gave John a cheeky grin and said, "I just hope you can keep up, *Papi.*" She laughed at John's scowl and then ran out the door as he gave chase.

That day was the most wonderful Nina could ever remember. They weren't leaving until Monday night so they had four whole days to enjoy the delights San Juan had to offer. Starting with the invigorating run on the beach, where John proved he was more than able to keep up with her, their first day on the island was more idyllic than Nina could have dreamed. They returned to the hotel and bathed each other in a long, sensual shower, after which they ate a delicious breakfast provided by room service. Once Nina was energized, squeaky-clean and well fed, she would have been perfectly content to stay in bed all day with John but he was too excited about showing her San Juan.

Okay, the seduction will have to wait. But just you wait until tonight, John . . . you won't know what hit you, she vowed with a tiny smirk. In the meantime, she got dressed in an outfit she knew would gain John's approval. It was a simple circle skirt in red with tiny white pindots all over it. With it she wore a white tank top and a gauzy white shirt tied at the waist. She had on red canvas espadrilles with long grosgrain ribbon ties around the ankles and she'd pulled her hair up into a chic knot with a couple of cherry red hair picks stuck through it. She looked sexy and sophisticated, like a young Lena Horne and she knew John would love it.

He didn't disappoint her either. His eyes lit up when she came into the living room of the suite. He went to her and took both her hands in his. "Miss Parker, you look beautiful. I can't wait to show you off to my island," he said, giving her a brief kiss.

John took her on a tour of San Juan and Old San Juan, which was once a military installation. He was as full of facts as a guidebook and Nina absorbed them as she drank in everything about the city which was teeming with tourists as well as local citizens going about their daily work. They saw museums, churches, and the shopping districts for which San Juan was noted. They went in several shops where Nina looked with great fascination, but didn't buy anything.

"*Chica,* don't you want something as a souvenir?" John asked curiously.

"I don't need anything to hold in my hand to remember this, John. I'll have it in here always," she said, indicating her heart. Even when her cheeks reddened and she tried to cover up her sentiments by saying something about tacky dust catchers, she didn't fool him for a minute. He didn't say anything, he just put his arm around her shoulders and they continued to stroll the avenue of shops. He led her into one called The Butterfly People and just watched as her eyes grew huge like a child entering FAO Schwarz for the very first time. Everything in the store had a butterfly theme from the sculptures to the jewelry to the exquisite items of clothing. He saw her look with great longing at a tray full of beautiful hair ornaments, then at some expensive silk lingerie covered with colorful butterflies. He had a hard time pulling her out of the store, but she maintained her hard line that she didn't need anything.

They returned to the hotel after an enjoyable day of sightseeing and a fabulous lunch at a seafood restaurant. They took a long nap in each other's arms and awakened relaxed and refreshed. John loved waking up with Nina in his arms. It just felt right; there was no other word for it. He kissed her softly and smiled lazily when she kissed him back.

"Are you having a good time?" he asked as he kissed her ear.

"I'm having the best time I've ever had in my life," she sighed, and took his long braid in her hand. She toyed with it absentmindedly and cuddled even closer to John.

"We should be getting up. We have reservations at a place I think you'll really like," he told her.

"Dressy or casual?"

"Kinda dressy, I guess, but not really fancy."

"Good, because I have the perfect outfit to wear," Nina said confidently.

After a long, sexy shower she and John parted to get dressed, Nina using the master bath and John the smaller one. John was almost ready, attired in a beautifully made blue raw silk shirt and a pair of double-pleated slacks with a braided leather belt. He was sitting on the side of the bed putting on his shoes when Nina emerged from the bathroom with her hair in a tousled updo with a few strands artfully escaping around her face and the nape of her neck. She was wearing one gold hoop earring and a little more makeup than usual, her lips were a honeyed shade of toffee that made John want to remove every article of clothing he'd just put on. She gave John a dimpled smile as she put on her other earring. "I'm ready," she said in a sultry voice.

She held her arms out to the side and executed a pivot turn that rivaled something right off a Paris runway. She was wearing a wicked pair of cobalt blue shoes with a thin braided strap across the toe and a heel strap that topped a sexy little French heel. John's eyes caressed her feet, which as always drove him crazy. There was something extremely sexy about Nina's long slender feet. As for the rest of her ensemble, she might as well have been naked. Nina had on a black satin dress that barely covered her butt. Nor did it cover her bust, for that matter. Her breasts, damn it, *his* breasts, he thought furiously, were on tantalizing display. The dress dipped low enough in front to allow a provocative glimpse of his personal paradise. It had black spaghetti straps and it was trimmed top and bottom with ice blue lace. It was provocative to the point of being erotic; John couldn't believe what he was seeing. She looked like something out of a Victoria's Secret catalog and John was damned if she was leaving the room looking like that.

"You can't be serious, Nina. That looks like . . . underwear," he growled.

Nina gave him a familiar look; the one where one eyebrow lifted and she dared him to say anything. She turned again, this time showing him the confection from the back. She even gave a satisfied little wiggle of her hips. Looking back over her shoulder she winked, slowly and audaciously. "It is underwear, *Papi*. This is my slip." She burst into merry laughter and ran back into the bathroom while John burst into rapid Spanish that even the untutored ear could deduce was no doubt quite profane.

Nina was still laughing when she returned wearing a sexy but decorous cobalt blue silk dress styled like a vintage Diane Von Furstenberg wrap dress. It was a Diane Von Furstenberg, in fact. Nina had snagged it at a yard sale in a posh San Francisco neighborhood and it was her favorite dress. John's bracelet was the only jewelry she wore, other than the earrings.

John's aggravation was completely forgotten when he looked at Nina. "You need to be spanked," he mumbled as he crossed the room and put his hands around her waist.

"Are you offering?" Nina asked sweetly.

John squeezed her waist and pulled her closer to him. "Don't tease me, baby, I'm barely controlling myself as it is. Come on and let's get out of here before I lose my mind." He abruptly released her, took a step back and stared at her intently for a long breathless moment. He muttered something in Spanish and, taking her by the hand, he all but dragged her out of the suite.

Nina couldn't stop smiling all night. John had taken her to a fabulous restaurant, one of the best-known ones in San Juan. The atmosphere was elegant, the food was delicious and her companion was beyond compare. John was a wonderful date; he did everything he could think of to make the evening memorable. Their table was secluded and there was a beautiful arrangement of flowers just for her in the middle of it. The menu had been personally selected by John and prepared to order just for them. The restaurant staff couldn't do enough for them; they treated them like visiting royalty. Nina loved every minute of it; she really did feel like a queen.

They were seated in a circular booth with a high back and without realizing what she was doing Nina moved closer to John on the richly upholstered seat. He put his arm around her shoulders and leaned in for a kiss. "Are you enjoying yourself?" he wanted to know.

She reached for his free hand and entwined her fingers with his before returning his kiss. "This goes way beyond enjoyment, John. This evening is so wonderful I never want it to end," she confessed. "No one has ever done anything for me like this in my whole life."

John looked at Nina with an expression so tender she felt her heart turn over. "*Mi corazon,* I'm glad you're happy but this is just the beginning. Don't you know by now I'd do anything for you? I plan to make every dream come true for you, Nina. Every fantasy you have is mine to make reality." He kissed her again, a soft little kiss that radiated through her body and made her dizzy with sensation.

All it took was that tiny, sweet caress to push Nina over the edge of reason. The hard shell of practical common sense shattered into pieces and like a butterfly emerging from a cocoon, she felt free for the first time in years. He might not be hers to keep but he was all hers right now and the only thing she cared about was making John as happy as he made her. She leaned against him with a soft little sigh that made John turn her face to his. "Are you tired, sweetheart?"

"Absolutely not," Nina assured him. "I couldn't possibly be better."

"How about something sweet? They have this incredible coconut flan that's supposed to be the best in the world."

"That sounds good, but that's not what I want," Nina said softly.

"What would you like for dessert, baby?"

"You."

"Check, please." John signaled the waiter and pulled his wallet out with one smooth motion while Nina collapsed in laughter. John, who never hurried for any reason, was moving like he was in fast-forward mode.

When they returned to the suite, John opened the door and was happy to see the lamps were already lit in the living room and his other instructions had been followed to the letter. An array of gift-wrapped boxes were placed on the coffee table in front of the sofa, boxes he'd arranged to have delivered while they were out. Nina's eyes widened at the sight and she turned to John. "Where'd these come from? What are they, John?"

John tried to look surprised as he took Nina's hand and led her over to the sofa. "I have no idea, *chica*, maybe you should open them."

Nina just stared at the boxes without moving to touch them. John had to sit down and pull her into his lap to make her pay attention to him; she seemed mesmerized. "Nina, aren't you going to open them?"

"But what are they, John? It's not my birthday," she said lamely.

John laughed gently and put his arms around her,

burying his face in her neck. "You are truly one of a kind, baby. These aren't for you birthday, they're just something I wanted you to have because I love you and I want to make you happy. That's all," he breathed.

Nina's eyes filled with tears. She blinked furiously, trying to keep them from overflowing but they coursed down her cheeks unchecked. John kissed them all away, crooning to her in Spanish and in English. "Aww, now, don't cry. I wanted to make you happy, I wasn't trying to upset you."

"Oh, don't be ridiculous, can't you see how happy I am? I thought you were supposed to be a genius or something. Can't you see when someone is overcome with joy?" she replied irritably.

John laughed out loud as he wrapped her more securely in his arms. "My bad, *chica.* I'll know better next time."

Nina rubbed her face against his shoulder and said, "Just see that you do. Now, what's in those boxes?"

Her voice was both curious and wistful and the sound of it tugged at John's already overloaded heart. He reached for one of the smaller packages and handed it to Nina. "Why don't you open this one and find out?"

She turned the box over and over in her hands, smoothing the exquisite wrapping paper with her fingers. Finally she began to remove the paper, opening it slowly as she tried to preserve the paper. When the wrapping was finally off she took the lid of the box off and revealed the colorful butterfly hair combs she'd looked at earlier. With a cry of surprise she turned to John. "John, I saw these today at that butterfly place! How did you know . . ."

John took over when Nina's voice faded away. "I know a lot of things, baby, although I have a lot more to learn. Just trust me enough to let me in, won't you?"

Nina was too busy trying to kiss him to answer. John

succumbed for a moment, then pulled away. "Okay, we need to slow down, Nina. Here, open this one."

John insisted that she open all the boxes and soon there was only one left. The things he'd selected dazed Nina. Somehow he'd made a note of everything she'd looked at with longing and he managed to purchase every piece and present it to her tonight. Besides the hair ornaments, there was a fabulous hot pink silk umbrella covered in colorful butterflies, a pair of dangling cloisonné butterfly earrings and a crystal bottle of her favorite perfume, L'Air du Temps. There was also another pair of earrings; these were diamond studs that looked like they were a carat each. Nina looked at him quizzically after opening the earrings.

"These weren't in the butterfly store. Neither was that perfume," she pointed out breathlessly.

John slid his hand up her warm thigh under the delicate silk of her dress. "I know baby, but I can use my own judgment from time to time, can't I?"

Nina didn't answer because she was too busy sucking his earlobe and trying to get his shirt off. "Nina, baby," John's voice roughened with desire. "Do me a big favor and just open that last one before we, umm, before we . . . we . . . oh *please,* Nina, open the box," he said desperately.

"Oh fine," Nina said with a mock pout. The last box was the biggest one and it contained beautiful lingerie, a half-cup bra and matching black thong with silk butterflies embroidered in strategic places. There was also a short, sheer gown that wouldn't conceal anything and a short matching kimono.

Nina was so pleased with the items she grabbed John around the neck and began kissing him all over again. "You are without question the most thoughtful man in the world," she said, her eyes filling with tears.

"Don't do that, Nina. My heart can't take it when you

cry," John entreated her. "Why don't you try that on for me, hmm?"

Nina wiped the tears away with her forefinger and smiled. "Okay. You just go in the bedroom and I'll be in shortly. And then your heart will really have a problem," she promised. She gathered up the lingerie and turned to go into the master bedroom. "I'll meet you in fifteen minutes so be ready, John," she purred and blew him a kiss.

John broke into a broad grin and held up his hand like he was catching the kiss. "I can't wait, baby." When she disappeared into the bedroom he waited until he heard the bathroom door close before going into the bedroom to collect a few things. He also called room service and ordered a couple of bottles of non-alcoholic sparkling wine, since he couldn't consume alcohol and he'd never seen Nina touch a drop. Then he went to the other bathroom to take a quick shower and to shave; he didn't want to scratch Nina's delicate skin. The fifteen minutes was turning into thirty minutes, but John didn't mind. Room service came and he had everything ready for Nina whenever she was ready.

He piled all the pillows up at the head of the bed and lay against them, his bare body covered with only a sheet. The lights were dimmed and John had opened the door to the balcony so the soft ocean breezes would refresh the room. There was soft Latin jazz playing and the atmosphere was sexy and inviting, just what he wanted for Nina. Any impatience he might have felt simply melted away when Nina finally appeared in the doorway that led to the bathroom. She looked like the embodiment of every fantasy he'd ever entertained in his life.

Her hair was released from the updo and looked like it was ready to be tousled by his hands. She was wearing the short gown he'd bought for her and as beautiful as it had been in the box, it was a hundred times more enticing on her body. It was made of silk organza cut on the bias to be more accommodating to the body. The nude fabric was a perfect match for Nina's skin. She looked like she was completely naked, expect for the silken butterfly appliqués that were so realistic they looked as though they were perched on her body. She wore nothing else except for a pair of high-heeled pink satin mules like the kind of slippers worn by glamorous movies stars back in the day.

She walked slowly across the room to John and sat down on the bed next to him. He held out his hands to her and she took them with an unreadable expression on her face. He gently pulled her towards him, coming forward to meet her halfway in a tender kiss. "You look beautiful, *mi mariposa.* That means my butterfly, Nina. You're so incredibly lovely, did you know that?" Without waiting for an answer he let go of her hands and threw the sheet aside, patting the space right next to him. "Come on, woman, don't make me wait. You were right, Nina; my heart can't take this much longer. I need you right now," he said in a low, passionate voice. His thick, engorged sex was proof of his need; he was magnificently aroused and ready for her.

Nina gave him a smile worthy of the Mona Lisa as she let the little mules slip from her feet and she got into bed. She knelt next to John and put her hands on his shoulders, gently stroking them as she looked into his eyes. Leaning forward, she kissed him, gently at first and then with a wild, sweet hunger that shook John even as it increased his need. He reached for her, only to have her stop him.

"Not yet, John," she whispered. "Tonight it's all about you, my love." She kissed his neck and his chest, holding him against the pillows so he couldn't reciprocate her strokes and caresses. When her warm lips reached his nipples, a giant tremor went through his body at the unexpected and very welcome assault on the highly sensitive area. "Nina," he rasped. "*Mi querida,* you're driving me crazy."

Nina didn't answer him; she was licking and sucking her way down his body, stopping to pay some sensual attention to his navel. She traced it with her tongue, and then kissed it the way she would his mouth, sending shock waves of sensation through John's body and creating a longing that was painful in its intensity. When Nina took his manhood in her hands, John became the slave of her passion. The feel of her soft hands stroking the most sensitive part of his body, the intoxicating scent of her perfume, the sight of her so beautiful and uninhibited brought all his senses together in an incredibly erotic dance of delight. When Nina's intentions became clear, John felt compelled to stop her.

"Nina, you don't have to do that," he told her, although the look on his face said otherwise.

"I want to do it, John. You do it for me, why can't I do it for you?"

It was getting harder for John to speak with Nina's hands caressing him and her body looking more and more exciting. The strap of the gown had slipped off her shoulder and her breast was almost completely exposed. She looked sexier than any woman he'd ever been with and she was letting him know in no uncertain terms she wanted to give him a precious gift of the ultimate intimacy. John was so aroused he was about to lose his mind. "Nina, baby, just because I do it for you, you don't have to . . ." he began, gasping when he felt her lips surround him and her heated mouth take charge of his need. He moaned from sheer pleasure and gasped her name again.

Nina raised her head and looked at John; she looked flushed with love and radiated sensuality from every pore of her body. "Do you like that, John? Does it make you happy?" she asked softly.

"More than you know, baby, but . . ."

Nina brought her mouth to John's for a kiss, and then put her finger against his lips. "Shh. This isn't just for you, John, it's for both of us," she murmured before continuing to show him the same kind of selflessness he'd bestowed upon her so often.

He had no choice but to abandon himself to the rapture of the moment, watching the woman he loved so dearly give herself to him so sweetly and freely. It was a moment he would treasure as long as he loved her and that would be forever.

Chapter 10

John seated Nina in the restaurant and leaned over to sample the sweetness of the nape of her neck while he did so. Sliding into his seat, he noted the look of contentment on her face and smiled in satisfaction. That was the way he wanted her to look always. "Well, *chica*, what would you like to do today?"

"What are my options? It's such a beautiful day, anything would be fun." She continued to read her menu, looking for something authentically Puerto Rican for breakfast.

John took her menu, saying he would order for her. "I'll order you what we used to have for Sunday breakfast," he told her. "Afterward, we can go to the beach, we can sightsee some more, we can go visit my relatives in Carolina, we can go horseback riding . . ."

"Horses?" The look of anticipation on Nina's face told him all he needed to know.

"Okay, horseback riding it is. Now, I'm going to get you something for breakfast so wonderful you're never going to want to leave San Juan," he teased her.

"Too late. I'm already smitten. I could stay here for the rest of my life," she admitted with the dazzling smile that won his heart anew every time he saw it.

In a short while the waiter brought their breakfast, which consisted of *huevos revueltos con salmon, guineitos ninos,* and *domplines.* There was also a chilled mixture of passion fruit and guava juices, and the excellent Puerto Rican coffee Nina was beginning to crave. John told her what each dish was, although she figured out the scrambled eggs with salmon on her own. "The *domplines* are little fried dumplings and the *guineitos ninos* are fried finger bananas. I hope you like it, *chica.*"

He needn't have worried as Nina had already taken several bites and was making a sound of delight. "This is absolutely delicious, John, just fabulous. You do take good care of me, don't you?" She reached across the table and put her hand on top of his in a gesture of complete trust and he caught the hand up and gave it a squeeze before releasing it.

"I try to, Nina. It's the least I can do since you take such good care of me. And as soon as we're done here we'll go riding. Have you done much riding?"

On their way back to the hotel, John conceded the answer to that question was a resounding yes. Nina was more than competent on horseback; she rode with a singular grace and beauty and a posture that was indicative of riding lessons at some point in her past. When they arrived at the stable, Nina was like an eager little girl; she couldn't wait to get started. Even the helmet the stable forced her to wear didn't detract from her beauty as she rode. It was an amazing experience for John. Nina was like a totally different person at the stables. She was animated and excited and totally at ease with the animals. Even the legendary smell of the manure didn't bother her. John was expecting a turned-up nose and some of her pithy comments, but to his amazement she took a deep breath and smiled happily. She looked a little embarrassed when John caught her at it.

"Old habit," she said sheepishly. "I know it's sick but I actually like this smell, it brings back good memories for me."

Nothing more was said about her olfactory peculiarities. They selected their mounts and took off on the trail laid out by the stable hands. John watched with admiration and adoration while Nina rode like a queen, posting perfectly like a trained equestrienne. She was full of smiles all morning and when the ride was over she showed genuine sadness at leaving her mount, a sturdy roan stallion named Gaucho. She was leading the horse back to the stables and talking to him as she did so.

John laughed out loud when she pulled Gaucho down to her level for a good-bye kiss. "Thanks for the lovely ride, Gaucho. You were magnificent," she said with a wistful sigh.

John looked fondly at her when they were on the way back to the hotel. "I don't think I have to ask if you had a good time," he remarked.

"I had the best time, John. I can't thank you enough for this. I used to ride a lot when I was little. My brother had a pony at his birthday party one year and we got so excited Mommy bought us one. We had to take care of him, but that was fine with us, we loved that horse. We learned how to groom him and walk him and we all took riding lessons so we'd know what we were doing. We didn't keep him at home, even though we had a really big house. Our house was in the city and it wouldn't be fair to Ranger to try to keep him there. So he lived at a riding stable that wasn't too far away from our house, and we went over there every day to take care of him. We called him Ranger but you know, I can't remember if we gave him that name or if he came that way," Nina said with a slight pucker in her forehead.

"He was a beautiful little horse and he loved us, especially me. I was his favorite," she said gleefully. Her face was alight with happy memories and she looked more carefree than John had ever seen her. She was wearing one of her ponytails and it was blowing in the breeze from the open window. She had on a crisp white shirt, jeans, which were, as usual, pressed and creased, and she had on her running shoes in lieu of riding boots. Even though they'd spent the last couple of hours riding, Nina looked like she'd just left the house. She had some kind of built-in dirt repellent, John decided. He didn't think Nina was aware of what she'd just revealed and to prove it, he asked her a question.

"So why were you Ranger's favorite, *chica?*" he asked gently.

It was like a veil dropped over her face. Her eyes grew dull and evasive and her smile vanished. "I don't know." She looked out the window and refused to utter another sound or look at John again.

He let her have her silence for a while but when they pulled into the hotel he turned to her before relinquishing the rental car to the parking valet. "Nina, you made me promise not to pry. I'm not going to try to get in your head or anything like that. But you have to understand you can trust me with your life. All I want is your happiness, I'd never do anything to cause you any pain, and I hope you know that by now. I just hope you'll be able to talk to me one day, *querida.* There's nothing you could tell me to make me love you any less, nothing that would make me think less of you. Remember that, Nina."

He got out of the car and walked around to Nina's side to help her out. He held both her hands and put a kiss on each one. "Don't forget, *mija,* I'm always here for you."

Nina might have been as fresh as a daisy after their ride, but John felt the need to clean up. "I'm going to take a shower and wash my hair," he said as they rode the elevator up to the suite. "I smell a lot like Gaucho, if you ask me." He looked down at Nina, hoping to get a smile out of her. It was a futile attempt, as she didn't react at all; it was as though she were in her own little world.

They entered the suite in silence and Nina went out onto the balcony and sat down in one of the big lounge chairs, staring in the direction of the sea. John watched her for a moment and went into the bedroom to prepare for his shower. He took off his clothes and tossed them in the direction of the bed, making a mental note to pick them up before Nina came into the room. He took the band from his long hair and unbraided it as he entered the bathroom.

Picking up his bottle of shampoo from the vanity, he turned on the shower and got in. While he lathered his hair, John pondered Nina's uncharacteristic outburst. It went without saying that she was hiding things about her past, and it was equally obvious the burden of the secrets was getting to be too much. That's why things kept slipping out, she wanted him to know these things or she'd have been able to maintain her silence. As much as he wanted to help her through this he couldn't, not unless she agreed to talk to him. He'd made her a promise and he intended to keep it, no matter how difficult it was for him to mind his own business. *I just want her to be happy. To be as free and relaxed as she was this morning.*

He groaned aloud as he pondered the difficulty of the situation. If he could get her to talk to him, it would unburden her mind and set her on the path to the kind of emotional freedom she so richly deserved. But if he probed at her in any way, she would hate him because she would consider his intrusiveness a violation of her privacy. As John rinsed the shampoo out of his hair and lathered his body with imported hard-milled soap, he laughed at the irony. Without even trying his little Nina had him hamstrung, unable to make a move. *Dios, she could wrap me around her little finger without even trying,* he thought, but it wasn't an unpleasant notion.

He reached outside the shower stall for a towel and stepped out of the glass enclosure as he wrapped the towel around his waist. He was about to leave the bathroom when a low and sultry voice stopped him.

"Come on in, the water's fine," Nina said softly. She was in the giant Jacuzzi surrounded by bubbles. There were candles lit on the vanity and soft music was playing. Nina looked beautiful. She was reclined in the tub so that nothing was showing below her neck, but when she issued her invitation to John, she sat up so her tempting breasts were fully displayed. "What are you waiting for?" she said flippantly, but her voice was trembling.

John dropped the towel without hesitation and stepped into the tub. In seconds he was in Nina's arms and they held each other for a long time without saying a word. Nina was the first to pull away and she slid behind John so that he was resting on her with her long legs around his body. Cradling him in this manner, Nina took his long wet hair and pushed it aside so she could massage his shoulders and back.

"This reminds me of when I was in the hospital, Nina."

"How so? I don't recall giving any nude massages, John." Nina had to laugh; the very idea of such a thing was absurd.

"Maybe we were dressed, but you did give me back rubs. You used to massage my back and my shoulders and when you thought I was asleep you would even massage my feet and my legs. Don't try to play it off, Nina. You were so good to me. You did everything you could to make sure I was comfortable and I'm never going to forget it."

Nina didn't answer him right away. She continued to

use her hands to relax John; she kneaded his broad shoulders and worked all the tension out of his neck and back. When she started speaking, it was in a voice so soft John had to strain to hear her at first.

"My mother was a singer. She was very well known, if I told you the name of the group she was in, you'd know it right away. We lived a very nice life. We lived *large,* John, very large. There was a big house and two or three cars, private school, Ranger; we had a housekeeper and everything. I don't remember my father, he and my mother were divorced when I was very little, still a baby, I guess. Mommy had to travel a lot but when she was home it was so wonderful, every day was like Christmas. When I was seven years old she died and it was never like that again.

"My brothers and I were split up after she died. Mommy's best friend took the boys to live with her, but she didn't take me. I went to live with Morgan, Mommy's manager. Morgan was very kind to me and he treated me like a little princess until social services came and took me away. They said it wasn't right for a single man to be raising a little girl and they hustled me out of there with a quickness. But I didn't have to go to strangers, one of Mommy's cousins took me in."

John was perfectly still while she talked. He didn't want to distract her in any way although there were some questions he was dying to ask. He forced himself to remain silent and she continued to talk.

"Her name was Marva and she was so much fun! She was really artsy and bohemian and we had all kinds of adventures together. She had lived all over Europe and she came home to take care of us. My brothers already had a home but she was right on time to take me in and she was glad to do it. She left all her bohemian friends and her apartment in Paris to come home to Chicago just for me," Nina said in a voice quivering with emotion.

John had to speak at this point; he had to ask a question. "What happened, baby?"

"My old friends at social services, of course. Somebody dug up the fact that she'd been in some kind of nude play while she was living in Europe and that made her an unfit guardian. Of course, they didn't tell me this, they just took me away from her and I never saw her again. That's when I went into foster care."

By now the water had cooled considerably and John suggested they get out of the tub. Nina agreed and soon they were clad in robes and sitting on the sofa in the living room. Actually, Nina was sitting on the sofa with John sitting on the floor in front of her. She had toweled his hair dry and combed it out and now she was massaging his scalp before applying a little pomade.

Nina worked in silence for a few minutes before making one of her usual comments about his tresses. "I really hate this hair, John. It's just criminal that it's growing out of your scalp and not mine. It's positively unnatural for you to have such pretty hair, you wretch."

John laughed loudly and took Nina's feet in his hands. He pulled them into his lap and started rubbing them while he talked. "Aw, baby, it's just hair. If it bugs you I'll cut it off, it makes no difference to me. You have really gorgeous feet, did you know that?"

Nina giggled at the unexpected compliment. "I take good care of my feet. The father in the first foster home I was placed in was an orthopedic surgeon and he believed in taking care of your feet. We didn't get to wear fancy shoes, we always had sturdy sensible shoes," she said.

"So they were really hard on you? Were they really strict?" John asked.

"Oh no, not at all. They were very, very sweet people.

They were very kind to me. They had a daughter and a son and they treated me like family. We had rules for the household but they weren't Draconian or anything. We had to make our beds and set the table and feed the dogs and walk them, things like that. We all got to read a lot and we were allowed to talk about our books during dinner. We were encouraged to, as a matter of fact. They were a really talkative family and we spent a lot of time talking and doing creative things. They didn't have a television but they had lots and lots of books, and a big room that was just for crafts, and we went to art galleries and plays," she recalled. "They were the most loving people in the world, John. They wanted to adopt me."

John kept rubbing Nina's feet, occasionally bringing one up to his lips for a kiss. "What happened, baby? Did they change their minds?"

Nina's voice caught and she had to clear her throat. "Social services told them a black family wanted me. They were white, see, and if there was any possibility of placing me with a black family, well, social services had to place me there. So the social workers came and got me again and off I went to more strangers. It was really hard to go because I'd been with them for almost two years. I was with Morgan for about three months, and I was with Marva for about six months, I guess, but I'd been with the Benrubi family for almost two years. It was horrible."

John let go of Nina's feet and stood up so he could sit down on the sofa. He stretched out on the end opposite Nina and held one hand out to her, patting his chest with the other one. "Come here, *mi preciosa corazon.*" When she was resting on his broad chest with his arms around her and their legs entwined, she sighed deeply and sadly.

"What happened with the new family, baby? Did you not get along?" he asked softly.

"There was no new family. To this day I have no idea

what happened, but there was no family waiting for me with open arms. I was living in Chicago where I was born, but after they took me from the Benrubis I got sent to Springfield, Illinois and dropped into foster care there. I went from place to place from then on. Sometimes I'd be in a good place and sometimes not so good. And that was that, I guess. I grew up and I wasn't in foster care anymore, I was on my own. And I've been on my own ever since," she murmured.

"Not anymore. You're never going to be alone again. I'm never going to leave you, you understand?" John tightened his arms around her and kissed her hair, waiting for her answer. All he heard was the soft even sound of her breathing; she'd fallen asleep in his arms. It was John's turn to sigh, a deep heartfelt sigh of pain for his beloved. This had been some day for her and for him, too. Now he understood so much more about Nina. He could only imagine what it must have been like for her to grow up in wealth and to have everything snatched away from her. To lose her immediate family and then to have everyone she cared for methodically removed from her life must have been hellish.

No wonder Nina was so standoffish and aloof. She'd had no sense of security, no stability in her life since her mother died. *Why didn't that friend take Nina, too? Why did she just take the boys? And where are they anyway? Don't they wonder what happened to their little sister?* The questions kept coming as John thought about the things Nina had told him. On the one hand, her revelations had enlightened him, but on the other they just led to more questions. What had been an enigma was now a mystery. Only his Nina could be this complicated.

The sound of her breathing and the feel of her slight weight against him were so natural and comforting he followed her into sleep.

Chapter 11

John leaned against the ornate door leading to the master bedroom of the suite The brilliant afternoon sun streamed into the room, bathing Nina in a golden glow. They'd spent the morning on the beach near the hotel and she'd gained a bit of a tan that enhanced her natural coloring. Puerto Rico obviously agreed with her, although it was hard to tell from the worried look on her face.

"You're sure I look okay? I don't look tacky or anything?" Nina frowned as she smoothed her dress over her slender hips. John rolled his eyes heavenward as he told her again she looked wonderful.

"Nina, you look perfect. You look sexy, elegant and very stylish. Way too good for me," he said cheerfully. "My family is going to love you, don't even worry about it. You could look like the bearded lady in the circus and they'd think you were special because you're mine."

They were going to Carolina, the neighboring township where most of his aunts and uncles lived. When John had first suggested going, Nina thought it a wonderful idea but now in the bright light of an impending departure it seemed a huge folly. What in the world was she doing, going to meet his family? She felt like the biggest faker in the world. She knew in her heart she couldn't have John in her life forever and acting like they were destined for a life together was stupidly, cruelly wrong on her part but she couldn't seem to stop herself. She was so crazy about him by this point she was willing to go along with almost anything he suggested. Even going to meet his relatives looking like a . . . *what*?

Nina continued to fuss with her clothes, ignoring every comforting word John said. She looked at her reflection in the mirrored closet door and frowned. "I think I should wear the black one," she said turning to pick it up from the discard pile. John picked her up under one arm and carried her into the living room, ignoring her protests.

"Baby, you couldn't possibly look any better, please believe me and stop tripping over this, would you? You look fantastic, why don't you believe me?"

Nina really did look radiant. Her delicate dress was made of rose-colored silk jersey with a deep scoop neckline. It had spaghetti straps and it fit her slender body perfectly. The knee length showed off her legs without revealing too much. She had on a pair of rose-colored silk flats with iridescent beading on the toes and the thick gold bracelet from John, as always. She was also wearing the diamond studs in her ears and one of the butterfly combs was anchored at the top of her ponytail, the wavy one. She looked summery and feminine and very much like a butterfly herself, as she seemed ready to fly out of the room.

"Nina, you need to chill. What's happened to my cool, impersonal Miss Parker? We're just going to see my aunts and uncles to say hello. I haven't seen some of my family in years, how could I come all this way and not even drop in for a visit," he crooned as he cupped her face in his hands. "We won't stay long, they just want to make sure I'm okay after my surgery. You're not really scared, are you?"

Nina wanted to tell him this was the first time she'd ever had occasion to meet someone's family and yes, she was terrified, but she couldn't bring herself to say it. She gently removed herself from his hands and smiled airily. "Oh, I'm fine. Are you sure this dress is okay? I don't want them to think I'm a hoochie," she mumbled as she smoothed the dress over her hips.

John gave her a sexy smile and assured her again she looked fabulous. "If it was a half-inch lower in the front I might have some doubts, but you look perfect, very pretty, *mija.*"

Nina looked down at her bosom and snorted indelicately. "Honey, this thing could be about four inches lower and nobody would see anything. I'm the chairman of the committee, you do realize that, right?"

John's brows came together in puzzlement. "Committee? What committee?"

"The itty-bitty titty committee. Charter member since puberty. Okay, let's go before I lose my nerve," she said, ignoring John's shout of laughter. She picked up her little clutch purse and a matching shrug to cover her shoulders if the evening air got cool. John put his hand at the small of her back as they left the suite.

"There is no more beautiful woman in all of Puerto Rico than you. Remember that," he said and kissed her on the cheek. Nina gave him a wicked smile and kissed him back.

"That must make you the luckiest man in Puerto Rico. Don't you forget that," she laughed, then gasped as John grabbed her bottom on the way out the door.

John's words came back to haunt Nina as she surveyed his family. They were on the patio of his *Tia* Maria and *Tio* Roberto's house and for the most part it was a lovely afternoon. She met his other uncles, Hector, Felipe, and Miguel, and his other aunts, Luz, Bonita, and Rosalinda. There were too many cousins for her to remember and they came in all ages and sizes from toddlers to teenagers to adults. They were all friendly and gregarious, speaking both Spanish and English and talking with great animation, even when other people were talking. A man who'd been John's best friend when they were younger was there, too. His name was Alejandro Reyes and he and John greeted each other like long lost brothers. It was a wonderful homecoming for John, and Nina was made to feel entirely welcome by the whole family with the exception of his cousin Lola.

Lola was a little younger than John and a lot curvier than Nina. She was average height with stunning caramel skin and cascading black hair flowing over her shoulders. She was built like a compact Barbie doll, with curves in places Nina didn't even have bones. *John obviously didn't know Miss Hot Pants was in town when he said I was the most beautiful woman in Puerto Rico,* Nina thought. *Nobody's going to think I'm beautiful with that wench around.*

Miss Lola obviously hadn't gotten the memo about dressing modestly, either. She was wearing a halter-neck dress in dazzling white with a plunging neckline that barely contained her bounty, and it was almost as short as Nina's infamous slip. *And I know she doesn't have on a scrap of underwear or it would show right through that thing she's got on. "Cousin" my foot.* Nina's thoughts may have been angrily territorial, but she hadn't missed the mark as Cousin Lola soon made plain.

The woman had latched onto John like a remora hanging on a shark from the time she made her dramatic entrance onto the patio. She'd made a beeline for him and planted a big red lipstick kiss on his mouth to the chagrin of her Aunt Maria.

"Lola, what is wrong with you," her aunt fussed. "What do you think you're doing, kissing your cousin like that?"

Lola had no shame in her game at all as she continued to cling to John. "*Tia,* that's just it. Johnnie isn't my cousin, is he? He was adopted, something no one bothered to tell us. You kept the information to yourself, didn't you, *Tia* Maria," Lola said in a nice-nasty voice that certainly didn't fool Nina. "I've been in love with my handsome cousin Johnnie all my life and now I find out he's not my cousin at all."

She beamed up at John who was looking more embarrassed than amused. He gracefully removed his arm from her grasping hand with its long curved fingernails painted scarlet with gold tips. He cleared his throat and acted like the perfect gentleman he was. "Lola, it's good to see you again after all these years. I don't think you've met Nina Whitney," he said, moving to Nina's side and putting his arm around her waist.

He may as well have been speaking to the birds in the trees for all the attention Lola paid to Nina. For the rest of the afternoon, while they moved around chatting with family, while they sat down to eat, while Nina was being shown all kinds of family pictures by *Tia* Maria, Lola was right there, showing all of her teeth and much of her anatomy to John. Maria was mortified and let Nina know it. The two women were in the cool living room of the house looking at photo albums. Maria looked at Nina appraisingly before speaking. "I apologize again for my headstrong niece, Nina. She's the only girl in her family and very spoiled. Since she started entering these beauty contests all she thinks about is how she looks and which man is going to take her someplace and buy her something pretty. She's lost her mind, I tell you. And as for this obsession with John, please just ignore it. She always had a little crush on her cousin and now that she thinks she's

Miss Puerto Rico, well, she's just out of control," Maria said sadly.

"But you? You're the perfect woman for him. John's parents Nestor and Consuela would have adored you, Nina. I've seen John with his share of pretty ladies but I've never seen him so happy and content, the way he is with you. You two are going to make a lovely couple and you'll have lots of pretty babies," Maria said confidently, and then gasped as Nina dropped the album that she was perusing. "All you all right, *mija?*"

"I'm fine, *Tia* Maria. I just need a little water," Nina said quickly. In a few minutes she was seated on the patio again, with John's long arm around her shoulder as she sipped a glass of sparkling water. John smiled at her and pressed his lips to her temple.

"Are you ready to leave, Nina? We can go anytime you like." Nina nodded and told him a tiny white lie. "I am a little tired, John. We can leave now if you're ready."

"Let me say a few quick good-byes and we're gone."

Nina nodded again and continued to sip her drink, trying to ignore the fact that Lola was staring daggers at her. Nina *hmmphed* to herself and prayed that Lola would stay out of her way. In the mood she was suddenly in, Lola was the one who needed to watch her back.

Nina was quite prepared to forget the whole thing the next day. It was another glorious day with blue skies and brilliant sunshine. She and John had made love all night like giddy rabbits and they'd had an excellent breakfast, which they were now digesting, next to the pool. At the moment, neither one of them had enough energy to head for the beach; although John promised they would spend the next day there. For the moment they were perfectly content to lie on the big chaise lounges by the pool and sip passion fruit juice over crushed ice. They had already rubbed each other with lotion to repel the rays of the sun and now they were just talking softly and enjoying each other's company.

It was a great revelation and turning point for Nina, when she realized she was actually jealous on John's behalf. When that over-endowed skank started making moves on John, Nina wanted nothing more than to rip the woman's meticulously placed false lashes right off her head and feed them to her. She wanted to plant her foot squarely in the woman's butt and kick her until her leg fell off. Who did she think she was, trying to push up on her John? If the woman had called him "Johnnie" in that syrupy voice one more time, Nina wouldn't have been responsible for her actions. The whole thing was surreal to Nina, who'd never had a reaction like this in her life.

Of course, that was because she'd never been in love like this before. As soon as Nina realized what she just acknowledged, she began to panic. Her hands got wet and clammy, her breathing became labored and she turned ice cold. Her old friend, the little voice in her head had some pithy comments to make about her condition. *Girl, you need to quit. Why do you do this to yourself? You knew you were in love with the man* way *before this and here you go acting like a schoolgirl. That man loves you like you're the only woman he ever met in his life and you feel the same way so it's a good thing. Quit being simple, girl, you're gettin' on my last good nerve.*

Nina had to laugh, she wasn't getting any sympathy from her inner voice, it seemed. She was on her own for this one. She sipped her fruit juice and looked over at John, relaxing next to her without a care in the world. Nina forced herself to look at the sparkling aqua of the pool as she relived the morning before she and John arrived poolside.

She'd just finished brushing her teeth and was looking in the mirror to see if her duplicity and scheming was evident to the casual observer. *How could I let myself get so caught up? This is wrong, it's just wrong. But it feels so good and so right, she thought miserably.* Just as she was trying to decide if a good cry in the shower was the best way to relieve her angst a knock came on the bathroom door. It was John, wearing a beautiful smile and nothing else. "Care for some company in the shower?" His deep, sexy voice never failed to give her a thrill. And the prospect of one of those long showers with his soapy hands all over her body, touching her with such adoring love made her warm all over. Her fears dissipated at once and she happily joined John for loving and lathering. Her dire thoughts were cast aside and she let herself be happy in his arms once more.

They had dried each other off and fed each other the breakfast John ordered from room service while having a wonderful conversation. All her anxiety and guilt was forgotten as they just reveled in each other's company. Now everything was just marvelous. She looked at John, so sexy and bronzed and was pleased to find him looking at her as though she was the most captivating woman in the world. "What are you staring at? It's this dumpy little suit, isn't it?" she said with an overdone sigh.

True to his word, John had bought her a bathing suit at the hotel. It was a one-piece maillot in a deep turquoise with a subtle gold shimmer to it. It was too modest, in Nina's opinion, but John thought it was perfect. It had high-cut legs and was deeply cut in the back, although not quite as scandalously low as her chocolate brown dress. The front was cut into a very deep V but it was intersected by a flat bow just under her breasts, which prevented it from showing anything John didn't want some other man seeing. He'd explained it to her before she allowed him to purchase the suit.

"Nina, this is just how I was raised, something that's been ingrained in me since I was a child. Latin men, even quasi-Latin like me," he said with a short laugh, "just don't like to see their women out on display like so much meat. It's fine to be sexy and fashionable, but when it comes to extra short, extra sheer and really low-cut things, it's just not how you want your woman to be seen in public. At home, that's one thing; you want to see your woman looking hot for you, *just* for you. But out in public, never. To be honest, it used to be that a woman who dressed like that was considered to be a *puta*, a woman who sold her body for a living," John said, frowning. He rubbed his finger over his moustache and admitted, "I don't think it's still that way, but I still don't like the idea of too much exposure."

After purchasing the bathing suit, a matching cover-up and a pair of beaded thongs, they returned to the suite and Nina tried the suit on again for John. He told her once more how sexy she looked. "But modest and elegant, the way a lady should," he'd added, ignoring the fact that Nina rolled her eyes and stuck her tongue out at him.

He'd crossed the room to where Nina was standing and came up behind her so they were both looking into the mirror. "I'm being old-fashioned and ridiculous, aren't I? Does that make me a big macho chump?" he whispered into her neck.

Nina turned her head so John could access her neck more easily. "Yes, it does, but you're *my* big macho chump, don't forget that."

The suit was very sexy and it accented Nina's slender form perfectly. In truth, she'd never had a suit so becoming and certainly not one as expensive, but she had to keep up her little pretense with John for a while. Now as they reclined under the hot sun and talked about nothing in particular, she felt somehow cherished and desired. She was about to say this to John when a shadow fell across them.

"There you are! We figured you might be out here and we were right," trilled a voice Nina hoped never to hear again in her life. She squinted her eyes and shielded them with her hand to look up into the painted face of Lola, who was standing over John like a hungry dog eying a thick juicy steak. Hovering next to Nina's chaise was John's friend Alejandro, wearing a frighteningly tight pair of bikini briefs and looking just a little bit too glad to see her. And for once Nina's little voice had nothing clever to say.

In the years to come Nina would remember that day as the one where she exercised more restraint than she'd ever used in her life. She'd been calm and polite all day, even when the sight of Lola wearing her microscopic lime green bikini and hanging all over John made her want to throw up. Lola and Alejandro had come up with the brilliant idea of renting a suite at the Wyndham so they could hang out with John and Nina. Why they thought their presence was a welcome one, Nina couldn't fathom. Then she realized it was just about Lola making a bold play for John. She had to say one thing about Lola: the woman was single-minded in the extreme. Nothing, including the fact that John was obviously involved with someone else, was about to deter Lola from her goal, which was to get John at all costs.

Lola followed John around like a poodle in heat all afternoon. She kept trying to get him alone and Nina could hear snatches of her fevered conversations in Spanish. *She's going to start humping his leg any second,* Nina thought angrily. To his credit, John was cordial but distant, putting himself next to Nina at every opportunity, using even more endearments than usual, and keeping his hands on her as much as possible. Anyone else would have gotten the message, but not Lola. Like a slutty version of the Energizer Bunny, she just kept on coming.

Alejandro, John's friend, finally apologized to Nina for her behavior. "Nina, don't concern yourself with Lola. I'm afraid she's been allowed to become spoiled and selfish, it's sometimes that way with very pretty children."

She ain't hardly a child, Nina thought as she tried to listen to what Alejandro was saying. He was a virile and handsome man, about an inch over six feet with golden brown skin and curly black hair. He had kind and merry eyes and a nice muscular body, although he was hardly in John's class physique-wise. Nina's eyes went over to John who was apparently explaining to Lola he already had some lotion on his body. She had two sloppy handfuls of highly scented goo, which she was trying to slather on him. Bless his heart, he wasn't having it.

"You see, Nina? She is still a child, with so much to learn. You, on the other hand, are a real woman," he said softly. "A woman and a lady," he praised. "You look so beautiful, modest yet enticing, the way any man wants his lady to look."

Nina's face froze as she tried to assimilate his words. *Is this joker trying to hit on me or is this just some kind of corny, macho Latin charm?* Luckily, John came unwittingly to her rescue.

"Nina, I think you've had enough sun, *mi corazon.* You're looking a little flushed. Why don't we go in?"

She agreed immediately and started to gather up her magazines and her tote bag. Alejandro's eyes followed her movements and he gave John a leering grin of approval. "That's a beautiful lady you have there, John. Not only beautiful but elegant and intelligent. You're a lucky man. You've always been lucky, haven't you?"

John wasn't really listening to Alejandro, he was too impatient to be rid of Lola and be alone with Nina. "I've worked very hard for everything I have, but I guess I've also had some very good fortune." He aimed a mock punch at his old friend and said, "It's my reward for clean living and a pure heart. I hear you've had more than a little good luck yourself. Your restaurants are doing quite well from what I've read. You're doing really well these days, Alejandro, I'm proud of you."

"I'm ready, John. Nice to see you two, maybe we can do this again," Nina said in a voice only John knew was totally false in its friendliness. She'd put on the matching cover-up to her suit and stood closer than usual to John's side. John draped his arm around her shoulders and they almost made a clean break when Lola chimed in with the last word.

"Oh, you can't get rid of us that easily," she chirped. "We're all going to dinner and to the casino tonight, doesn't that sound like fun?"

No, it actually sounds just like the ninth level of Hell. Nina only hoped her dismay didn't show on her face.

John couldn't remember Nina looking lovelier than she did right now. She always looked wonderful, but tonight her pure natural beauty stood out in sharp contrast to Lola, who looked even more scandalous than she had by the pool. The microscopic bikini was embarrassing enough but now she had on an alarmingly short gold outfit that put everything she possessed on vulgar display. She looked to John like a hostess in a third-rate Vegas club.

Nina, on the other hand, looked understated and elegant in an ivory outfit of wide-legged pants and a short jacket with a lacy camisole underneath. Her hair was freshly shampooed and conditioned and she was wearing her wavy ponytail with her new diamond studs and her gold bracelet. She looked sophisticated but sexy and desirable in the nicest way. John was so proud to be seen with Nina. And from the looks she was getting from the other men, there were several dozen who'd like nothing better than to take his place. He deliberately pulled her closer to him and the look on his face dared anyone to try to come between them. It was a look that every man in the place knew to obey, but to John's intense irritation, Lola had no such intention.

They'd enjoyed an excellent dinner in the hotel's main restaurant, at least three of them had; Lola was the kind who claimed to always be dieting and she merely picked at her food. Now, according to Lola, it was time to hit the casino. "This will be so much fun," she gushed for the tenth time. "You all like a little game of chance, don't you?"

Nina felt compelled to speak up. "That's when you take your hard-earned money and put it on a table so the casino can take it away from you, right? No thanks, I prefer to keep my money in my pocket."

She had an unexpected ally in Alejandro who agreed that he wasn't in the mood for gambling. "Would you like to dance, Nina? There's an excellent dance club right here in the hotel."

As much as she loved to dance, Nina wasn't about to go anywhere with Alejandro. He might be a friend of John's but there was something about him she didn't quite trust. "Thanks, but no, I'll just watch," she said with a tight little smile.

Lola insisted on dragging John off to the black jack table, which gave her an opportunity to plead her case. "John, you have to know I have feelings for you," she began. John decided to pretend he had no clue what she was talking about, hoping it would save some of her almost non-existent dignity.

"Of course you do, I'm your cousin, part of your family."

"But that's just it, John, you're not really my cousin. You're adopted so that means we're not truly related," she said breathlessly. John doggedly studied his cards and refused to look at her, but when she put her hand on his thigh, he had to act.

"Lola, you can't just set aside my family relationship because we're not blood kin. Nestor and Consuela were my parents, the only parents I knew and they considered me their son. My aunts and uncles, who include your parents, also consider me family. So it's pretty hard for me to blithely say we're not related after all these years," he said gently but firmly. She had to know he meant business and stop this foolishness. "And besides, you have to realize I'm involved with someone else."

Lola tossed her hair back, not realizing she loosened a track in her weave when she did so. "That little bird woman? Oh please, Johnnie, she's not woman enough for you. If she's your woman, why isn't she over here fighting for you?" Lola said hotly.

The ice in John's voice finally penetrated Lola's stubborn head when he said, "Because she's a lady, *my* lady and she knows she doesn't have to fight for my heart, it belongs to her."

Meanwhile, Nina and Alejandro were seated at the bar where he was trying to ply her with alcohol. After refusing several drinks, Nina finally had to give him her stare of death. "I do not drink alcohol." She enunciated each word perfectly and very slowly, as though speaking to a hearing impaired person who didn't know much English. "Is there another language I might use to get that message across to you?"

Alejandro burst into laughter, apparently tickled to death by her stern demeanor. "Nina, you are indeed a treasure. I love a woman with spirit. You know, my dear," he said, lowering his voice to a lecherous whisper, "I have means. Ample means, so you will never have to work again. I can take care of you in the style to which you should become accustomed. I can take you places and give you things you've never dreamed of, Nina."

Nina was so stunned she didn't trust herself to say a word; she just got off her stool and started walking in the direction she'd seen John heading with Lola the Limpet clinging to his side. She finally saw him looking at Lola with a horrified expression and she caught the last few words of Lola's impassioned speech, something about her having womanly needs only John could fulfill. Nina put her hand on John's arm just as Alejandro arrived after chasing Nina through the crowded casino. She looked at John, then at Lola and Alejandro and all she could do was shake her head.

"Look people, I'm going to make this really simple for all of us." Turning to Alejandro she pointed at Lola. "She has needs. Womanly needs." She turned to Lola and pointed at Alejandro. "He has means, ample means and he can probably take care of all those *needs* of yours. You two should really get together because John has a woman and I have a man and we're leaving. Goodnight."

She turned on her heel and didn't have to glance around to know that John was right beside her, although he was laughing so hard tears were forming in his eyes. Nina stabbed the elevator button a few times and gave him a look of disdain. "I thought you Latin men were supposed to be so particular about how your women went out in public. Why hasn't somebody clued Little Miss Half-Naked in on that trend?"

Still laughing, John replied, "Hey, you see she ain't got

a man of her own, that's probably why." He reached for Nina who neatly evaded him.

"And by the way, your friend isn't a very good friend, if you ask me. He was trying to hit on me," she said indignantly. John's face instantly went from highly amused to deeply furious and he pushed the lobby button furiously. "What are you doing?" Nina asked in alarm.

"I'm going to go down there and punch his lights out," John growled.

"You'd rather beat up a sap like that than be alone with me?" Nina asked with a raised eyebrow. By now the elevator had reached their floor and the doors opened. Nina waltzed through the open door and took off her jacket so that John could get a good look at the lacy camisole it had been concealing. His expression changed completely as he got a look at her high, enticing breasts in a tiny sheer half-cup bra.

"Oh it's like that, is it? Okay, that's an ass-kicking I owe him, but right now you're coming with me," John growled playfully as he scooped her up to carry her down the hall.

"Now that's more like it," Nina sighed.

Chapter 12

Paris slipped her Blackberry into its case and dropped it into the leather tote bag she carried in lieu of a brief-case. She looked at her dining companion and flashed the dazzling smile that charmed her viewers five days a week. This smile was a little different, though, it was for Titus Argonne and no one else, therefore there was even more sweetness to the curve of her lips.

They were having coffee in the nicely decorated cafe-teria of The Deveraux Group offices. Titus had just re-turned from a few days out of town and now Paris was leaving, too. "I'll be in Detroit for three days taping. I need to get some footage for the interview, which is actually going to be taped in the studio here in Atlanta. It's going to air the night before Thanksgiving, because of sweeps," she told him. Paris was giving him more detail than was warranted, but she just loved talking to him. She'd been so tongue-tied around him for so long, it felt wonderful to be able to have regular conversations with him.

Titus smiled and the bluish gray hue of his eyes became bluer, as it always did when he was in a good mood. "Sweeps? That's Nielsen ratings isn't it? They do that so many times a year, right?"

Paris beamed at the handsome man across the table. "Yes, they do. I'm surprised you know that," she said.

"I know a little bit about a lot of things and a lot about a few things. I'm trying to learn more about you, though. Tell me again when you'll be back," he said, placing his hand over hers on the table.

"I'll be back Friday afternoon," she told him.

"Then I'll take you to dinner on Friday night, how does that sound?" Titus rubbed the back of her hand in small circles as he spoke.

Paris had to force herself not to giggle; the feel of Titus's hand on hers did crazy things to her. "It sounds like every date we've had. It sounds wonderful. Where are we going?"

"It's a surprise," Titus whispered.

Paris felt the usual pink flush spread across her cheekbones. "I almost wish I didn't have to go to Detroit," she admitted. "But this interview is really important to the family as well as to the show, so I want it to be as perfect as I can make it. It's a compelling topic that I'm trying not to sensationalize. I just want to tell the story as honestly and as humanly as I can."

Titus suddenly stopped stroking her hand. "Yeah, it's kind of a delicate situation. But you're the best person to do this interview, you're close enough to the family to do it compassionately, and you're very professional, so it will be a big success for you. I have every confidence in you, Paris."

"Titus, what a nice thing to say," she said sincerely.

"I'm a nice guy," he said in a low, sexy voice. "Now how about if I take you to the airport this afternoon or is someone on your staff going to handle that?"

"I'll either drive over there or ride with the crew, you don't have to do that," she protested.

"I *want* to do that," Titus corrected her. "How else am I going to get a kiss good-bye?"

"We can leave at three," Paris said quickly, and then her

face grew flaming hot as she realized how eager she'd sounded.

Titus just smiled and took her hand again. "I'll be waiting for you."

Of the two of them, Nina was by far the more nervous about the upcoming interview. She was trying to be her normal calm, unflappable self, but someone who knew her well could tell she was on edge. And by this time, John knew her very well indeed. In the two weeks since they came back from Puerto Rico, their relationship had deepened and become even sweeter. As far as John was concerned, the only thing that could make it any better was shared living space, but Nina wouldn't let herself be pinned down. Closer they might be, but Nina was still elusive when she chose to be.

"Okay, tell me again how this is supposed to go? Why is Paris here now? Can't she just wait until you go to Atlanta for the real interview?" Nina asked fretfully.

They were in the living room of John's apartment, relaxing on the sofa with Nina cuddled into John's side, covered with her cashmere throw. The weather had cooled off considerably with the advent of fall. The two Californians were adjusting well to the change of season, especially Nina who was, after all, a native of Illinois. She wouldn't have admitted it for the world, but she liked the cooler weather because it gave her more opportunities to be close to John who felt it was his responsibility to keep her warm. All she had to do was give a tiny shiver and John was right there, putting his arms around her. Nina loved the attention, although she supposed one day she would have to confess she really wasn't that cold-natured. Not today, though.

"*Chica,* it'll be fine. She just wants to get some footage

of the family and us interacting, things she can use to create an image of our new relationship. Nothing weird or sensational, just us," John said comfortingly.

Nina was silent for a minute, inspecting her short, neatly manicured nails before speaking. "I guess I'm still having trouble getting my head around why you have to do this in the first place. Okay, so Big Benny is your biological father, why is it necessary to broadcast it to the whole world? Isn't it enough that everyone involved is cool with it? I don't see why it has to be so public, is all." Fearing she'd said too much, Nina buried her face in John's chest and refused to look at him.

John laughed gently and tried to get Nina to meet his gaze, eventually giving up. "Sweetheart, my family is pretty prominent, well, *very* prominent. It's not like people don't know who we are. When the book is published I'm going to have a certain recognition factor, too," he said modestly. So modestly, Nina raised her head and frowned at him.

"You're not exactly Joe Nobody, John. You're one of the most respected men in your field and in academic circles you're considered to be brilliant, innovative and courageous," she said hotly.

John laughed at the indignation in her tone and used the opportunity to pull her into his lap so he could see her face. "That's exactly my point, Nina. People are going to talk about this. They're already talking about it, gossiping about it, there've been things in the tabloids, terribly wrong things, I might add. The reason we want to do this is to get the right information out there not just to satisfy morbid curiosity, but also to have a clean record for the family. Dad and I want to tell the story the way it really happened so all my nieces and nephews will understand where I came from, and understand how I feel about being part of the family."

Nina was silent for a moment, playing with the buttons on John's shirt. Finally she spoke. "It really doesn't bother you, does it? I mean, being adopted, being raised by people other than your natural parents, finding out you have this whole other family, you're just taking everything in stride. You really amaze me, John. I have to admit, I'm in awe of you."

John was watching Nina more than listening to her. He was becoming more attached to her every day; he sometimes wondered if she understood the depths of his feelings for her. As far as he was concerned, the only thing missing in their relationship was a wedding ring, something he planned to remedy soon. In the meantime, he had to content himself with her daily presence in his life. The book was almost finished, though, and there would be no logical reason for her to remain in Michigan with him unless they were committed to marriage. And the first step in that direction would be to find a suitable residence. He couldn't very well ask her to live with him in University housing, they needed a place of their own, a place to start their life together.

He rubbed his face against Nina's soft hair and just when he felt her breathing begin to slow into a pattern of slumber, he asked her a question. "Nina, will you help me pick out a house?" He had to smile at her reaction. Her eyes got big and she didn't utter a sound. He had rendered Miss Parker speechless, something that had to go down in the record books.

Nina really had no reason to distrust Paris or complain about her. She really was professional and pleasant and she didn't seem to have any sensational agenda. Nina watched her taping and the younger woman seemed to be working very hard to present everyone in his and her best light. She'd taped John giving a lecture at work; she'd done some footage of the Cochran Building where Cochran Communications, the family business, was housed, and some at Adam and Alicia's architectural firm. Now she was taping a family dinner at Donnie and Angelique's big house. Nina had come with John, but she was basically trying to stay out of the way.

To that end she was keeping an eye on little Lily Rose. They were sitting quietly in Lily Rose's room, which Angelique had decorated lovingly and creatively. Nina was trying to get the baby to go to sleep, but she had other plans. Lily Rose was wide-awake, laughing and babbling in a combination of her own little language and the words that made up her growing vocabulary. Nina was sitting in a big soft armchair patterned with flowers, holding the baby and encouraging her to go to sleep. "How about if I sing you a song? Will you go to sleep if I sing to you?"

Lily Rose nodded her head enthusiastically and said "yes" as she patted Nina on the cheek. "Okay, snooks, here you go." Nina cuddled the baby close to her heart and began to sing "Someone to Watch Over Me" in a soft voice. Lily Rose immediately quieted down to listen, but she wasn't as sleepy as Nina hoped. Instead she slid down into Nina's lap and fastened her big pretty eyes on Nina's face as though she were the most fascinating creature she'd ever seen. And that's how Paris found them when she walked into the room.

Nina didn't see Paris right away; she finished the song and laughed when Lily Rose clapped her hands for more. "Oh, no you don't! You get no more songs from me, you little faker."

Paris added her applause to Lily Rose's as she sat down on a slipper chair in the corner of the nursery. "I'm sorry to intrude but I was on my way to the guest room and I heard you singing. You have a phenomenal voice, girl. I didn't know you could sing like that." She stared at Nina with her usual open frankness. Paris, by her own admission, was the most curious person in the world.

Nina coolly acknowledged the compliment with a nod. "I have a passable voice, I guess. I never think about it one way or the other." Paris was looking at her so hard Nina was beginning to feel uneasy. Lily Rose came to her aid by letting out a loud shriek of joy and demanding to go to Paris.

"Aww, you remember your Cousin Paris! Come here, sweetie, and give me some sugar," Paris cooed. Rising from her chair she took the baby from Nina.

Nina mumbled something about helping Angelique and fled the room. Paris took her place in the armchair and continued to kiss the laughing baby. "You know something, Lily Rose? That lady reminds me of someone. I just can't remember who it is. Someone from a long time ago," Paris said thoughtfully. "I'll think of who it is, though, I always do."

Chapter 13

John looked at Nina's face and didn't like the tension he saw reflected there. They had just returned to her suite after having an early dinner at a Japanese steakhouse she liked. She'd eaten with good appetite, but seemed preoccupied and John wanted to know why. He took the remote control out of her hand as she was mindlessly flicking from one channel to another, something she did only when she was deep in thought. Normally Nina was methodical in her thoughts and actions; she selected a program and watched it all the way through without interruption. John was beginning to know a lot of Nina's little quirks and habits and found them all endearing.

She was the tidiest person he'd ever met, for example. If she took something like lotion or perfume out and used it, it went right back to its assigned place as soon as she was finished. She was meticulous in her wardrobe; every piece was laundered or dry-cleaned as soon as it was soiled in any way, although to be honest, John couldn't remember ever seeing anything that looked stained or even slightly wrinkled. Nina was so immaculate, her clothes looked the same when she took them off as when they went on. He knew she liked old movies, she had a penchant for decorating shows and she liked crossword puzzles and word games of any kind. And she had a real fondness for junk food, which she tried mightily to squelch. She loved music and had extremely eclectic tastes, including a passion for disco, of all things.

He recalled how embarrassed she'd been when he found her out, catching her dancing with mad abandon to "Sylvester's Greatest Hits." "Marva used to love disco music and we would dance all over the house together," Nina admitted. "I never outgrew it, I guess."

Yes, John knew a lot more about Nina than he ever thought he would and the information was gratifying, but there was still so much to learn about her. Rubbing the remote across his chin, he asked her point blank why she was so restless. "What's the matter, baby, you seem lost in thought."

Nina issued a soft sigh and bit her lower lip, looking lost. The look passed immediately and she gave John a reasonable facsimile of her normal expression. "I'm fine. I'm just a little tired is all; I've been working some late nights to get the manuscript finished. It's almost done, you know."

John knew it only too well and the thought of Nina going away after its completion was too painful to contemplate. He pushed the thought aside and concentrated on Nina's needs. "You've been working really hard, sweetie and I think you need a break." He stood up and held out his hand to her. "Come with me. I have something special for you, something you'll like a lot," he promised. She took his hand and followed him into the bedroom without saying a word.

In a very short time John had fulfilled his promise and Nina was lying face down on top of a thick towel John had placed on the bed. They had taken a long hot shower together and John had used his considerable skill to make her forget her problems. The hot steam, the fragrant lather and John's long, skillful hands all melded into an intensely pleasurable experience, but he had even more in store for her. He covered her with a towel and whispered that he'd be right back. While he was gone, she almost drifted off to sleep; she was so comforted by the tender care he had given her. Her eyelids were so heavy that even when she felt the stream of warm oil down the center of her back she didn't open her eyes, she just moaned with pleasure.

John began the massage at her shoulders, working down her back until she felt like her bones were dissolving. His strokes were strong and sure, releasing every bit of tension and leaving her limp with enjoyment. He poured more oil on her delightful derriere, palming each cheek with his big hands and kneading them slowly and gently until the tension gathered in another part of her anatomy entirely. The warmth of his hands got her more and more stimulated, until she began to writhe against the towel for relief. "John," she whispered urgently. "What are you doing to me?"

"What do you mean, angel? I'm giving you a massage, that's all," John said softly.

Nina moaned, clenching her hands on the bedclothes. John wouldn't relent in his sensual assault on her body. He continued to caress her cheeks, moving his hands in heated circles that encompassed her hips and increased the heat that was building inside her. "John, oh John, you have to do something," she gasped. With every touch she was becoming more aroused to the point she feared she would explode.

John's fingers slid down to find her moist and needy, her body quivering for his. With his free hand he removed the towel around his waist and made sure the condom he'd put on earlier was still properly in place. "What do you want me to do, Nina?" he teased her gently.

He knelt over her, taking her slender hips in his hands. "What do you want?" he repeated.

Nina raised her hips until she was kneeling in front of John, her thighs open and ready for him. "I want you to make love to me John, right now," she moaned. "I want you inside me, deep inside me." She cried his name aloud as John entered her, holding her hips and taking what was his, plunging into her warmth over and over until their rhythm was set. Then he moved his hands up to her breasts, caressing them and manipulating her tight, erect nipples while she lost herself to the waves of pleasure washing over her body. John continued to squeeze her breast while he brought his hand down to her most intimate part, stroking her pulsing clitoris to make sure they reached the ultimate climax together. He pumped faster and more furiously while her body clenched and held him, taking all he could give and demanding more until their moist and sex-slicked bodies convulsed in an explosion of delight that left them both weak and shattered, breathing hard and reaching for each other.

Nina was still trembling when she turned to go into John's embrace. "John, that was . . . different," she said shyly, when she regained her ability to speak.

He kissed her face, gently and tenderly, while waiting for his heart rate to slow down enough to allow proper speech. "I hope you liked it, *querida*. You bring out so much passion in me, Nina. I've never made love to anyone as exciting as you."

"You're just saying that because you love me," she said in a playful voice.

"Yes, Nina, I do. Totally and completely," he declared solemnly. The look in his eyes was Nina's undoing. Her eyes filled with tears that threatened to overflow. With trembling fingers she touched his face, the handsome face that meant more to her than anything in the world.

"That's nice. Because I seem to be in love with you, too," she said solemnly. "More than I can tell you, more than I can show you, more than I ever knew. I think you may be stuck with me."

"This is good news, Miss Parker, so why don't you look happy?" John teased her as he kissed her neck.

Nina tried to smile, but her mind was racing too fast. *If you only knew,* she thought sadly, *if you only knew.*

After their second shower, John and Nina were once again in bed, but this time she was cradled on his shoulder, trying to find a way to tell him what was troubling her. He presented her with the perfect opportunity when he started talking about the big interview. "They're sending the corporate jet, which will be nice. Adam and Alicia are coming, as well as Donnie and Angel and the baby, Dad and Martha and you and me. That's a huge crowd of people to be entertaining for the Thanksgiving holiday, but Benita says she can't wait to have us all there."

"Well, she'll have one less person to pick up after because I'm not going," muttered Nina.

John reacted immediately, sitting up so fast Nina almost fell out of bed. "What do you mean, you're not coming? What's this all about, Nina?"

"John, there's no reason for me to be there," she said lamely, startled by the intense look he was giving her. "I'll just be in the way," she added feebly.

"Nina, don't be ridiculous. In the first place, you're not going as an appendage, or part of my luggage, you're my woman, the person who means more to me than anything or anyone in this world. Why *wouldn't* you come with me to spend the holiday with my family? And what in the world makes you think I can get through this without you? One of the reasons I've been so calm is that you're always with me, chilling me out, keeping me sane and grounded, and now you just want to bail on me? There's something else going on here, Nina, what is it?"

"Wow. You do have a temper, don't you?" Nina was impressed, John could be so levelheaded and understanding it could make a person nuts but this side of him was unexpectedly interesting.

John looked apologetic. "I didn't mean to yell, but you kind of ambushed me with this. Talk to me, *chica,* what's the real reason you don't want to go?"

Because I'm scared half to death of Saint Benita of Atlanta, she thought miserably. *That sister of yours is more intimidating than all the Cochran women put together and I can barely hold my own with them. And I'm supposed to spend a whole four days with the queen of perfection. Ha, no way buddy.*

John looked so concerned and so upset Nina had no choice but to try to explain, but in a way that wouldn't make her seem like a simp. "Well, John, for one thing there's the question of our accommodations. I don't want to advertise our sex life in front of the whole world; I'm just not modern enough for that. Are we supposed to sleep together or apart or what? How is all that going to work? And I don't know these people from the man in the moon, what am I supposed to talk about while I'm there? I don't want to feel like an outsider and I don't want to look like the town tart because I happen to have a healthy sex life with the man I love. I just think it'll be easier if I don't go, that's all." Nina took a deep breath after her long speech. It wasn't total honesty but it was close enough. To her surprise, John looked relieved instead of upset.

He leaned forward and arranged the pillows at his back so he could lean back on them. Holding out his arm to Nina, he patted his chest to encourage her to rest against him. When she was safe in his embrace, he kissed her gently and told her to put all her fears out of her mind. "First of all, *chica,* Benita and Clay have a big guest house which has four suites, each one has a couple of bedrooms. We'll probably be staying out there so its not like we'll be flaunting ourselves under her roof with the children around. But if you want, we can stay in a hotel, I couldn't possibly care less although I have to admit I don't like the idea of not sharing a bed with you for even one night. I can't sleep without you next to me. You've gotten me really spoiled, you know that?" He kissed her again before continuing.

"You are a permanent part of my life, Nina. Benita and her family, well, they're my family, too. I hope you realize they like you just for you, not because you're my woman. All my brothers and their wives have each told me at some point that I'm lucky to have you; they think you're wonderful. My dad thinks you're perfect for me, even though you're not too crazy about him."

Nina had the grace to blush. "He doesn't know that, does he? I don't want to hurt his feelings or anything," she mumbled.

"Dad has skin like rhino hide, I don't know if he realizes you're not in his fan club, but I doubt it bothers him. He lives in his own little kingdom as you well know, nothing much penetrates the wall surrounding the throne," John said with dry humor. "But that's not the point. The point is these are my people, my family. They like you, Nina and if you give yourself a chance, I think you'll like them, too. Please don't make us spend our first Thanksgiving apart. Please come with me so we can make some more memories," he said softly, kissing her again and again.

"You don't play fair. Of course I'll come," she sighed before abandoning herself to his love.

* * *

The trip to Atlanta was much less taxing than Nina anticipated. The Cochran jet was luxurious and comfortable and big enough for her to hide from people, like Big Benny Cochran, but she wasn't that big a coward. She found herself seated next to John and across from Benny and Martha, whose seats faced theirs. Big Benny just turned on the charm and the four of them enjoyed easy conversation during the flight. The conversation was made even more pleasant by the addition of Lily Rose who took turns sitting with everyone; she plainly adored her grandfather and spent quite a bit of time playing happily in his lap. She was about to celebrate her first birthday and had acquired many new words and wasn't at all shy about using them. She demonstrated this when she took a turn sitting in John's lap. Leaning towards Nina she pointed a finger at her and said, "Sing! Sing, Neenee!"

Nina felt her face grow hot, but she obliged the baby with a song. She held out her hands and Lily Rose went to her at once, settling down when Nina sang "Skylark" to her.

Martha was particularly entranced by the sound of Nina's voice. "You know, you have a truly beautiful voice," she said thoughtfully. "It reminds me of a singer I used to love, now what was her name?" She tapped her finger against her lower lip and tried in vain to recall the name of the singer. Benny also commented on the purity of Nina's tones.

"You've been holding out on us, Miss Nina. What other talents are you hiding, I wonder?" His eyes were twinkling but there was a piercing assessment of Nina in the look as well.

Even John was captivated by her voice. "You know, I've only heard you sing one other time and that was when Adam and Alicia eloped."

Nina blushed again. She'd completely forgotten that she'd sung "The Lord's Prayer" *a capella* at the impromptu ceremony. John looked at her intently, seemingly oblivious to her discomfort. "You really do hide your light under a bushel, *chica*," he said in a low voice for her ears alone.

Nina breathed a silent sigh of relief when the attendant came around to tell them to fasten their seat belts, as they would soon be landing. Donnie collected Lily Rose for the landing and no more was said regarding Nina's voice. *I have got to stop doing that*, she fretted. *I need to be more careful, especially around these people.*

Chapter 14

John was right about their accommodations. There was a certain degree of privacy afforded them in Bennie and Clay's guesthouse. The main house was the one where Clay had been living when he met Bennie and they just couldn't bear to leave the house. Over the years they'd made additions to it as their family expanded, but they conceded they'd probably be living there forever.

"We tried getting a new place a few years ago but it was disastrous. We just couldn't get a real estate agent who understood the dynamics of our family," Bennie said ruefully. "There was one mansion with enough bedrooms and it was certainly large enough, but there was a *catwalk* upstairs connecting the master suite with the other bedrooms," she said, making a face. "Clay took one look at it and started laughing hysterically. Honey, what our boys would have done with a catwalk in the house . . ." Bennie's voice trailed away and she shuddered.

"Anyway, when the people next door moved and put their home on the market we bought it and converted it into a guesthouse with Adam and Alicia's help. It just seemed like the simplest thing to do because I just can't see us leaving this place. Too many memories," she smiled.

The two women were in the big sunny kitchen of the

main house, sharing a pot of tea. John, Adam and Clay were off golfing with Clay's brothers, and Alicia was with Vera Deveraux, who wanted to feature Alicia on her show, *Personal Space.* Donnie and Angelique were staying with her mother and stepfather, which left Nina alone with Benita. She could have hidden out in the guesthouse until John returned, but her fear of Benita was outweighed by her curiosity. Nina wanted to know what the big secret of Benita's mystique was and the only way to do that was to check her out closely.

Benita Cochran Deveraux was gorgeous, that much was obvious. She was quite tall, six-feet-one in her bare feet. She had beautiful caramel skin and thick black hair with the beginnings of a burst of silver in the front. Her figure was firm and voluptuous, even after five children, and there wasn't a single line in her face. Nina had to admit that she didn't seem to have one physical flaw. And she was friendly and down to earth, too. Nothing seemed to bother her, not even when her rambunctious boys ran in and out of the room to distract her attention. While they were drinking tea, Bennie was also going over a list with her houseman, a tall, very good-looking middle-aged man named Braxton. Braxton seemed the perfect addition to this huge household. He was good-humored, unflappable and possessed boundless energy.

"So there's going to be about twenty adults and fifteen children, right? Okay, I'm thinking four turkeys, two hams, and all the trimmings. What do you think about oysters in the dressing?"

"I don't think so, Braxton. Clay will eat anything, and so will Trey, but Marcus won't touch them and neither will Marty and Malcolm. Let's just skip those," she mused, checking more things off another list.

Just then, a frantic Labrador covered with lather raced though the kitchen and was tackled by Bennie as he was headed into the dining room. She grabbed his collar after being covered with suds and really funky smelling water and led the panting dog to the patio. Without so much as a glance at her ruined clothing, she let out a yell for her twins, Martin and Malcolm, who were standing like statues in the kitchen doorway trying to look angelic. Bennie made a vain swipe at the suds clinging to her top and fixed the boys with a steely eye.

"Why did you decide to give Patrick a bath? Didn't I tell you he was going to the groomer this afternoon?"

Both boys nodded rapidly. "Patrick don't like to go there, Mommy," little Marty said earnestly.

Malcolm agreed, and said, "He cries when he has to go there. So we washed him."

"We washed him good, too," Marty added with a cherubic smile.

Bennie pursed her lips and tried not to smile, which was hard because the boys looked so cute, even though they were wet from head to toe and covered with lather and dog hair. "Where did you attempt to give him this bath?"

"In your bathroom," they replied in unison.

Bennie slapped her forehead and pulled her hand straight down her face, mumbling as she did so. "Okay, this is what's going to happen. You two are going to clean up every bit of water from the bathroom all the way down the stairs and through the kitchen. Braxton, don't help them unless, well, you know, things get ugly. Then you two are coming upstairs to clean my bathroom and you're going to take a bath. If it wasn't so cool out I'd put you in the yard and hose you down," she said sternly.

Her words were lost, as they had already dashed off to get cleaning rags and paper towels from the long-suffering Braxton. Bennie sighed deeply and looked at Nina, who'd been observing all of this activity with a bemused look.

"I wish I could tell you this is a rare occurrence, but this is pretty typical around here. Come on upstairs with me while I change and we'll run away from them," she said with a smile.

Nina followed Bennie as she went up the back stairs to the second floor of the huge house. She had to admire Bennie and Clay's home, it was clearly a place where love ruled. It was beautifully decorated, but it was also warm and homey and surprisingly unpretentious for a couple with as much money as Bennie and Clay had. They stopped on the second floor to check on Kate and Bella, the twin girls, who were still taking a nap. Watching Bennie with her children gave Nina an odd feeling; she couldn't put a name to it.

Finally they arrived at the master suite on the third floor of the house. Clearly it was meant to be a haven for the couple to relax and escape from the rest of the world, and just as clearly, their children had usurped it. Toys were here and there in the sitting room; the bathroom with its freestanding circular Jacuzzi was also home to an assortment of rubber ducks, scuba gear and children's bubble bath. And of course, the remains of Patrick's bath were evident in the water splashed all over the floor and the fragrant suds everywhere. "At least they have good taste," Benny said with a wry twist to her mouth. "They used my last bottle of Mariella Burani bath gel to bathe the dog, bless their disobedient little hearts." Still shaking her head she turned to Nina. "Have a seat and I'll get out of these lovely things and we can hit the road."

Nina gingerly took a seat in the pale green and ivory sitting room and looked around, admiring the furnishings and to a degree, Bennie. She was a lot more laid back than most mothers would be; the antics of those boys would have driven a lot of women, especially rich women, into a screaming fit. As if she could read her mind,

Bennie wandered into the sitting room in fresh clothing, just a simple pair of slacks and a lightweight cashmere pullover. She was putting on a bracelet and talking at the same time.

"I'm much too lenient with the boys, I know I am," she said with a sigh. "Clay has to be the disciplinarian or they'd be robbing piggy banks and knocking over toy stores. They have a fatal combination of dynamic energy, high IQs and utter fearlessness," she laughed. She sat down on a loveseat and smiled at Nina. "I wanted to be a mother more than anything, especially after I met Clay. It was love at first sight for me. I walked around the corner at our headquarters in Detroit and there stood the handsomest man I'd ever seen in my life. When he said hello, it was all over but the shoutin'. I was like 'stick a fork in me, I'm *done*'. I had to chase him down like a bounty hunter but he finally admitted he loved me and we got married which was the happiest day of my life."

The memories made Bennie glow as she related the tale to Nina. "The next happiest day of my life was when I found out I was carrying Clay's baby. Nina, I still get goose bumps when I think about it. Clay was so happy he cried when I told him. So when I lost the baby, it almost killed us both. I came very close to losing my mind, you know. If it hadn't been for John, I'd probably still be in the mental hospital," Bennie said quietly.

Nina couldn't think of anything to say in response to that. She knew what Benita was talking about. Years before, when Benita and Clay Deveraux were first married, Benita had been in California on a business trip and had been involved in a car accident that tragically caused her to lose the baby she was carrying. She'd been consumed with guilt over the miscarriage, swearing that it was her fault. Her guilt and her grief caused her to sink into a depression so profound the only person who could get through to her was John, who'd been called in as her therapist. Nina pulled herself out of her thoughts and listened to Bennie who was still talking about her gratitude to John.

"John saved my sanity, my life and my marriage and I loved him like a brother even before I knew we were related. So that's why it's so hard for me to sweat the small stuff. I feel so privileged to have my babies, when they cut up it just doesn't bother me that much," Bennie admitted with a sheepish look.

"And quiet as it's kept, I think I want another one. I know it seems crazy with five children, but I love being pregnant so much! It's an amazing feeling," she sighed. "Believe it or not, I feel sexier and more desirable when I'm carrying Clay's babies than at any other time. I'd love to have just one more, but I don't dare bring it up, Clay would think I've lost my mind for sure." She sighed again. Bennie glanced at her watch and said it was time to get the ladies up from their nap. "Then we can boogie on out of here for a minute, if you'd like."

Nina followed Bennie into the nursery to get Kate and Bella, marveling at the obvious depths of her emotions regarding her children. For the first time in a long time she tried to understand why she couldn't have those same feelings like a normal woman. And she wondered what John would think of her if he ever found out.

In spite of her initial misgivings about Benita, Nina had an enjoyable afternoon with her. She helped her get the little girls into their clothes and was impressed by how many words they knew. They were almost two and very chatty. The four of them went out for the afternoon and did a little window shopping, had a little lunch and a lot of conversation as they tooled around Atlanta. Finally,

Bennie turned to Nina with a conspiratorial look and asked a most unexpected question. "So, Miss Nina, how long have you been in love with my brother John?"

Nina was so shocked her face didn't even get hot. She looked at Bennie who was deftly steering her Volvo station wagon through the mean traffic and seemed to have been waiting for an opportunity to pounce on her. "Am I that obvious?" she asked grumpily.

"Oh, shoot yeah, girl. And if it's any consolation, John is worse than you are, so don't feel like the Lone Ranger. So tell me, when did it happen?" Bennie was as eager as a teenager dishing on a cute boy with her best friend. Nina couldn't believe she was doing it, but the words just came pouring out.

"Well, if you must know, I fell in love with him the first time I laid eyes on him. My publisher was hot to get this book from this *uber*-shrink and I was hand picked to do the ghostwriting. I had to schlep down to L.A., a town I despise, to meet this nerd and I was not a happy gal. I go to his office, his assistant sends me in and there stands this . . . this . . . bronzed *god*, that's the only way I can describe him. He was so fine he didn't even look real; he looked like a photograph of a man, if that makes any sense. Then he said my name and shook my hand and I swear I didn't hear another word he said. I got hot, I got cold, I was sweaty, my mouth was dry, I was a mess, you hear me? To this day I have no idea how I got the assignment because I can't remember saying or thinking one single coherent thing that day."

Bennie burst into laughter and patted Nina's hand. "I can relate, that's just about how I reacted to Clay. So what happened then?"

"Well, I was commuting at first, we'd meet about once a week to go over things and set up a writing schedule. Then I agreed to stay in L.A. for a week because his assistant had to go out on maternity leave. That's when I overheard the conversation about him being sick and that's when I really knew I was in love with him because I almost died when I heard the words describing his illness. I knew if he died, part of me would die, too. There was no way I was going to let him out of my sight until he was well, because I just couldn't stand the thought of him not being alive. I know that sounds crazy and melodramatic, but it's true," Nina said quietly.

Bennie touched Nina's hand again. "It doesn't sound crazy to me, Nina. I married my college sweetheart and he died from Hodgkin's disease. I thought I wasn't going to survive. I wanted to die with him, it hurt so badly. So believe me, it doesn't sound crazy. It sounds like love to me."

This time Nina did flush with emotion, a lovely warm feeling that suffused her whole body. "It is love," she affirmed. "It really is."

Paris's interview with the Cochran family turned out brilliantly. It was taped two days before Thanksgiving and aired the day before. It was all she hoped it would be, with heartfelt talk interspersed with the taped scenes of typical family life and photographs of the Cochrans and of John's family. As a special surprise, she'd arranged for Big Benny's relatives from Idlewild to be flown in and there wasn't a dry eye in the studio audience when his Great-Aunt Emmaline and his aunts Dahlia, Daphne and Reba walked onto the set. With careful questions from Paris, the story of Benny's long estrangement from his family and the loss of his first love, Cassandra, was told. Even when it was revealed that Cassandra was John's mother and it was obvious that the liaison took place while Benny was married to Lillian Cochran, it didn't seem sordid, it was told tenderly but frankly.

Paris looked at John and asked him point blank how

he felt about being found by his biological father. John didn't hesitate. He smiled as he looked at his father and said, "Blessed. I feel honored to be accepted as a member of this family and blessed to have a brother who gave me back my life." This was directed to Adam, whose eyes looked suspiciously moist when he heard John's words.

After conversation with Bennie and Clay, Adam, Alicia, and the other Cochrans who were present, Paris couldn't resist a final question. "So John, do you think you'll be following the pattern of your family and getting married? Is romance on the horizon for you?" she asked with disarming frankness.

"Yes, I plan on getting married and very soon. I was lucky enough to meet the love of my life and I can't wait until she's my wife," John answered firmly. While he was speaking his eyes were on Nina, whom he could see as she stood offstage. Paris's eyes lit up and there was a collective "ooh" from the women in the audience. "I don't suppose she's here," she said archly. "Is there a possibility we could persuade her to come onstage?"

"Absolutely not," John replied. "She's a very private person and I'm sure I'm already in trouble, so let's leave it at that."

Nina was beyond blushing at that point; she was simply rendered motionless from sheer shock. She couldn't have moved a muscle if she was offered a large sum of money to do so. Surely John wasn't talking about *marriage* on national television without discussing it with her first. She put her hand on her chest to help still the rapid pounding of her heart but it didn't help. She was so caught up in the moment she didn't notice the speculative looks she was getting from the backstage crew, which was just as well. Should she be angry, elated, scared, what? Suddenly John was standing over her and she had no more time to ponder the proper reaction because he put both hands around her waist and bent down to kiss her.

"Go ahead, let me have it," he whispered. "On a scale of one to ten with ten being consumed with rage, how mad are you?" His handsome face looked so concerned and so full of caring, Nina felt herself fall in love all over again.

"As long as I'm the woman you were talking about, you get to live," she smiled. She moved closer to his warmth and returned his embrace with one of her own.

"Well, Curly, are you ready to go home?" John was toying with a strand of her hair while he spoke.

Thanks to Bennie, Nina had an adorable new hairstyle, one that she could shampoo every day and still maintain. After their outing Bennie had invited Nina into a room she'd set up as a salon. "When Renee and I decided to go into the spa business, we went to cosmetology school, which is how we met our friend Ceylon. She was our instructor, but that's another story altogether. I only do my husband and the boys regularly, but Ceylon and I often do each other's hair," she explained.

She'd stopped talking and looked at Nina closely. "You know, this would be a fabulous look for you," she told her as she showed her a hairstyle in one of her trade magazines. "All you need to do is shampoo it, put some non-alcohol styling gel on it and scrunch it so the natural curls come through. And you can still style it in lots of ways. Wanna try it?"

Nina looked at the magazine picture and back at Bennie. "Are we talking about *my* hair here? I don't think that would work on my stuff."

Bennie wasn't listening to her; she was feeling Nina's hair and trying to figure out how much hair to trim. "Nina, this will be prefect for you. Since you run so often, you can shampoo your hair every time you run and you won't have to put heat on it. And people don't seem to realize that a relaxer just takes out some of the natural curl of the hair, it doesn't make it permanently straight. You're going to be amazed at what your hair will do, trust me."

Nina got caught up in Bennie's enthusiasm and let her have her way. In a few hours she was thrilled with the end result.

Bennie had meticulously shaped Nina's shoulder-length hair into a bob that stopped between her chin and her shoulders. The cut added volume and depth and Nina was shocked to see that Bennie was right; with an application of a little silicone based frizz-free serum and a styling gel, she could scrunch her hair and let it air dry and the result was a mass of tight ringlets that looked so adorable John about lost his mind when he saw her. He was entranced with her hair now, he was always stroking it, playing in it, wrapping a curl around his finger or just inhaling the scent of it.

Now she smiled up at him and brushed a flirtatious lock off her forehead before answering. "Yes, *Papi,* I'm ready to go. I think I'd like to be alone with you for a while," she whispered.

John growled something savage in her ear because she knew good and well they weren't going straight to Bennie's. They were all expected at Clay's mother's house. Heedless of the people milling around them, he tightened his arm around her waist and kissed her hard, resulting in a cascade of wanton-sounding giggles from her. They finally left the backstage area to rejoin the family, holding hands and looking crazy in love with each other.

Meanwhile, Paris, who was observing them from her vantage point some feet away, sighed with happiness. Poking Aidan in the arm she said, "See? I knew they were perfect for each other. I knew it. I'm never wrong about these things, I know a perfect couple when I see it."

Aidan gave an exaggerated 'ouch' and rubbed his arm dramatically where Paris had poked him. "Big whoop. So two people who have the hots for each other end up falling in love. *That's* a stretch," he said in a heavily ironic tone. His eyes widened for a second and he added, "I still say you need to concentrate on your own love life. What's the forecast for you and that big ol' detective? Just when is something scandalous and juicy going to happen with you two?" he asked with a mischievously raised eyebrow.

Before Paris could answer a deep voice sounded behind her. "That's a good question, I've been wondering about that myself."

Paris whirled around and looked into Titus's mesmerizing eyes. Before she could say anything he spoke again. "I'd really like to hear *your* prediction for us," he said with a devastating smile.

Aidan excused himself at once, saying, "You can thank me later," in a stage whisper. He took one glance over his shoulder as he departed, gratified to see the couple moving into each other's arms for what promised to be a passionate kiss.

"My work here is done," Aidan said smugly.

Chapter 15

John couldn't resist teasing Nina after they returned from Atlanta. She'd had so many reservations about going and so much fun while she was there he had to poke a little gentle fun at her. "When are you going to realize that I know what's good for my baby? I know what you like and I know how to make you happy, so you need to just put yourself in my hands, Nina. Let *Papi* run the show," he said, preening like a macho peacock.

Nina put her hands on her hips and dropped one shoulder in the universally recognized "Negro-you-must-be-joking" stance. "Do you realize how that sounds? Either you're completely deluded or we need to lower your dosage. You must be out of your mind if you think I'm going to sit around and let you make my decisions for me, are you kidding?"

They were in Nina's bedroom; John sprawled across the bed and Nina standing in front of the closet putting away her clothes. John turned on his side and gave Nina his most winning smile. "Of course I'm kidding. I'm not about to try to run your life; I was just giving you a hard time. But I'm very happy you had such a good time with Benita and the family. She's something else, isn't she?"

After spending a few days with her, Nina could agree that his sister was a special person. Bennie was the least pretentious, most laid-back person Nina had met in a long time and she'd made Nina feel like a friend, not just someone who was along for the ride. And her children were adorable, even the irrepressible twins. The babies, Kate and Bella, were sweet and loveable, but Trey was in a class by himself. She said as much to John. "Have you ever seen a child as much like his father as Trey? He's the coolest child I've ever met," she said fondly.

John agreed. "That party was hilarious. I haven't laughed that much in years. And it was all Trey's idea. Pretty amazing. I think he has the makings of a great producer in him."

The party to which John referred took place the day after Thanksgiving. It was to celebrate all the November birthdays, which belonged to Clay, Trey, who was born the same day as his father, and John and Adam, who were born five days apart. Trey decided it should be what he called a singing party. The family was still seated about the enormous dining room table digesting Thanksgiving dinner when Trey made his announcement. "Everyone has to sing in order to eat. If they don't sing, they have to pay and we'll give the money to church," Trey had declared. When his parents asked why a singing party, Trey had a simple answer. "Because people like to sing. Singing makes them feel good. It makes them happy. And we're all happy because we have Uncle John and Aunt Nina in our family so we should have a big singing party and have fun."

The party at Bump and Lillian's house the next night was fun for everyone. True to his word, Trey manned the door and whoever was foolish enough to refuse to sing had to fork over the money if he or she wanted to eat. Paris didn't even debate the issue; she just thrust a big wad of bills at Trey. John also emptied his wallet and offered Trey a blank check besides. Most of the family participated eagerly, like his cousins Amariee, Jill and Jasmine, who sang a Destiny's Child number. Trey was unsuccessful in getting his dad to perform, which garnered him a huge donation. He had mercy on his elders, though, and said his Grandpa Benny didn't have to perform. "You don't have to make a donation either, Grandpa, you can just take it easy," Trey said kindly.

Big Benny snorted and strode to the microphone. He nodded to Bump, who was accompanying everyone. It was hard to say who was the most stunned when Benny began singing the Quincy Jones classic "Everything Must Change." His rich baritone caressed each note, turning the song into a work of art. His voice lingered in the air like the heady fragrance of a thousand red roses and left everyone breathless, except Benita who'd grown up with her father singing her to sleep, and his wife Martha, because Big Benny sang to her all the time. She whispered to Lillian that he'd seduced her with his voice. "I kept telling him no until he started singing one night and it's been yes, yes, *yes* ever since."

Nina and John laughed together as they recalled the evening, full of surprises, laughter and love. "I'd forgotten how nice it was to be with a family," Nina said quietly. She was sitting on the side of the bed with a faraway look in her eye and John simply pulled her into the shelter of his arms and held her. "You're never going to have to wonder again, Nina." He kissed her lips softly and smiled. "I don't think the twins will let you get away from them. They're in love with you now."

She leaned into his comforting warmth and laughed. It was true; she'd won their hearts forever. Nina had gone to the kitchen to get a glass of water and found little Marty and Mal looking glum. When she asked them what was wrong they said they wanted to sing but they didn't know any songs except Jingle Bells. Nina asked them if they wanted to sing with her and in about fifteen minutes they made their debut singing Pip-style backup to Nina's "Midnight Train to Georgia." They had mastered a couple of simple dance steps and the "toot-toot" part perfectly and had an absolute ball performing.

"They said I was their best friend and they loved me." Nina laughed again at the memory.

John wrapped a curl around his finger and kissed the end of Nina's cute nose. "Just don't forget who loves you the most. You're mine and I mean to keep you," he vowed. Instead of the smile he expected, Nina's response was a lowered head and trickle of tears down a face stricken with sadness.

"Nina, don't do that, baby, you're killing me. Talk to me. What is it that's troubling you?"

Nina could only shake her head and try to stop the tears from coming. She dashed the tears away with the heel of her hand and muttered something about P.M.S. "It's just my hormones. I get like this once a month or haven't you noticed," she said grumpily.

"Actually, no. I thought it was just your usual grouchy mood, not the traditional monthly one," John teased her. He groaned as Nina poked him in the chest and demanded an apology. He was happy to give it, as long as the tears stopped and she was back to her normal self. He held her closely and rubbed his face against her tight, springy curls, but he knew this wasn't the end of it. Nina was still hiding something from him and until he found out what it was, their future happiness was in jeopardy.

John watched Nina sleep for a few minutes as he pondered some other events of the weekend in Atlanta. One evening while Nina and Bennie were having girl time with Alicia, John was in the kitchen with Adam and Clay. Each one of them had a twin clad only in his underwear standing in front of him. They were parting the children's hair and staring at their scalps. The men were so engrossed in their work John hated to interrupt them, but his curiosity got the better of him.

"Um, I hate to be nosy, but what are you doing?" John asked with unconcealed curiosity.

Clay looked up with a grin. "Checking them for ticks."

John looked skeptical, but Clay assured him he was serious. "They play outside almost all the time and there's no telling what kind of vermin they could get into. So this is a daily routine. Bennie is adamant about it, she's read too much about deer ticks and Lyme disease and whatnot."

The twins were surprisingly cooperative, although the routine examination was punctuated with their incessant questions. In addition to being very active children, they were very talkative, something that didn't seem to bother Clay in the least. He was patient and good-humored with them and plainly enjoyed his role as a father. John watched them without saying a word. Clay had smiled at John's silent observation and when he sent the boys upstairs for their bath, he turned to him.

"The best thing I ever did in my life was marry Benita," Clay said in his deep, gravelly voice. "When I met her I was totally knocked out, so much so I tried to run for my life but it didn't work. I was so in love with her I couldn't see straight and I still am. The next best thing to happen to me was becoming a father. I had no idea having kids could be so fulfilling. As long as you have a good lock on the bedroom door, of course," he added wryly.

Adam, who was still sitting at the kitchen table with John, burst out laughing. Clay smiled and pointed at Adam. "Go ahead, laugh. Wait until you're under the covers with your wife getting some much needed intimate time with her and you hear a little voice asking, 'What are you doing?' You'll be calling a locksmith within the hour, trust me."

All three men laughed together, but Clay recovered first. "Believe it or not, I'd like to have another one but your sister would probably have me committed if I brought it up. I love having babies with my wife. Benita is the most beautiful woman on earth as far as I'm concerned, but when she's expecting it just drives me crazy," he admitted. "I'm trying to work up my nerve to suggest another one, but I couldn't do that to her. She has enough on her plate as it is," he sighed.

John couldn't think of anything to add to this heartfelt declaration, and Clay had looked at the two men and smiled. "Your turn is coming, though. You Cochrans like having babies as much as the Deverauxes do, you'll be popping them out pretty soon," he predicted.

Adam, not surprisingly, had agreed. "Alicia and I want a big family, at least four. We plan to get started next year."

John was saved from answering by a loud thump from upstairs followed by Patrick's frantic barking. Clay raised his hands and stared at the ceiling briefly before taking off to find out what was going on. Adam left in search of Alicia and John was left sitting in the kitchen contemplating the conversation that had just taken place.

Even now, back in Ann Arbor with Nina curled next to him in the bed, the words still echoed around his head. Everyone took it for granted that babies followed marriage like night followed day. But it didn't always happen that way and for John, it wasn't going to happen. He looked at Nina again and a tremor raced through his body. How would she react when she found this out? He grimaced at the irony. Nina wasn't the only one with secrets. Would she still want him when she found out what he was keeping from her?

* * *

Paris tapped on the door of Bump's studio and waited for permission to enter. She peeked around the door after hearing his voice and gave him a big smile. "Hey, Uncle Bump! Thanks for making time to see me," she said brightly as she entered his studio.

He was seated at his uncluttered desk but stood when she came into the room and held out his arms for a big kiss. "You know I always have time for you. Now what were you being so mysterious about? You made it sound like you found the Holy Grail or something. What have you been up to, you nosy rascal?" he asked fondly.

Paris made a comic face and said in a voice totally devoid of guile, "I keep telling people I'm *inquisitive*, like any good researcher. Nosiness is just snooping, getting in people's business for no good reason. I, on the other hand, am trying to acquaint myself with all aspects of the human condition to better serve humanity." She looked so pious Bump laughed in her face.

"Sit your nosy butt down and tell me what's on your mind, Snoopy."

"Ooh, Uncle Bump that's just wrong," she muttered as she sat down on the comfortable chair across from Bump. She reached inside her Coach tote bag and pulled out a document envelope. "Something's been nagging at me since I went up to Detroit for the preliminary taping. I was at Donnie and Angel's house and I found Nina in the nursery with the baby, singing to her. There was something about her voice that was just odd to me and I couldn't put my finger on it. Then, when we were at Trey's singing party, something else just kinda went "boing" in my head and I couldn't let it go. I started digging around on the Internet and in the archives at The Deveraux Group. Take a look at this and tell me what you think," she said, handing him a few black and white photos.

Intrigued, Bump reached for the pictures and examined them carefully. In just a couple of minutes, he saw what Paris had seen. "Well, I'll be damned. You know, I thought I was getting senile, but when I heard her voice it was like listening to a ghost. I didn't say anything at the time, but I knew I wasn't *that* crazy," he muttered as she continued to stare at the pictures.

"So you think I'm right? You think she's the one?" Paris asked eagerly.

Bump looked long and hard at the first picture, a snapshot of the late, long-lamented songbird Rita Shannon. The picture was at least twenty-five years old, but the image was timeless. There was Rita Shannon sitting in a big armchair serenading her little girl, flanked by her young sons. The woman looked so much like Nina it could easily have been her in the picture. "Why didn't I see the resemblance before?" Bump wondered out loud.

"It wasn't so much the resemblance as the way she looked holding Lily Rose. There was just something so familiar about the pose, it made me think I'd seen it before. And I *had* seen it, in a book about girl groups from the sixties. But the other one, that was the clincher for me. Look at it, Uncle Bump."

Bump turned to the other photograph and let out a low whistle. This one was a picture of Rita with a head full of short ringlets, looking over her shoulder with an infectious smile bracketed by dimples, the same dimples they'd all seen when Nina was singing with the twins at the party.

"This can't be a coincidence, Uncle Bump. Everyone knows Rita Shannon had three children. After she died there was a big thing about her singing partner Donella Divine adopting the children. They were supposed to be such rivals, but Donella stepped up and took the kids to give them the kind of home Rita wanted them to have. Then she left their group, The Sensations, and kind of disappeared. I read all this from different sources, of course. There were some variations, but they all agreed on one thing. One, there was no love lost between Rita and Donella. Two, Donella took guardianship of the children and three, after that she just vanished from public life." Paris rose from the chair and started walking around the big studio, a habit when she was deep in thought.

Bump laid the pictures on his desk and got a faraway look on his face. "You couldn't know this, but I knew them. I knew The Sensations and their manager. I always liked Rita. She was a sweet little thing, full of talent. Now that Donella? Piece of work, that's what she was. Couldn't half sing and she had all the coordination of on ox on roller skates. I worked with them a couple of times and it was a trip. The worst time was when I was the musical director for the Oscars." Bump shook his head, lost in the memory. "They had a big hit that year, the song was nominated for an Academy Award and they were going to perform it at the ceremony. Rita was pitch perfect every time and Donella kept screwing up. They finally had to make her stand there and move her mouth and they played a track with Rita singing her part, too. That girl was just pitiful," Bump recalled with a shake of his head.

"So why was she in the group at all?" Paris asked. "Why didn't they drop her, replace her with someone else?"

"Because, my poor innocent Snoopy, Donella was the mistress of the man who owned the label. She married him right before they hit the real big time. And I'll tell you something else, Paris. She may have adopted those boys but she didn't take that little girl. Whoever Nina grew up with, it wasn't her brothers and Donella. I saw them in Toronto where they moved not too long after Rita died and Donella had *two* children, not three. The little girl in that picture was nowhere in sight."

"So who *is* Nina and where did she come from?" Paris asked in frustration.

Bump gave her a long, serious look. His tone was equally grave when he addressed her. "That's something we may never know, Paris, because that's a line you can't cross. This is one you've got to leave alone."

The old Nina would have seen it coming. The other Nina, the wary and distrustful one who knew life was full of ugly surprises, would have been ready for it. But this Nina, the one who'd been wooed and courted and romanced into happiness, was blindsided. The new gentler, sweeter Nina was the one who was jerked back into reality by a phone call. It came a couple of weeks after their Thanksgiving sojourn to Atlanta, two weeks in which she and John grew closer than she could have believed possible.

She had just finished printing off the second copy of the completed manuscript and instead of the depression she thought she'd suffer at the end of the project, she felt elated. She stroked the precise stack of paper that represented months of hard work and was proud of what she and John accomplished. *We really do work well together,* she thought with a loving smile. The tiny mechanical voice of the printer announced her job was complete and Nina clapped her hands in delight. She jumped up from her chair, took the last sheets off the printer and added them to the stack, then put a CD into her portable player. In seconds she was dancing madly to "The Hustle," the seminal disco anthem of the ages. She felt weightless and joyous, ready to fly. The book was finished, John was healthy and happy and most amazing of all, he loved her. Nina finally collapsed on the sofa, laughing and exhilarated.

Her cell phone rang and she answered it at once, her smile evident in her voice. "Hello!" she said happily. She had to turn the stereo off in order to hear clearly, the voice on the other end was the last one she expected to hear. "You're *what?* No, I don't understand, I don't understand at all! How can you do this to me?" Nina's voice shook with rage. "This isn't right, you know it isn't. How can you treat me like this after all I've done?" Nina was ice cold and trembling from head to toe. When the brief conversation ended she wrapped her arms around her middle and stood with her head bowed for a long moment. When her head raised her eyes were cold and resolute; she knew what she had to do.

She picked up her phone and punched in a familiar number. "It's me. Where is she? Does she know about it?" Nina paced back and forth while she listened to the voice on the other end. "She *what?* Well, when were you going to tell me about it? Okay, I'm on my way. I'll be there late tonight or very early tomorrow morning. You have my cell number, if something else happens I expect you to use it." Her voice was firm but there was a gentle restraint there, too. "I'm sorry I yelled at you. I'll be there as quick as I can."

She made reservations while she packed her bags. "No, I don't need a return flight. Just one way," she told the ticket agent.

She put one copy of the manuscript into a neat white box and addressed it to John's editor. The other copy she put into a box along with all John's research materials. She would leave it at his apartment on the way to the airport. She had to make four trips to load the rental car but now she was finished. She looked around the suite and was strangely calm. She felt no pain, no tears, no anger, she felt nothing. Turning to the door, she walked away from her dreams and returned to her reality.

John frowned as he flipped his cell phone shut. He'd been calling Nina all afternoon and got no answer. His face relaxed as he realized she might be at the track; she never left her phone on when she was running. Deciding to surprise her, he glanced at his watch and checked his appointment book. He was free for the rest of the day and he wanted to do something very special for Nina. He was singing to himself as he left the building, bracing himself against the early winter chill. It was almost totally dark, even at this relatively early hour. It had been two weeks since the Thanksgiving holidays and the end of the term was almost here, along with the beginning of the winter break. He smiled as he got into his SUV, thinking about the holidays with Nina. He'd been trying to wait until Christmas to give her something, but he knew he couldn't hold out any longer.

His first stop was a florist, where he picked out two dozen Tropicana roses. Their deep coral color reminded him of Nina, feminine and exotic at the same time. He then stopped at Trader Joe's market for some non-alcoholic sparkling wine and other delicacies he knew would delight her. John was in an even better mood when he got to the University apartment. He opened the door singing and almost broke his neck when he stumbled over a large box that hadn't been there earlier. "What the hell is that?"

He set his purchases in the chair by the door and inspected the box. He took out the manuscript, which Nina had secured with large elastic bands and stared at it thoughtfully. Realizing the rest of the box contained his research John ignored it, turning his full attention to the manuscript. It was finished, all complete. John felt humbled and awed when he saw the results of all Nina's hard work. *This is all thanks to Nina. This would have never happened without her.* John's heart swelled with gratitude and love as he flipped open his phone again to call her. *Answer the phone, woman!*

He looked out the window at the inky sky; now it was totally dark outside. Glancing at his watch, he left the apartment with long purposeful strides. He had no idea where Nina was and she wouldn't or couldn't answer her phone. Something strange was going on and he didn't like it one bit.

Chapter 16

John looked like hell. His entire posture bespoke depression and anger. He was sitting with his legs extended in front of him, and his elbows resting on his knees. He was staring at his feet, his unshaven face a mask of pain. All of his brothers looked concerned.

Finally Andre spoke up, needing to get clarification. "So what happened, John? You got to your place and found the box, then what did you do?"

John continued to stare before speaking. When he did his voice sounded raspy and unused. "It was getting late and I was worried about her because I hadn't heard from her and she wasn't answering her phone. I decided to go to her place to see what was up and when I got there . . ." He stopped talking for a second as pain flashed across his face. "When I got to the residence motel, I went to her suite and there was housekeeping, changing the linen and vacuuming, cleaning the suite up because she'd checked out." The anger and bitterness in John's words were at war with his pain and bewilderment.

Alan gave a low whistle. "So she just left without a word to you? You have no idea what made her take off?"

"None whatsoever. Everything was fine, better than fine. I bought a ring for her in Puerto Rico and I was going to pop the question last night, I couldn't wait until Christmas. And she just vanished," he said bleakly.

The men were gathered at Adam and Alicia's loft in council. John had called Adam that morning, frantic with worry and all the men met at Adam's to lend their support and help. Donnie said what was on all the men's minds, the worse case scenario no one wanted to address. "John, man, you can't rule out foul play. I mean, have you considered the fact that something could have happened to her?" he asked gently.

"Yeah, I thought about nothing else but that for the first five or six hours. But everything was just too methodical and precise, too much like Nina. I called my publisher this morning and guess what, the manuscript was delivered. She sent it in express overnight delivery and it arrived today. So that told me she planned this, or at least that she was in her right mind before she left.

"I felt like a real idiot doing it, but I had to ask them what her address and telephone number in Oakland is. There's so much about Nina I don't know, things we just never got around to talking about," he said with a shake of his head. "Get this," he said looking up at the worried faces of his brothers. "Nina was out here on her own dime. I thought the publisher was paying her expenses while she was here, but she was paying them out of her own pocket," he said, the disbelief evident in his voice.

John grew hot all over again as he remembered the brisk, chatty voice of the editor working with him and Nina on the book. "Nina's quite something, isn't she? I kept telling her she could work from home on this, but she insisted she had to be in Michigan with you. I told her we couldn't reimburse her expenses and that she'd basically have no income until the completion check was cut, but she was fine with that. She's always been the most productive ghostwriter we have and it looks like she's done a wonderful job with you. Congratulations on an excellent project, John. I think this book is going to have a home on the best seller list for a long, long time," she said warmly.

Now it was Andre's turn to give an awed whistle. "You mean to tell me she came out here to be with you and she was paying for it herself? That had to be costing her a bomb, man. And she was probably keeping up her regular expenses back home, too. What in the world would make her do that?" he said wonderingly.

Donnie looked at his twin brothers in disgust. "You really are the romantically deficient ones, aren't you? Love made her do it, you idiots."

Andrew agreed. "She knew you were sick before you left California and she wanted to be with you to keep an eye on you. It wasn't about the money, it was about her looking out for you."

John leaned back on the long leather sofa and put his arms behind his head. "How could I have been so blind? Why didn't I figure any of this out? I feel like the world's biggest fool."

Adam gave his brother a sympathetic look before repeating Donnie's earlier concern. "But we still don't know why she took off, or where she is. I don't want to be an alarmist, but I don't think we can rule anything out yet. She could be anywhere, man."

John looked slightly sheepish for a moment. "Okay, she did leave me a note. I finally found it after losing my mind for a few hours because it wasn't like she'd put it where I could find it right away. There were just a couple of lines: 'I'm sorry to do it like this but it had to end sometime. It may not seem like it, right now, but this is the best thing for both of us. I really do love you.'" John recited the words angrily and raked his fingers through his goatee.

"I still can't get over her thinking she could just leave me a little note like that and then disappear on me."

"So now you just have to figure out where she could be. We can call Titus Argonne, his people could track her down in a New York minute," Adam said.

John had a surprising response. "Actually, she's in Oakland right now, unless she's taken off again. I called her home number and she answered the phone. It was her voice, no question about it. So I really don't have a choice," he said grimly.

"What do you mean, no choice," Adam asked with a raised eyebrow.

"I mean I'm going out there and get her. I have no idea what happened to make her think she could just drop out of my life with no warning but she's about to find out what time it is," John replied angrily. "I always knew Nina was difficult, but to be honest, that's what I like about her. She's not like most women, all sweet and sugary, Nina is *spicy*, man. She keeps me on my toes constantly and I love that. But this goes beyond all understanding, it really does. I don't know whether I want to love her forever or lock her up."

He was shocked when all his brothers started laughing. The shock subsided when Andrew was finally able to speak. "Welcome to the family, John. Now you're a real Cochran. You're not really one of us until your woman drives you crazy," he said with a wry smile.

The brothers all spoke in unison. "Amen to that." Adam took it a step further and grinned at John. "You're definitely one of us now."

When Alicia came home and found her loft full of the Cochran men wearing gloomy faces and looking forlorn, she did what any smart woman would do. She fixed a huge pot of *arroz con pollo* and a big salad of avocado, oranges and sweet onion in citrus vinaigrette, and fed the delicious meal to them while the flan she was making for dessert baked in the oven. In a little while, they all felt better, even John. He felt well enough to ask what they meant about him really being one of them now.

Alan took pleasure in elaborating. "All of our wives gave us a hard time from jump street. A Cochran wife has to be dragged kicking and screaming down the aisle; otherwise it might not be true love. None of us had an easy time with the women we love. Believe me when I tell you, Nina's behavior is typical of this family."

John laughed, but his brothers all looked at him with total seriousness. Andrew started by telling him what he'd gone through with Renee. "Man, she hated the sight of me for *seventeen years.* Seventeen years of being in love with the woman and she wouldn't give me the time of day. We fought like tigers for years, ask anybody. Even after we finally got together there was plenty of drama and I'm talking serious life-altering stuff. I almost lost her forever because of my macho stupidity," he told him.

John still didn't quite believe him. "Andrew, that's deep. You and Renee seem like the perfect couple. Anybody can see how much love and respect you have for each other."

Donnie laughed. "Yeah, *now* they do. But back in the day, man, they used to throw down. Almost as bad as Angel and me. We fought from the day we met, back before Clay and Benita got married. In fact, the only reason we got married in the first place was because we drank too much champagne in Vegas one night and lost our minds." At John's look of shock, he laughed again. "It's all true, John. Of course we realized we were in love and we were smart enough to stay together, but we had some pretty lively years before we got it right."

By now John was really enjoying his brother's tales. Nodding to Alan and Andre, he said, "Okay, your turn."

Alan shuddered. "Man, Tina couldn't stand the sight of me. Andre and I went to Harvard Law School and we thought we were the shizz-nit, hear? Young, fine, educated and rich. We just knew we had it goin' on. Well, Tina thought I was the biggest jerk in the world. She called me a blight on humanity and that was when she was being affectionate. It took me a long time to get next to Tina," he said ruefully.

"So when did she warm up to you?" John wanted to know.

"About a year ago," Alan said with a straight face.

Andre nodded in agreement. "Faye wasn't much better than Tina. Actually, she was worse. Her family has serious money, enough to buy and sell us ten times over, and she wasn't impressed with me no kinda way. She used to look down her nose at me like I was a street hustler or something. It took an entire semester of dedicated, systematic begging to get her to give me the time of day. That woman had me beggin' like Babyface for weeks, man."

Adam had nothing to add during all this, he was busy clearing the work island where they'd eaten and was filling the dishwasher. John called him on it, and wanted to know his tale of woe regarding Alicia.

Voices were raised as the brothers all denied Adam and Alicia having any such problems. "Oh, no, he didn't go through what we went through. They were always best friends, all sweet and kind to each other," scoffed Alan.

"He hasn't suffered like a real man," Andre agreed.

"John, see what you missed out on not growing up with these fools? These jokers have no idea what they're talking about. I suffered plenty, believe me," Adam retorted.

"Like how? Did you two fight about who was the best looking or something? Y'all were so close it was sickening, that's not what I call suffering." Alan looked disgusted at the idea.

Adam looked serious as he defended himself. "Let's say you meet the woman of your dreams, the one woman you know is your soulmate, the perfect person for you. And let's say you get a little glimpse of paradise and then you get tossed into the friend zone and you have to stay there for *ten years*. Ten years of being her pal, her buddy, her best friend. How would you like that, having to watch her going out with other men? Would you like to think about other men touching her, wondering if you were going to lose her forever? I had a hard time, all right, and don't tell me I didn't."

The respectful silence lasted for about ten seconds before the men started making derisive noises and throwing their napkins at Adam. Even Andrew, the most genteel of the bunch, got on Adam. "Nobody's buying it, bro. I'm sorry, but your story doesn't compare. We went through hell and you're complaining because you were just friends? You had it easy, man."

"Hey, man, Tina put out a restraining order on me one time, Alicia never did that to you," Alan said indignantly. "Just admit it, you had it the easiest of all of us."

"Okay, I guess I did. Probably because I have more *skills* than the rest of you," he said with a wicked grin.

The loud, raucous reactions to that statement almost made John forget his agony. Almost, but not completely as he contemplated what he had to do next.

John was putting the last of his personal items in his suitcase when he heard a knock on the door of his apartment. He left the bedroom and entered the living room to open the door. He couldn't conceal his surprise when he found Adam and Alicia standing there.

"Come in," he invited, although his voice betrayed his curiosity. "What brings you all the way out here?"

Adam got right to the point. "I'm going with you, John. I can't let you go out to California by yourself, there's no telling what kind of trouble you might get into."

"And I'm going with him to keep *him* out of trouble," Alicia said wryly. "And to give poor Nina some support, she doesn't need you two ganging up on her."

John was speechless, but Adam wasn't. "Hurry up man, let's get going. You can have your say on the plane. Let's just get out there because you know you're not going to rest until you see Nina and make sure she's okay."

Amazed by Adam's perception, John did just as he suggested and finished packing at light speed. Soon they were on their way to Detroit Metro and the plane that would take them to Nina. He had no idea what he would find when he got to Oakland, but anything was better than this uncertainty. *Nina, mi corazon, I'm coming for you. And you'd better have a good reason for all this craziness. God knows you'd better be able to explain this madness to me.*

Chapter 17

Nina's legs were past tingling. The pleasant exertion that normally accompanied a run had long gone and her legs were almost numb. She didn't pay it any attention; the lack of feeling in her limbs matched the emptiness she'd felt since the day she got the phone call. She forced her body forward in the gathering twilight, gradually slowing down to a walk under the canopy of trees lining the streets of her neighborhood. She tried not to look at the small houses on either side of the quiet lane, but she couldn't help herself. They were all painted in pastel colors with contrasting trims, the yards neat and green with borders of shrubs and flowers. Several of her neighbors called to her and she waved and spoke to them, calling them by name. She could feel her eyes filling with tears and she dashed them away with the back of her hand. This was no time to get weak; she had too much work to do.

She set her jaw resolutely and increased her pace to a quick jog as she neared her house. She was looking down at the little clusters of flowers that bordered her driveway, thinking they needed a trim. If she hadn't been so absorbed with the flowers she wouldn't have been so startled. As it was she ran up the stairs to her porch and was about to open her front door when a figure loomed out of the hanging swing, which was partially obscured by bougainvillea vines. Nina screamed bloody murder and gave the intruder a blast of the pepper spray she kept on her key ring.

"*Dios, chica,* it's just me! Oh, damn, what was in that crap, battery acid?" John covered his eyes and bent over as the stinging pain of the spray overcame him. Nina frowned as she realized the identity of her visitor. "Serves you right for sneaking around. Get in the house so I can wash that stuff off your face, you idiot."

She ushered him through the front door and took him right to the kitchen. She made him bend over the sink and used the hose attachment to rinse his face and eyes. She directed the warm water at him and rinsed over and over until he finally begged her to stop. "Okay, baby, that's enough. I'm sure it's gone now," he gasped as he choked on the excess water.

Nina didn't answer; she made him sit down at her kitchen table. "I'll be right back. Don't rub anything, it makes it hurt worse," she warned him. Her hands were shaking and her heart was still pounding from the mighty surge of adrenalin his presence caused. She couldn't even speculate about why he was there, she had to concentrate on getting that stuff off his face. She got towels from her linen closet and a jar of Vaseline from the medicine cabinet. She went back into the kitchen and screamed again as she saw Adam and Alicia standing there. "What is this, Scare Nina Day? Where did you people come from?"

Alicia answered her, speaking in a soft voice in deference to Nina's obviously rattled nerves. "We got in a couple of hours ago and your neighbor saw us knocking at your door and invited us over."

Nina had collected herself enough to put a towel around John's shoulders and begin to pat his face dry with a soft cloth. She was absorbed in her task, but not so much that she ignored Alicia. "Miss Velma is a good neighbor, but a little too trusting for her own good," she murmured. *And a little too talkative. There's no telling what that sweet old lady told the three of you,* she thought resignedly. Suddenly remembering her manners, Nina looked at Alicia and Adam with an apology in her eyes. "I'm sorry I'm being so rude. Please have a seat. May I get you something? It's a long flight from Detroit, are you hungry?"

They both assured her they were just fine. "Miss Velma insisted on feeding us," Adam said with a smile. Nina didn't look up from her task of applying a very thin film of Vaseline to the reddened areas on John's face, but she smiled all the same. "Miss Velma feeds everybody," she said fondly. "It's a wonder I'm not as big as a house, as much of her food as I've eaten."

"I'm just fine, thanks for asking," John said with obvious irritation. "I'm the one who's been attacked and you're ignoring me."

Nina was finally satisfied with her work and took her hands away from John's face. She went to the sink and washed the residual ointment from her hands, then turned to face John as she dried her hands on a paper towel. "Okay, you've got my full attention now. What are you doing here, John?"

John rose from the chair and almost knocked it over in his haste. "What am I doing here?" he shouted. "Nina, you left me! You packed up and disappeared without a word except that stupid note that told me nothing. You may as well have left a Post-it note! You didn't write one word about where you were going or why you were leaving and now you ask me why I'm here?"

Nina tried to turn away from John but he was too quick for her. He put his hands on her shoulders and kept her from moving. His voice was hoarse and raspy as he demanded answers. "Nina, what happened? Why did you leave me?"

"I don't owe you any explanations, John. You don't own me and I can come and go as I please, you got that?" Nina radiated defiance as her voice rose to meet John's but he wasn't having it.

"You're gonna have to do better than that, baby. How could you leave me, Nina? After all we've been to each other, how could you walk out and not say a word to me?"

Adam and Alicia left the kitchen to give the couple much-needed privacy. Nina didn't notice them leave, her eyes were fixed on John's. "I'm sorry," she whispered. "Everything happened so fast, I had to get out here right away. The bottom dropped out of my world and all I could think about was what I had to do next."

"It didn't even occur to you that I might be concerned, that I might be able to help you, that you didn't have to handle whatever it is all by yourself?" John couldn't believe what he'd just heard.

Nina had to look away from him, she couldn't stand the pain in his eyes another second. "No, John, it didn't cross my mind," she admitted. "I got a phone call and I didn't have time to plan anything, all I could do was react."

John relaxed his iron grip on Nina's shoulders and massaged them gently. He could feel her tension; her body was as taut as a steel band. "React to what, Nina? What happened to make you come out here so fast?"

Nina pulled away from John and walked around the kitchen table. She wrapped her arms around her waist and looked around the cheerfully decorated room before answering him. "I had to come out here to pack up my things and find a place to live," she said sadly. "I'm being evicted."

* * *

John couldn't take his eyes from Nina's face as she explained the sorry situation. They were now seated in her living room, a pretty, surprisingly feminine space. The walls were pale green and there were draperies in cotton sateen with thin ivory and green stripes at the windows with matching shades. The sofa and loveseat were covered with ivory slipcovers and there was an oversized armchair covered in a flowered chintz fabric that matched the array of throw pillows. There were two big comfortable ottomans and the room was filled with plants both flowering and green, which gave it a homey air. Alicia was sitting on an ottoman next to the armchair where Adam was sitting and John and Nina were on opposite ends of the sofa.

"I've lived here for about ten years," said Nina. "It was a wreck when I first saw it, the whole neighborhood was a wreck, but I liked this house, there was something about it that spoke to me. So I made the owner a deal. If he'd cut the rent, I'd fix it up with the understanding I could buy the house from him, and he said okay. So I fixed it up, room by room. It took a long time, but I finally got everything looking just the way I want it to. I did the work myself because I couldn't afford to pay anybody. When it was something big, like electrical wiring or something, Mr. Giddens would do it because he was the owner, of course. But everything else, I did all by myself. I learned how to paint, plaster, stain, strip, whatever it took to get the job done. Even the furniture," she waved her hand to indicate the living and dining rooms, "came from yard sales, secondhand stores, even stuff other people just threw away. I got to be a pro at trash picking," she said with an embarrassed laugh. "I think it all turned out pretty well though. I love this little house. I always get a sense of accomplishment when I walk in the door," she said in a quiet, dull voice.

Following her gaze around the room, John could see

why. Nina had created a beautiful home. It looked like a doll's house. Everything was selected with great care and positioned just so. The love and creativity and hard work were evident in every corner of every room. "What happened, Nina? Why are you being evicted?" John wanted to reach for her hand, but she seemed so remote he didn't dare.

"Mr. Giddens thought I'd done a really good job on the house. So good, in fact, he decided to give the house to his mother. He changed his mind about our deal, says he's not selling the house because the value has gone up so much it just wouldn't make sense for him to let go of the property. I have until the end of the week to get out so he can move his mother in," Nina said flatly.

"He can't do that," John said angrily. "That has to be a violation of something, some kind of statute or law or something. You had an implied contract with him and he can't renege on it at this point. You can take him to court and sue for the rights to this house." John didn't seem to realize that if Nina kept the house she'd also stay in Oakland instead of returning to Michigan with him. All he cared about at the moment was Nina's happiness. The fact that she was being treated badly was enraging him.

She surprised him totally when she said no. "I suppose I could try to sue him, but I'm not going to. If I've learned anything in this life it's that when something is over, it's over and there's no point in crying over it. This house wasn't meant to be mine and there's nothing I can do about it, except get my stuff out of here and move on," she said dully.

John couldn't believe what he was hearing. "Nina, you can't let this guy get away with this. He can't just walk all over you and get away with it; he has to pay for what he's done. You can't just walk away from your home and everything you've built here, that would be criminally wrong. You can't do it, Nina, it's not fair to you."

Nina laughed bitterly, standing up as she did so. "John, you don't know how naïve you sound right now. Since when is life *fair*?" She searched his face for an answer and sighed softly when she didn't see what she was looking for. "Look, I need to take a shower, I've polluted the air long enough. There isn't much here in the way of food because I've been gone so long, but help yourself to anything you find. I'll be right back," she added as she turned to leave the room.

John watched her leave, and then turned to Adam and Alicia. "I don't care what she says, he's not getting away with this. I need to call Alan and Andre and find out what to do about this Giddens character."

Adam agreed at once. "You have to do what you have to do. You can't let him get away with what he's done, you have to stand up for Nina."

"But suppose Nina doesn't want all that drama," Alicia said reasonably. "This is her life after all, and she's the only one who can make those decisions. You have to stay out of it, John, unless she invites you in."

"That sounds really civilized and mature, Allie, but sometimes you gotta go with your heart. If I were in John's position I'd be doing the same thing," Adam admitted.

Alicia looked at him in surprise. "Adam, no you wouldn't. You're much more level-headed than that," she protested.

"Not when it comes to you. You never knew this but the reason Preston finally left town was because I beat the crap out of him. I should have done it the night we found him in bed with what's-her-name, but you were too upset. One night I ran into him and he said something smart and it was on like Donkey Kong. I beat him like he stole something and told him he'd better stay away from you if he knew what was good for him and he took me at my word, I guess, because he left Boston the next day."

"Adam! I don't know what to say," Alicia exclaimed. "If people had told me you did that I'd have called them liars."

"Why? You should have known me well enough to understand I don't play when it comes to what's mine and you were mine even then, Allie."

Alicia tore her eyes away from Adam's long enough to explain what they were talking about to John. "Preston was my fiancé and we caught him and Adam's girlfriend in a truly compromising position, which is why we dumped the two of them. But this is the first time I'm hearing this sad story. I'm stunned, I really am," she said, looking at Adam with a disapproving frown.

"Give him a break, Alicia," said John. "I know just how he feels and believe me, the guy would have lost some teeth that night. It may be macho, ill advised and stupid, but a man has to take care of his woman. And regardless of what Nina says, this guy is going to be sorry he ever decided to mess with mine."

Alicia threw up her hands; there was no point in trying to reason with either one of them. "Look, Adam and I think you guys need some privacy. We're going to stay at a hotel tonight and we'll be over first thing in the morning. If she really intends to pack up and leave here, we have a lot of work to do," Alicia said as she rose gracefully from the low ottoman. Adam also stood and put his arm around her waist. John walked them to the door and shook Adam's hand before kissing Alicia on the cheek. He tried to thank them, but Adam wasn't hearing it.

"Please," Adam said, holding up a hand to stop the stem of gratitude, "you're my brother. This is what family is for. See you in the morning," he said as he and Alicia went down the front steps to the rental car.

* * *

After he locked the door behind them, John walked around the house, waiting for Nina to finish her shower. The dining room was traditional but very personal. There was a china cabinet from the 1930s with Nina's colorful china and several pieces of Depression glass. There was a big multi-paned window with a wide sill and several lady vases from the 1940s, so-called because they were women's heads romantically posed with half-closed eyes. Nina's collection was both beautiful and rare because all of hers were African American. John looked at the shining surface of the table and chairs before going into the kitchen, which he hadn't really looked at before. Knowing all the effort she'd put into her home made it seem even more attractive. He smiled as he looked around at all the colorful touches in her kitchen. The curtains were made of a vintage fabric patterned with cherries and there were touches of red everywhere. There were replicas of fruit crate art from the 1920s and 1930s in bright red frames, and all the drawer and cabinet pulls were red ceramic. Even her pots and pans were of bright crimson enamelware, suspended from a pot rack that hung from the ceiling over the stove.

Nina came into the kitchen wearing a pair of loose-fitting lavender cotton knit pants and a long-sleeved top with little lavender thongs on her feet. Her hair was wet from the shower but it still looked adorable. "Where are Adam and Alicia?" she asked, looking around as though they might pounce on her.

"They went to a hotel. They thought we needed some time alone," John answered.

Nina didn't say anything as she went to the refrigerator to get a bottle of water. "They were right, Nina. We need to talk." John held out his hand to her and waited, holding his breath, to see what she would do next.

She stared at his outstretched palm for an agonizingly long time before slowly putting hers into it. Finally she spoke. "Okay, let's talk. But why don't you take a shower first, you've had a pretty long day. I need to go see about Miss Velma anyway, make sure she knows you haven't knocked me on my head or something," she said with a crooked smile. "Come on, I'll show you the bathroom and the bedroom."

She tugged his hand a little and led him into the hallway. He followed her meekly as she pointed out the bathroom. "I put some towels out for you." Her bedroom was next and John followed her in, looking around with undisguised interest. Nina suddenly turned shy, as she seemed to realize John was standing in the middle of her most private sanctuary.

"Umm, you can sleep in here tonight, I guess. It's only a queen-sized mattress and it probably won't be too comfortable, but the other bedroom only has a double bed and that's not nearly big enough for you, so you can have this one," she said, speaking rapidly as if she feared interruption.

John sensed her unease and put his arms around her. He could feel her trembling and it bothered him, hurt him to his heart actually. "Nina, baby, it's okay. Everything's going to be okay," he crooned. "Let me get cleaned up a little and we'll talk this all out, I promise. It's okay, Nina, I'm here for you, don't you know that?"

She didn't say anything although John was gratified when her trembling stopped and she relaxed against his body.

It wasn't much, but it was a start.

Chapter 18

By the time John emerged from the shower, Nina's hair was dry and she was a little less shaky. At least she was ready for the interrogation she knew was about to come from John. She knocked on the bedroom door before entering with a tray. On it were two bowls of homemade peach cobbler with ice cream, a thermal carafe of hot tea and two of her flowered china cups and saucers.

"Miss Velma thought you might like what she calls a 'little somethin' before you went to bed," Nina said casually as she set the tray on the decoupaged wooden chest at the foot of her bed. She looked almost like her old self as she added, "Miss Velma also thinks you're hot. She may be sweet and neighborly but she's a dirty old lady, as she will be the first to admit it."

She was trying hard to conceal her reactions, but the sight of John's broad, muscled chest was bringing up memories she didn't want to have, memories of the passion they shared and the love he'd given her so freely. Nina's eyes roved hungrily over his golden brown skin, still slightly damp from the shower. Everything about him ignited a fever in her; the finely delineated sculpture of his torso, even the neat scar from the transplant. Everything about John appealed to her in every way. She could feel her control slipping and forced herself to act normally.

"Sit down before this gets cold," she instructed. John complied, sitting down on her bed and making himself comfortable against the pillows piled at the head. He was wearing nothing but a pair of loose fitting, cotton drawstring pants and he looked as appetizing as the cobbler. Nina handed him a bowl and a spoon and his eyes lit up as he inhaled the spicy sweetness of the dessert.

He put a spoonful in his mouth and groaned. "Miss Velma can throw down," he said appreciatively. He ate a couple of mouthfuls in silence while acclimating himself to Nina's bedroom.

It was like Nina, incredibly feminine but unique. The bed was a big four-poster painted creamy ivory. The dust ruffle was also ivory, pleated instead of gathered, and the duvet and pillow shams were a vintage tropical print, as were the curtains. There were window shades in this room, too, but these were the same creamy ivory as the bed frame. A dressing table was situated between the two windows and a small armchair was in the corner near the big armoire. This drew John's attention as it was filled, amazingly enough, with teddy bears. He smiled at the sight; it meant he was right all along about Nina. She might try to be tough, but only a sentimentalist of the first order saved all her childhood toys. He was about to say this when Nina sighed softly.

"What is it, *querida?*" he asked gently.

Nina looked around the room and sighed again. "I'm going to miss this place," she admitted. "I worked so hard on it, John. My hands had calluses and splinters and you can just imagine what my nails looked like. I didn't care, though. I was so happy because I had a home of my own, finally. I had my own place and it was really mine because I fixed it up and made every single room look just the way I wanted it to," she said. "I loved this house, I really did."

John felt a pang as he realized she was speaking in the

past tense. He looked around for a place to put his now-empty bowl. There was a small table next to the bed but he didn't dare mar its finish. He was relieved when Nina put out her hand to take it from him and elated when she handed him her portion. "I'm full," she said.

John ate another spoonful of the incomparable cobbler before jumping in with both feet. "Nina, I'm confused. This place obviously means a lot to you and that man has done you an incredible wrong. So how can you just walk away from it like nothing happened? And how could you turn your back on me? You left me like I didn't matter, either. Talk to me, Nina, and help me understand."

Nina was at the foot of the bed, pouring them each a cup of fragrant sassafras tea. She added sugar to both cups and stirred while she struggled to give him the answers he sought. "John, I don't know how to explain it. I guess I owe you an apology and an explanation, but I don't know if it's going to make sense to you," she said solemnly. She took the second empty bowl from him and handed him a cup of tea.

"All my life anything I've ever loved has been taken away from me. My brothers, my mother, Morgan, Marva, the Benrubis, anything or anyone I got attached to was gone, just like that," she said, snapping her fingers. She sounded more lost than bitter. "Nothing lasts in my life, John. I don't get to keep anything. And when it's over, it's over and all I can do is pick up and start a new life. I've done it enough times to know the drill. There's no point in trying to change things or prolong them. I just deal with them, that's all I can do," she ended dully.

"But Nina, even if you believe this, why didn't you say something to me? How could you just turn your back on me and walk out the door like I meant nothing to you?" John was trying to be as matter-of-fact as Nina, but he couldn't keep the pain out of his voice.

Nina's hands began to shake as she saw the depths of John's feeling for her on his face. She was shaking so she couldn't hold the cup properly and she barely managed to put it on the tray without spilling its contents. "John, I never should have let things get this far. I should have been stronger; I shouldn't have given in to you. But you were so wonderful to me, you treated me like such a lady, I got weak and stupid. I tried to convince myself it would be okay, that somehow my past wouldn't matter. When I got that phone call, though, it was like all the walls just caved in and I knew it was a sign, I had to get far away from you as fast as I could. And besides, Miss Velma collapsed. They had to take her to the emergency room and I had to come see about her, she needed me," Nina added softly.

She was supposed to be talking to John, but it was as if she was talking to herself. The words that poured out of her sounded like her deepest secrets, the things she'd never meant to say. John held out his arms to her and she hesitated only a moment before moving into his embrace. She let out a long, trembling breath and allowed John's arms to comfort and strengthen her. She would have been content to stay there in his arms forever, but he softly urged her to continue talking.

"Why did you want to get away from me, Nina? What could possibly make you think we don't belong together, *mi corazon?* I love you and I know you love me. Nothing's going to change that, Nina, it's only going to get better and better between us, you should know that, baby."

Instead of comforting her, John's tender words made Nina's heart ache. "You don't understand, John. I can't be the woman you want me to be. I'm not the kind of woman you think I am. I'd never fit into your family, I'm not like one of your brother's wives, nice and sweet and perfect. I can't be like that. I knew it when we went to Atlanta, there's no way I could ever be a part of your family."

John could feel her agony but he was mystified by its origin. "Nina, why do you say that? Just because you grew up in foster care, that doesn't make you less of a person," he began only to be cut off by a short, bitter cry of laughter from Nina.

She pulled away from his arms and sat up straight, looking at him with equal parts defiance and fear. "I didn't grow up in foster care, John. I grew up in the streets. I went from home to home and I didn't fit in anywhere. When I got treated really badly I would just run away and they'd always find me and put me somewhere else. The last place they put me was the worst. It was with a so-called minister and his family. He really wasn't a preacher; he was a con artist who rooked old ladies and desperate single women out of their money. He had a wife and two really bad little kids and I was like the household slave. I did everything in that house from scrubbing floors to washing clothes and I better not complain because 'the Lord's gracious goodness had delivered me into their sheltering arms from a life of sin'. That's a direct quote, by the way, I heard it several times a week," she said acidly.

"Then he started beating me."

For the first time John understood what people meant when they said something about their blood freezing. He went completely cold as Nina uttered the words that broke his heart in two. "He did what?" he said slowly, praying he'd heard her wrong.

Nina couldn't look at John as she spoke; she fixed her gaze at a point past his head, looking at her teddy bears. "He was a mean drunk, John. He used to take it out on his wife and kids and to some extent he still did, but I became his favorite punching bag.

"It didn't last very long, though. I started going to bed

fully dressed with my shoes on and I made up my mind if he did it again I was getting out of there once and for all. And sure enough, he came staggering home one night kicking the furniture, and cussing at the top of his lungs. I swear I could smell the liquor even with my door closed. He beat up everybody in the house and then it was my turn. He came in there and grabbed me by my hair, calling me all kinds of names. I had something for him that night, though. As soon as he started I took a knife out from under my pillow where I'd hidden it and I stabbed him in the shoulder. Then I jumped up and I ran. I ran as far and as fast as I could and I never looked back. And this time they didn't come after me. That was the last foster home I was ever in," she said with finality.

John was so filled with rage from hearing about her abuse he could barely hear what she was saying, but he made himself concentrate on her and not his blinding anger. "How old were you, sweetheart?"

"I was fourteen," she said, looking at him for the first time. "Fourteen years old and living on the streets. That's how I grew up, John, I was a little street thug. I stole, I lied, I cheated, I did any and everything I could to survive. I didn't go to pep rallies and football games, I didn't go to parties and proms and shopping with my girlfriends. I lived in runaway shelters, in bus stations, abandoned buildings and crack houses. It's really a miracle I survived at all, John, now that I think about it. I actually don't think about it. My past, I mean. I try very hard to never think about where I came from and what I had to do to survive. That's something else I learned the hard way. When you walk out a door, close it and lock it tight. Like Satchel Paige said, 'Don't look back, something might be gaining on you.'"

She was aiming for sophisticated amusement, but her delivery fell far short of its mark. She was trying so hard to be brave, but his Nina was terrified and he could sense it emanating from every pore in her skin like a cheap, cloying perfume. He reached for her again and refused to be denied as she made a faint attempt to elude him.

"Nina, you don't want to try me right now. Are you telling me this is why you left me? Because you decided that you weren't good enough for me? Woman, I ought to have you committed," he growled. "And don't forget I can do it in the state of California. One word from me and off to the loony bin you go. You ought to have your head examined, Nina. Nothing, and I mean *nothing* about your past matters to me. All that matters to me is that you are the most wonderful thing that's ever happened to me in my entire life.

"No woman has ever cared for me the way you do, no woman's ever challenged me the way you do and no woman has ever come close to satisfying me the way you do," he informed her. Seeing the look on her face he was happy to elaborate. "That's right, Nina. You are the most exquisite sex partner I've ever had. You turn me out every time we're together, baby, you make me feel like a king. I've never made love to a woman with as much passion as you and I never will. You make me happier than I ever dreamed I could be. Ever since my parents died I felt empty inside. And now, with you, my heart is overflowing with love, I feel excited to be alive and grateful for every day. I don't give a damn about what happened before we met. I regret any pain you've ever felt and it's going to be my pleasure to make the rest of your life wonderful. Just remember, Nina you're all that matters to me. You're a magnificent woman, far better than I deserve. Just let me love you for the rest of our lives, that's all I ask, baby. Just let me love you."

John cradled Nina against his shoulder and felt an immense relief when the tears came. It was like a dam had burst and all her anguish was pouring out. "Go ahead and cry, sweetheart. Let it all out so there's nothing left but our love," he murmured.

She sobbed openly for a long while and the tears eventually subsided until she was hiccupping and sniffing like a little girl. "Oh, God, I'm a mess," she wailed and tried to pull away from John.

His eyes crinkled in a loving smile and he admitted she'd looked better. "But you're still beautiful to me, my love."

"What a liar you are, John Flores. I know how I look when I cry which is why I try never to do it. I look like a tree frog, my eyes swell up and my nose turns red and I look like I should be sitting on a lily pad croaking. Let me up so I can go wash my face," she said crossly.

"Say you love me."

"I love you. I love you with all my heart, God help us both," she muttered. "Now let me up so I can do something about my face."

John was happy to oblige at last. While she dashed off to the bathroom, he gathered up all the dishes and the tray and took them into the kitchen where he rinsed them well and put them in the sink. If they were going to be together forever as he planned, he'd have to clean up his act. Nina wasn't the type to put up with his sloppiness for long and she shouldn't have to. That task done, he went to his suitcase in Nina's spare bedroom and got something out.

By the time he returned to the bedroom, Nina was already there wearing a very short, very sheer mint green nightgown with thin ribbons for straps. She had turned down the duvet and was under the blanket and sheet waiting for him. Her face did look better, she'd applied cold water to her eyes and the swelling had all but gone. She looked radiantly lovely and was smiling.

John stood over her for a moment, enjoying the sweet picture she made. "Close your eyes, I have a surprise for you," he crooned.

Nina made a face. "Haven't you surprised me enough for one day? I don't know how much my heart can take," she said drolly.

John assured her she would like this surprise. "Close your eyes," he said again. When her eyes were shut tight, he knelt beside the bed and took a small black velvet box out of his pocket. He opened it to reveal a glowing four-carat oval cabochon stone set in yellow gold, bracketed by brilliantly sparkling diamonds. "Now open them, *chica*."

When her long lashes fluttered open he put the box in her hand and said, "Nina, before I met you I was going through the motions. Now I know what love is because I know you. Please do me the honor of becoming my wife so I can show you what love is for all time," he said, his voice deep and full of emotion. "It's a fire opal. It reminded me of you because it's full of color and life."

Nina covered her mouth with one hand while she stared at the ring. She looked at John, looking so handsome and virile yet so vulnerable and she fell in love with him all over again. Finally she said the word that would change their lives forever. "Yes." Her eyes bright with tears, she said it again, just because it felt so good to say it. "Yes, John, yes a thousand times."

"Oh, no you don't. Put this on before you change your mind, then you can cry all you want," John said happily. He got into bed with her and they both admired how the ring looked on her hand. "Now kiss me so we can make this official. I love you like crazy, Nina."

"And I love you right back, John. Thank you for the ring, it's so beautiful," she said softly.

"You know what, my love? You talk too much," he said as he lowered his lips to hers. Their mouths opened at the same instant, renewing their passion in a long, sweet and intimate kiss. When Nina finally pulled her lips away from John's, her eyes were heavy with desire and she gave him an incredible smile. "John, I missed you so much, I thought I was going to die," she confessed.

"We're never going to be apart again, Nina. Never," he vowed and began to make love to her like it was the very first time.

The next morning, John awoke to the appetizing aroma of bacon and coffee. With his eyes still closed he mumbled, "Sweetheart, is that coffee I smell or am I dreaming?"

The rich, enticing aroma grew more intense and Adam's voice replied, "Yes, darling, it's really coffee and you're not dreaming. Get up and let's get to work."

John's eyes flew open to find Adam standing next to the bed with a cup of coffee that he had no doubt just waved under John's nose. He was wearing jeans, a T-shirt and a big grin. "C'mon, you lazy rascal, we have work to do. Nina's making us breakfast and we're tired of waiting for you," he said as he turned to leave the room. He turned back and added, "Nice legs, though, you really are one of us aren't you?"

John got out of bed quickly and took a fast but thorough shower. His hair was still damp when he entered the kitchen, dressed for a day of hard labor in jeans and an old denim shirt. What he witnessed when he entered the room stunned him, to say the least.

Nina was standing at the stove making a big fat fluffy omelet, and from the looks of rapture on the faces of Alicia and Adam as they devoured theirs, it tasted as good as it looked. They were also consuming big golden biscuits oozing with butter, and creamy grits. There was a plate of sliced fruit at each place setting and a cup of coffee. Alicia looked up as John came into the room and gave him a big smile as she spooned something onto her biscuit. "John, wait until you taste these. Delicious homemade fig preserves and Nina made them herself," she gushed.

John loomed over Nina and stared down at her accusingly as she quickly and expertly put two kinds of cheese, sliced mushrooms and sautéed onions and red peppers on one half of the omelet and flipped the top over it. "I thought you couldn't cook," he said accusingly.

Nina gave him her most beguiling smile, the one he was beginning to recognize as her get-out-of-jail-free smile. "I said I *didn't* cook, I didn't say I *couldn't* cook," she hedged. Giving the pan a couple of shakes, she slid the completed omelet onto a heated plate and waved it under John's nose. "Aren't you hungry?"

He growled, "I'll deal with you later. Feed me, woman." He kissed Nina on the forehead and took his seat at the table. Soon he was groaning his pleasure along with Adam and Alicia. "Nina, I can't believe you were holding out on me like this. All those pots and pans should have been a dead giveaway, though. All this time you could cook like this and you had me believing you can't cook. Shame on you, *chica,*" he scolded as he made short work of the delicious meal.

Nina patiently defended herself. "I never said I couldn't perform the act of meal preparation. I said I *didn't* do it and how could I in that hotel suite or your apartment? I need a real kitchen to do what I do. I wasn't deliberately trying to deceive you, not really," she said demurely, looking at him over the rim of her coffee cup.

She looked so cute in a neat little T-shirt with horizontal red stripes and a pair of carpenter pants, that he couldn't find it in his heart to be angry with her. Besides, he'd just devoured three biscuits, six slices of crisp, maple-cured bacon, and the fluffiest omelet he'd ever eaten. John made a mental note to ask Nina how she did it later. "And you really made those preserves from scratch?"

She nodded her head. "Yep, I really did. A lady taught me how to do it a long time ago," was all she would say.

John raised his cup of perfectly brewed coffee and gave her a smile of utter contentment. "*Salud.*"

Nina sat back and watched in amazement as the last of her belongings were put into a huge moving van. As incredible as it seemed, Adam had made a few phone calls and was able to get a mover there to not only pick up her things, but to pack them all. Her most fragile belongings were given first class treatment and she had no cause to worry about things being broken en transit. The transit part gave her a little concern at first because it was just assumed that her things would be shipped to Michigan instead of remaining in California. She started to protest and then realized there was no place else for her things to go. She was about to start a new life with John and that life was in Ann Arbor. So there was nothing for her to do but watch, as the highly efficient movers packed everything she owned into what seemed to be hundreds of corrugated boxes.

While the burly movers methodically emptied every room, Nina and Alicia went next door to say good-bye to Miss Velma. As soon as they were out of earshot, John turned to Adam to confirm he'd meant what he said the day before. "That guy Giddens, I want him dead, Adam."

At Adam's raised brow, John gave a short laugh and clarified. "I don't mean not-breathing dead, but I want him dead financially. If he's done this to Nina, he's done it to a lot of other people. This has to be his modus operandi and he needs to be stopped once and for all. A nice little class action suit might be just the thing for him," John said grimly.

Adam agreed. "Alicia and I took a walk around the neighborhood last evening and we talked to a few people who knew Nina. It seems like Nina was really instrumental in turning this neighborhood around. When people saw how hard she was working on her house, they started doing the same thing to their houses. And guess who owns eighty percent of the houses in this area? Why, Mr. Oscar Giddens, of course. And it seems as though he plans on doing to same thing to them that he's doing to Nina. Promise them they can buy the property in return for renovations and then pull the rug out from under them and leave them homeless. I have a feeling he's been doing this kind of dirty dealing for years but nobody's called him on it," Adam said angrily.

"I called Alan and Andre this morning and they're on it. They called Titus Argonne who's probably the best investigator in the country. Whatever little secrets Mr. Oscar Giddens is hiding are about to come out in the open."

"Good," John said with satisfaction. "I haven't said anything about this to Nina yet because I don't think she's going to like the idea. In fact, I'm pretty sure she's going to hate the whole thing. She has this stoic philosophy about life. If something catastrophic happens just walk away from it and don't look back. She's like a phoenix; she just rises from the ashes and starts all over, stronger than before. She's like no other woman I've ever met, Adam."

"Yeah, well she's gonna react like every other woman you ever met when she finds out what we're doing, so just get ready for it," Adam predicted. "Eventually it's all going to come out and she's going to give you holy hell for going behind her back, but you can deal with that.

Whether she likes it or not, and she won't, by the way," Adam said with a twisted smile, "you have to protect what's yours. What's the point of being a man if you can't take care of the woman you love?"

"Man, it's a good thing Nina and Alicia can't hear us right now or we'd be in a world of trouble," John laughed. "But I don't care, that's something I can handle. I just can't tolerate the idea of anyone mistreating Nina. That I won't stand for, not while I'm living."

Nina gave Miss Velma one last hug. She'd presented her with one of her prized lady vases and several of her plants. "You took such good care of them while I was gone, it's only fair you have them, Miss Velma. And you have to promise to come visit me in Michigan," she entreated.

"Oh, sugar, it will be my pleasure. I want to be there when you and that big man get married. I never saw a man so crazy about a woman in my life," she said fondly. "You just let him love you, sugar, and you're going to have a beautiful life, the two of you."

Nina looked around the immaculate parlor of Miss Velma's little bungalow with a pang in her heart. As excited as she was to be starting on a new phase of her life, she would truly miss her neighbor. Miss Velma was really the only person who knew everything about Nina's past and she'd never judged her, never done anything but give her love and support. Nina felt her eyes filling with unexpected tears at the prospect of not seeing her dear friend again. They were sitting on Miss Velma's comfortable sofa, holding each other's hands tightly. Nina was trying to memorize everything about her friend's face so she wouldn't forget her smile or the way her eyes twinkled when she was telling one of her fascinating stories.

Miss Velma's coffee brown skin was smooth and

unlined, her hair had very little gray and her figure was plump and shapely. And she always smelled fabulous. Miss Velma dressed every day as though the man of her dreams were about to drop by and take her somewhere wonderful. As a result, she was always ready for the many gentlemen callers she still entertained. She smiled at Nina with great love and told her not to worry.

"You're doing the right thing, sugar. This is the man created just for you and you're the only woman in the world for him. I'll always be here for you, Nina; you don't ever have to worry about losing my friendship. But it's time for you to have some real happiness. Go on now, and don't forget to send for me when it's time for the wedding," she said softly. "And don't forget to e-mail me. I have DSL now so I can really rock on the keyboard," she added impishly.

Both Nina and Alicia burst out laughing. It was so easy to forget that older people weren't just about crocheting and arthritis, they were exciting and vital and many of them embraced technology in a way that even the Gen Xers and Baby Boomers didn't.

All too soon, it was time for the visit to end. They rose from their seats and hugged tightly. Miss Velma stroked Nina's face and smiled. "It's going to be just fine, sugar. Better than anything you could imagine. You're going to have a beautiful life," she told her with such sincerity and love Nina's eyes filled up again.

As Nina and Alicia walked back to her house, Alicia asked her about Miss Velma. "She almost seems like she's making predictions when she talks. Does she have second sight or something?"

Nina smiled. "She wouldn't call it that. She doesn't consider herself a fortune-teller or anything. But she is by far the most intuitive person I've ever known. I'm not sure if it's because she has the wisdom that comes with age or because she really has some kind of special gift of insight.

But you know what?" She looked at Alicia in total seriousness. "I've never known her to be wrong about anything. If Miss Velma says something is going to happen you can count on it to come true."

By now they'd reached Nina's home just in time to see the movers making a final check of every room to make sure they had everything. Nina walked through the house slowly with John at her side. She looked sad and preoccupied as she looked around the place where she'd invested so much time, so many of her dreams. She stopped in the middle of the dining room and looked around for the last time. Suddenly she looked at John with a brilliant smile and put her arms around his neck for a big kiss.

"I just realized something. A house really isn't a home. My home is with you, wherever we are."

John held her tenderly and kissed her back. "Then let's go home, *mi corazon*."

Chapter 19

The only point of contention between John and Nina regarding the trip back to Michigan was her car. John was all for having it shipped, but Nina insisted on driving. They had stood in the garage and debated the topic forever. Nina was leaning against the tarp-covered car ticking off points on her fingers.

"You're on winter break from school and your classes don't start until after the new year. It's only a thirty-hour drive from Oakland to Detroit, we can do it in a couple of days," she said reasonably. "Besides, she hasn't been driven in months and she needs the exercise. Come on, what are you worried about?" she asked with her beguiling smile.

John groaned when he saw that little smile. "I hate it when you look at me like that, *chica*. You look so adorable I can't say no to anything you want from me. It just turns me to mush, that smile." He wrapped his arms around her and bent his head for a kiss. "You drive me crazy and you know it," he said softly.

Nina purred with contentment and rubbed against John. "So does that mean I can also drive you to Michigan?" she asked brightly.

John kissed her again and sighed with resignation. "Okay, you win. But I'm doing most of the driving. I still get nightmares over the way you drive."

Nina tried to pout but failed; she was too tickled by John's assessment of her driving. "I drive assertively, not aggressively and I've never gotten a ticket," she informed him.

"That's because they can't catch you," John muttered. When Nina pulled the tarp off the car he covered his eyes and groaned. "*Madre de Dios* what have I just agreed to?"

Nina's car was a sporty red Crossfire convertible and it was obviously made for speed. The prospect of driving all the way to Michigan in that thing was daunting to say the least, especially with Nina's lead foot on the gas pedal. "Okay, that settles it. I'm doing all the driving and no arguments from you."

Nina looked as innocent as possible and meekly said, "Of course, John."

Actually, the drive was much better than John could have anticipated. Although he would have much preferred flying back with Adam and Alicia, there were a number of advantages to the long drive. The main advantage was the fact that he and Nina had a lot of time to talk and she was in a talkative mood. If he asked her a question, she answered it without evasion. She even volunteered information, for which he was truly grateful. It meant she really trusted him.

"I never went back to school. High school, I mean. I finally got a GED and when I made it to California, I found ways to go to school. There're all kinds of grants out there for low-income people, or there used to be. And since I was basically *no*-income, I qualified for most of them. It took about six years but I managed to get a bachelor's degree."

John took a quick glance at Nina who looked completely at ease and happy. She was comfortably slouched in her seat, which was partially reclined. Her bare toes were resting on the dashboard and she was sorting through CDs, trying to find music they would both enjoy since John had a low tolerance for disco. Every time he looked at her she won his heart again. She'd been so buttoned-up and repressed when he first met her and now she was sensual and free. She actually looked younger as well as happier. And John couldn't be happier that they were together.

"Listen, *chica,* how about we spend the night in Salt Lake City? We'll get a good night's sleep and head out early in the morning." He reached over to take her hand as he spoke.

"That sounds wonderful. Do you realize you've been driving for almost eleven hours? You're going to need a good rubdown when we get to the hotel," Nina said, squeezing his hand.

Without realizing it, John sped up when he heard those words from Nina's lips. She laughed out loud at his eagerness. "Now who has a heavy foot? Slow down, baby, we'll be there in a little while."

John mumbled something in Spanish as he slowed the car down. Nina was right. In less than a half-hour they were pulling up to a four star hotel. Leaving the car with the valet, John and Nina checked into a beautiful room with an imposing king-sized bed and a Jacuzzi.

Nina looked around the room and kicked off her shoes. She pulled her lightweight cotton sweater over her head and gave John a wicked grin. "Last one in the Jacuzzi gives the first massage," she said as she dashed into the bathroom.

Even though Nina was technically the winner, she was merciful to John because of all the driving he'd done that day. She'd started running the tub before they got into the glass enclosed shower and it was ready when they got out. They slid into the pleasantly warm bubbling water and sighed in bliss, especially John who had the benefit of Nina's clever hands kneading his back and shoulders until the stress and tension of the long day dissolved in the bubbles of the giant tub. Nina worked until John was like putty in her hands. When he was almost asleep, she coaxed him out of the tub and helped him dry off, then turned down the covers on the bed and made John lay down on his stomach.

She drew a deep breath as she looked at John's long, muscular body. He was the sexiest man she'd ever seen and he was all hers. The thought gave her a sweet shiver of anticipation and her body, always ready for John, began to blossom in expectation of fulfillment. She took out her tube of baby oil and rubbed some between her palms before applying it to his thigh. Kneeling beside him on the bed, Nina rubbed his legs with the lightly fragrant oil, massaging each leg from the soles of his feet up to the top of his thigh, caressing his buttocks every time she reached that area. She finally made him turn over on his back to complete the massage and smiled when he moaned his satisfaction.

"No more, *querida,* or I'll never be able to walk again. I feel so good right now, I feel like I'm floating. You're too good to me, Nina," he murmured. His eyes could barely stay open. "Come here, baby, I need to feel you," he whispered.

Nina obliged him by removing her towel and lying down next to him, breathing deeply as he wound his arms around her and entwined their legs so they were as close as possible. "Your turn next," he promised as his breathing deepened and he fell asleep in her arms.

"I'll hold you to it, my love." Nina yawned once and followed John into a deep and restful sleep.

* * *

The next day Nina couldn't stop smiling. She was, in fact, giggling like a newlywed. Every time she looked at John, she'd blush uncontrollably and bite her lower lip. It was her turn to drive and it was just as well, it gave her something to think about other than the way John woke her up that morning. He'd more than made good on his promise to make up for falling asleep. He'd taken them to yet another level of fulfillment.

Nina had been sleeping soundly, dreaming about John, which happened a lot these days. It seemed like another nocturnal fantasy at first, a wonderfully erotic one with him touching her body, stroking her breasts and following the touch of his hands with the caress of his lips. His tongue cherished each nipple, making them swell and throb in response to the tender torture. His hot lips trailed down her torso, lighting a fire that only he could extinguish. When he reached the apex of her thighs he massaged her mound, coaxing her legs apart to allow him access to the heart of her femininity, the center of her womanhood.

Nina grew hot all over as she relived the exact moment she realized it wasn't a dream. A sweet shock resonated through her body, followed by another, then another and another as John's loving mouth worked its magic. Just when Nina thought she was going to lose all consciousness John gave her a final hot caress before working his way back up her body. He was already wearing a condom and he slid into her yearning warmth and proceeded to bring her even more exquisite sensations. Their hands clasped together over her head and she met his every demand, their bodies moving in an urgent dance born of their love and need for each other. When the moist heat from her body and her moans of delight told him it was almost time to finish, he whispered to her, "Good morning, baby. I told you I'd make up for last night." The sound of his deep voice, deeper from his passion for her, sent her spiraling off into a pulsing, explosive climax that went on and on until she moaned his name without stopping.

Even now she could feel the aftermath of their loving. Tiny sensual seismic shocks echoed through her body as a reminder of just how good it was. She dared to take a peek at John and frowned when she saw the way he was looking at her. "Stop it," she said crossly. "Do you want me to drive into a ditch or something? You'd better leave me alone if you want to get to Denver in one piece."

John laughed gently and reached over to squeeze her thigh. "Take the next exit, baby. I'll drive the rest of the way. You seem a little distracted, *chica.*"

Nina stuck her tongue out in his direction and changed the CD to punish him. Gloria Gaynor's voice came booming out of the speakers and Nina joined in. "I Am What I Am" was loud and joyous and sure to drive John crazy, or at least she hoped it would. Unfortunately, it had the opposite effect. She took the next exit and pulled into a gas station to fill up the car. While John was pumping the gas, she used the facilities, bought a couple of bottles of icy cold water, and cleaned the already immaculate interior of the car. Nina had already forgotten her little musical tantrum, but John hadn't. As soon as they were buckled into their seats and back on the expressway, John asked the question she'd been dreading.

"So why aren't you singing professionally, Nina?"

In the past that question would have put her into a sullen silence, but she was surprised to realize she didn't mind answering it this time. "There are a lot of reasons, John. First of all, I never thought my voice was all that great, to be honest. And even if I did, singing professionally was the last thing on earth I'd have pursued. I saw what it was like for my mother and that was enough for me. I didn't want any part of it.

"She was away from home all the time, she never got to spend as much time with us as she wanted to. And it wasn't a question of her just not going on tour or not going to the studio, she had to make money; she had to keep a roof over our heads. Like I said, she was our only parent, I really don't know what happened to my father. And there were the other members of the group to worry about, too; it wasn't like my mother could just do what she wanted just because she was the lead singer," Nina said thoughtfully.

"It was a hard life, at least it was for her. We loved it when she was home. We would hug her and kiss her and we'd all pile in the bed to sleep with her that first night. We missed her so much when she was gone, my brothers and I," Nina said looking out the window of the car until the lump in her throat subsided.

She looked at John with the first real sadness he'd seen in a few days. "I never wanted to have that life, John. It wasn't glamorous and exciting to me, it was torture because it took my mommy away from my brothers and me. It was never anything I wanted."

She turned back to him with a wry smile. "Of course, considering some of the jobs I did have, working as a singer would have been a nice change of pace."

John couldn't stop the next question, although he feared the answer. "What kind of things did you do, Nina?"

"I washed a lot of dishes, mainly because they weren't fussy about identification, they'd usually pay cash and you got to eat for free. One thing I figured out early on was the dirtier the job, the less questions people asked. I was tall and skinny and I looked older than I was, so everybody took me at my word. I worked at a lot of car washes, because the pay is crap and everybody hated doing it, so there's always a job open. I picked crops, I worked in a meat-packing plant for a while, I did a little bit of everything."

She reached for her bottle of water in the built-in holder and took a long swallow of the now tepid contents. "It was a rough life, John. I'm not even going to front. It was hard," she said quietly.

"Baby, didn't you ever try to find your family? Your brothers, didn't you ever try to track them down?"

"Yes, I did for a while, when I was kind of settled and I had time to do that kind of thing. When you're living on the road you're pretty much concerned with the everyday stuff. Keeping clean enough to get a job, keeping away from the police, trying not to get raped, not get robbed, not get ringworm or lice or crabs. It's a pretty full agenda. It doesn't allow you a lot of time for research," she said dryly.

John was appalled. He couldn't stand the thought of his Nina having to live like that. She should have had a life of comfort and security with a family who loved her and treasured her. That she'd survived at all was a miracle, and in his opinion she'd done more than just survive. She was an intelligent, elegant and lovely woman who could hold her own with anyone in the world and it was all her own doing because she essentially raised herself. Hearing her story was humbling, to say the very least. He wanted to say this to Nina, but knew without being told she would hate hearing the words. She'd think they were just drippy sympathy. He made a vow then and there that every day of the rest of Nina's life would be wonderful. She was more deserving of happiness than anyone he knew and he was going to see to it she had everything she'd ever missed out on.

After spending the night in Denver, Nina and John got on the road extra early. They drove straight through to

Missouri, which would be their last stop before heading to Michigan. When they stopped for dinner, John looked around the restaurant Nina had selected with interest. It was near downtown St. Louis, and the neon sign boasted the best BBQ in the state. It wasn't a fancy place; it was more of a diner. It was immaculately clean, with black and white tile flooring and black vinyl in the booths that lined the long front window and on the stools along the front counter. The part of town it was in was commercial, more industrial than anything else. The restaurant, which was named Big Al's, occupied one corner. Directly across the street was a strip club and there was a carwash on the other corner, along with a convenience store. Not the worst area in the world, but hardly genteel. Their waitress came over and while John was looking at the menu, Nina placed an order.

"I'd like a grilled chicken breast without the skin and a green salad with no dressing. And some low-fat cottage cheese. Can you do that for me, dear?" Nina spoke in a perfectly pleasant tone of voice, but the woman expressed doubt.

"I don't think we have that, miss."

"Could you check for me?" Nina asked sweetly.

The woman glanced at the kitchen and took a deep breath before going in that direction. She was back in what seemed like seconds. "We don't have any of that," she reported grimly. "Only what's on the menu. Care to order, sir?"

John obligingly ordered a cheeseburger with the works, but Nina seemed determined to get her way because she placed another order, this time for a duck salad with balsamic vinaigrette on the side. Their waitress now looked really put out and told Nina again that only menu items were available.

"Well, perhaps the chef would like to tell me that himself," she said silkily. The waitress raised her eyebrows and put her pencil behind her ear. "Okay, ma'am, I'll send him right out," she huffed, and stomped away mumbling.

"Nina, what are you doing? This doesn't look like the kind of place that can supply that kind of food and what it does supply looks pretty good," John said, totally puzzled by her behavior. The place did have an appetizing aroma rolling through it and there were plenty of people eating who seemed to be enjoying every bite, so John didn't understand why was she was doing this.

Just then a large, angry black man wearing white pants and a white T-shirt with a chef's apron on came barreling over to their table with a look of death on his face. "Look, y'all ain't got to eat here, but when you are here, you got to eat what I cook. If you don't like it, hit the road, damn it," he roared.

Nina looked up at him with a smile. "I see someone's disposition hasn't improved," she said calmly. "It's nice to see some things don't change."

The man's face went from enraged to enraptured as he recognized Nina. "Birdie, is that you? Get out of that seat, girl, and let me look at you!"

His words weren't necessary, as Nina had already scrambled out of the booth and wrapped her arms around the big man's waist. He hugged her so hard that John feared he'd break her in half. When things calmed down, Nina returned to her seat and the man, Big Al, who was the owner of the place, sat down next to her.

Nina introduced John as her fiancé, blushing happily as she realized this was the first time she'd said the words to anyone. "John, Big Al took me in when I was sixteen and if it wasn't for him I'd probably be dead now," she said matter-of-factly. "He gave me a job and a place to live and made sure I got my GED. I owe a lot to him that I could never repay." She was beaming at Big Al and rubbing his arm when she spoke. The big man looked pleased by her words, but terribly embarrassed.

"Just seeing you all grown up and about to be married is thanks enough. You turned out real nice, Birdie, real nice. I knew you had it in you," he told her, the pride in his voice unmistakable.

"How did you two meet?" John asked. "And how did she get the name Birdie? It's very cute, *chica,* but you never told me you had a nickname."

Nina made a sound of disgust and opened her mouth, but before she could say a word, Big Al was happy to tell John where the moniker originated. "I called her Birdie because of those little bird legs of hers. Skinniest child I ever saw in my life," he added. "And we met when she brought them little bird legs into the gentleman's ballet there," he nodded at the strip club, "thinking she could be a dancer."

He looked at Nina and they both burst out laughing. "If that G-string had stayed on, I might have made it," Nina laughed. "I was a good dancer."

"Yeah, but not a *pole* dancer, Birdie. Those men don't care how good you dance, they just wanna see . . . well, you didn't have what they wanted to see."

Nina took pity on John who was looking from one to the other with a stupefied expression on his face. "I was working in that car wash over there, which is a miserable place to be in the dead of winter. I'd heard how much money the dancers made at the club so I decided to give it a try. Let's just say it was the worst audition in the history of exotic dancing and leave it at that. Big Al owns that place, too, by the way. Anyway, he took one look at me, standing there looking like an idiot and he threw a coat over me, picked me up under one arm and brought me over here. He gave me a job, taught me how to cook and let me stay with him in his daughter's bedroom. She was away at college at the time." Nina turned to Al and asked how she was doing.

"Real good. She has her master's degree in electrical engineering and she works for Lockheed Martin in Atlanta. She and her husband will be here for Christmas."

They stayed and talked to Big Al for a long time while eating his superbly prepared burgers and fries. Nina hated to leave, but she and John had a schedule to keep. They were going to spend the night in St. Louis and be driving to Ann Arbor the next day. "Yes, I will definitely invite you to the wedding, whenever it is. And I promise to stay in touch. I've missed you over the years," she told the older man.

"And I missed you too, Birdie." Turning to John, he said, "I don't think I have to tell you to take care of her. She's a very special woman and she deserves the best."

"I plan to give it to her, sir."

"You better or you'll have me to answer to." The look on his face gave John no doubt but that the man meant every word. Big Al had no way of knowing it, but John meant every word, too.

John teased Nina as they drove away, calling her his little Birdie. "How long were you with Big Al, Nina? He obviously cared a great deal about you. Why did you leave him?"

Nina sighed briefly. "He was like a father to me," she said sadly. "But he had a big mean girlfriend who couldn't stand the sight of me. And I was there before she was, mind you. He met her after I'd been staying there for almost a year. She tried to pretend like she liked me at first but that didn't last. She tried everything in the world to get rid of me and I finally had enough and moved on. Al was so crazy about that ol' heifer he couldn't see straight, and if she was what made him happy so be it." She shrugged, through with the topic.

John glanced over at Nina, looking relaxed and happy in the passenger's seat. "I'll bet you were an adorable little girl, Nina. Were you as cute as you are now?"

Nina gave a short, mirthless laugh. "We'll never know. I don't have any pictures of myself from childhood."

John was stunned. "None at all?"

Nina shrugged. "I don't have anything from my childhood, John. No pictures of me, my brothers," she drew a shaky breath, "my mother, nothing. Not a doll, a book, nothing from when I was a child. It's like that part of me just vanished forever."

Ironically, it was John who looked stricken. Nina had to take his hand to comfort him. "John, that's just the way life is. You go from foster home to foster home, from here to there and everywhere and things get lost, they get stolen, they just disappear. Living on the street isn't exactly conducive to treasured memorabilia," she said with dry, bitter wit. "In a way, it's better this way. I remember everything about living with mommy as being perfect and I don't have anything to prove me wrong. It's weird but it works for me."

John wanted to crush her in his arms and tell her again how much he loved her, but with the car going 75 mph, he settled for kissing the back of the hand he was still clasping. "It's okay, Nina. From now on we'll make memories, just you and me," he promised.

Chapter 20

The weather had changed by the time John and Nina returned to Ann Arbor. It was seasonably cold and although the snow hadn't begun in earnest, there were periodic flurries. It seemed amazing to Nina that so little time had actually passed. She was sitting in the middle of John's bed wearing an old shirt of his with her hair wrapped in a towel. John came out of the bathroom clad in a beautiful navy blue velour robe lined with terry cloth and observed Nina's pensive face.

"Why are you so deep in thought? You look like you're millions of miles away," he said.

"I was just thinking about how fast this year has gone by. We came here in April, you found out about your family in June, you had the surgery in July, Adam and Alicia eloped in September, and got married again in October, and now here it is December and we're . . . engaged. And shacking up," she mumbled.

Ah ha, so that's it, John thought. He got into bed behind Nina; pulling her up against his chest while his legs cradled hers. She leaned back against him with a little sigh.

"I don't like how you said 'shacking up'. That implies a permanent condition and this is a temporary situation with us, you know that," he murmured, angling his head so he could kiss her neck. "We're getting married, don't forget that."

Nina smiled dreamily as she held out her hand with the magnificent ring sparkling at her. "When, John?"

"Whenever you like. Do you want a big wedding?"

Nina sat straight up, knocking the towel off as she did so. She turned around to face John. "No, I don't. It seems crazy to spend all that money. Let's just get married at the courthouse or something," she said anxiously.

John played with a strand of her damp hair and looked at her pretty face. He'd never get tired of looking at her. He liked her best this way, half-naked with messy hair and no makeup. He slid down a little and put his arms around her so she was resting on his chest and he could feel the weight of her on the lower part of his body. She rested her head on his shoulder and waited for his answer.

"At the courthouse? I think we can do better than that, Nina. How about we get married on New Year's Eve, something nice and intimate for just the two of us, how does that sound?"

Nina raised her head and kissed his chin. "I think it sounds perfect. Just perfect."

"So we're not going to hear the phrase 'shacking up' again? Because it just doesn't make sense to rent a place for you for what, two weeks, three? What does make sense is to buy a nice big house for us, which is why we're going to look at some places tomorrow," he murmured, moving his hands up and down her body. He never got tired of touching Nina. He started tugging at the shirt, wanting to feel all of her, and she started pulling away.

"Oh, no you don't! Once you start that it's all over for me as you well know," she giggled. "I have to finish my pedicure, John, stop it. *Stop* it."

"How about if I do it for you," John offered.

"Do what? My pedicure?" Nina looked skeptical, but

John gently moved away from her body, leaving her on the bed while he stood up. "Of course I can do your pretty toes. Where's your stuff?"

In a few minutes, Nina was propped against the headboard and John was sitting cross-legged in front of her with her feet resting in his lap. He had one slender foot in his hands, rubbing it with a sweet-smelling lotion. He did it just perfectly, too. His touch wasn't too hard or too soft, but a firm pressure that both relaxed and aroused Nina. She lay against the pillows and looked at John with half-lowered eyelids and sighed. His long hair was unbound and he looked exotically sexy as he focused on his task. A soft sigh issued from her lips, making him look at her.

"Am I doing this right, *querida*?"

Nina tried to answer him, but speech was difficult. The feel of his big warm hand caressing her foot was too distracting. He manipulated each toe and rotated his thumbs in circles on the sole, sending waves of pleasure up her leg. Nina began to feel hot moisture gathering in her lower body and she moved sensuously against the pillows. When John repeated the procedure on her other foot, her control slipped even more. She rubbed her hands over her thighs and sighed again, a yearning sound that made John look at her again, this time with a knowing smile.

"Do you like this, baby? Maybe I should do this more often. You have such beautiful feet, Nina. I love your feet, they're so sexy." He brought one to his mouth and kissed the arch, rubbing the sole against his cheek. At Nina's gasp, he smiled and took her big toe into his mouth, swirling his tongue around it and sucking gently.

Nina's arms rose gracefully above her head and she clutched the pillows with both hands. The sound that came from her lips only served to make John increase his efforts. He continued to kiss and caress her foot, her ankle, and then her calf, until he was kissing and licking his way up to her silken inner thigh. Nina's eyes were closed and her breath was coming in little fevered pants. The anticipation was excruciating. The slow, deliberate way he was touching her was almost too much for her to take. He was no longer sitting cross-legged; he was kneeling as he stroked her thigh with his hands and his face. When he reached the spot he was seeking, he paid it a sensual tribute with his lips and tongue, devouring her sweetness like an exotic dessert.

The buttons on Nina's shirt gave way one at a time as her body writhed in sexual bliss, leaving her exposed as John continued to ravish her with exquisite passion. His big hands held her hips so he could give her more and more pleasure, sensations that were driving her to the edge of reason. Her head tossed from side to side on the pillows and she reached for him blindly, screaming his name. He finally relented and began kissing his way up her body, stopping only once so her navel wouldn't feel neglected. He buried his face in her breasts as she wrapped her trembling arms around his neck. Finally he raised his body and turned over onto his back, pulling her into his arms so he could hold her next to his heart.

"If you're going to be screaming like that every night," he teased her, "we're going to need a very big house, *querida.* Otherwise we'll scare the neighbors."

Her answer was a cascade of giggles that sounded like chiming bells. "I love you, John," she whispered.

"And I love you, for always," he vowed.

John was in a terrific mood the next day. He had the good fortune to be in love with the most incredible woman in the world, he had a warm and loving family, and Christmas was coming. What could be better? John had always loved the holiday and for the first time since the death of his parents, he really felt like celebrating. Even though he and Nina had decided against decorating, it would be very festive as the whole Cochran family was going to the new vacation house Adam and Alicia had built in Idlewild, the community where his father was born. He had no reason to be anything but happy as he left the apartment to get the paper and pick up a few things for breakfast.

He'd just pulled into the parking lot of the Whole Foods Market when his cell phone went off. It was Titus Argonne, checking in with a preliminary report. "So what have you found out about Oscar Giddens so far?" John wanted to know.

"Plenty. This guy is one of the sleaziest operators on the west coast. There's so much dirt on him and his operations it's hard to know where to begin. There's certainly enough for Nina and her whole neighborhood to start a class action suit," Titus informed him.

"That's good news. Great news, in fact. This is just what we're looking for," John said. "Thanks a lot, Titus, you do good work."

"Yeah, well, sometimes I think I work too well," Titus said gravely. "Look, John, I'm not good at sugarcoating things, I just say them outright. I think you need to know Nina Whitney isn't who she says she is."

John took the phone away from his ear and looked at it incredulously. He put it back to his ear and said, "I don't think I heard you right. What did you say about Nina?"

"I said Nina Whitney isn't who she says she is. That's not her real name, John. Not only that, someone is looking for her. How do you want me to handle that?"

Titus leaned back in his oversized leather desk chair and looked at the phone he'd just hung up. He wasn't sure if John Flores was the most astute person he'd met in some time or the most gullible, but he was certainly the most confident. Titus replayed the conversation they'd just had and heard once again the unwavering tone of John's voice.

"John, when I was investigating Oscar Giddens for the class action suit, I came across some information about Nina Whitney and I followed it up. There are no school records, no birth certificate, nothing regarding a Nina Whitney. Whoever she is, she didn't exist until about twelve years ago." Titus had given it to John straight; he wasn't known for his tact. He was paid for results, not hand-holding. John's response had been immediate and decisive.

"Thanks, Titus, but I already know everything I need to know about Nina." He spoke with calm assurance but there was a ribbon of steel in his tone. Without saying it outright, he'd just let Titus know Nina was off limits.

Titus raised his eyebrows and twisted his mouth in a half-smile. He crossed his arms behind his head and stared intently at the Romare Bearden print on the wall across from his desk. He often did this while he was deep in thought. He'd reiterated his earlier statement to John about someone else investigating Nina and John's response had been tersely emphatic. "Find out who it is and bring him to me."

Titus dropped his arms and rubbed his hands together. Yes, John Flores was decisive if nothing else. *I just hope he's not dead wrong.* Titus stood up and glanced at his watch. He decided to take a walk while he digested his conversation with John. A walk through the complex would be just the thing, particularly if it ended in Paris's office. He smiled at the thought as he entered the reception area. Popping a couple of Altoids in his mouth, he told his secretary he'd be gone for about thirty minutes.

* * *

Paris had just returned to her office after a meeting with her staff and was studying her planner. One thing Paris had learned from grad school and her two years of interning for Cochran/Deveraux was the importance of planning and she was organized to the hilt. With the Christmas holidays so near, she had dozens of functions to attend, which required precise scheduling if she was going to make them all. In addition, she was going home to Louisiana for part of the holidays, and to Michigan for the rest. She was looking forward to both trips, although she'd have dropped everything to spend the holidays on a remote beach with Titus. *Stop that, you horny ol' girl,* she scolded herself. There was no point in denying it; she wanted Titus in the worst possible way. But what she was going to do about it, that was another question entirely.

"Miss Deveraux, a Mr. Argonne is here to see you."

Paris smiled. One day she would convince her secretary to call her Paris, but in the meantime, the object of her desire was here. She took a quick glance in the mirror she kept in her desk drawer to make sure her nose wasn't shining like a beacon and pushed the intercom button on her desk phone. "Thank you, Deirdre, please show him in," she said, happy her voice sounded normal.

She stood and walked around her teakwood desk and held out both hands to Titus as he entered her office. He took them and leaned in to kiss her on the cheek. "Hello, Paris, I hope I'm not disturbing you. I was in the neighborhood and well, you know the rest."

"Hello, yourself. Have a seat and tell me how your day is going," she invited, waving a hand at her long rose colored Ultrasuede sofa. Titus sat with his long legs stretched out and gave Paris an admiring look.

"You look very pretty, Paris. Although you always do, so I guess compliments are superfluous to you."

Paris did look sophisticated and sexy, albeit professional in a pair of cuffed, wide-legged taupe trousers and a cable knit cashmere turtleneck in soft pink. "Thank you very much, Titus, and any woman who thinks compliments are superfluous needs her head examined. I'll take them all, thank you," she said with a smile.

Titus returned the smile and was about to ask if she had plans for dinner when some pictures on her bulletin board caught his eye. Paris had a huge easel near her desk and it was covered with all manner of things. She had a habit of tacking things up that captured her attention or sparked an idea she might develop later. Titus stood and went to the board, taking the pictures off the board and examining them closely.

Paris was too surprised to be offended by his action, but not too surprised for curiosity. "Do those mean something to you?"

"Hmm?" Titus looked at Paris and realized what he'd just done. "Paris, I apologize. I just got a glimpse of this picture and I had to get a better look at it. Rita Shannon was a fantastic singer, wasn't she?"

Paris agreed with him. "Yes, she had a beautiful voice. I like old-school R&B and she was like the queen of the girl groups back in the day." She pointed at the picture she'd put with the one of Rita. "That, of course, is Nina Whitney, John Flores's fiancée. Doesn't she look just like Rita Shannon?" Without waiting for a response, Paris continued. "I have a theory about the resemblance. I'm not sworn to secrecy or anything, but it's such a delicate matter I haven't discussed it with anyone. Anyway, I'm convinced Nina Whitney is Rita's daughter." Gratified when Titus didn't look at her like she was nuts, Paris took his hand and led him back over to the sofa. She sat down and turned to the side so she was facing Titus with one leg curled under her. She told him what Bump had shared with her about Rita's children.

"There was all this hoopla in the papers about Donella Divine, who was also in The Sensations, adopting her children, but it turns out she only took the boys and they all moved to Toronto. There isn't any information about the little girl. And I mean no information at all, because I looked. I couldn't find one thing to tell me what happened to Rita Shannon's little girl. It was kind of weird anyway, Donella taking those children, because she and Rita didn't get along," Paris mused.

"But wouldn't it be tragic if Nina was somehow Rita's daughter and she got separated from her family after the only parent she had died? Wouldn't that be sad?"

Titus was listening to Paris intently, but his mind was clicking away like the tumbler in a combination lock being turned to the correct numbers. He studied the pictures carefully and suddenly gave Paris a brilliant smile. Without warning he grabbed her and kissed her hard.

"Listen, sweetness, I have to go out of town for a couple of days. But when I come back, we're going to do something really special, I promise you. Something really memorable."

Paris nodded mutely and wondered if she could get him to shut up and kiss her again. *Darned right I can,* she thought just as she pulled his head down to hers for a long lingering good-bye kiss.

When they finally broke apart, Titus seemed slightly dazed. "Now that's memorable, sweetness."

Chapter 21

John kept taking sideways glances at Nina on the ride to Idlewild. She was quiet and withdrawn, speaking only when he addressed her directly. She didn't seem to be angry, but something was making her unhappy and he couldn't have that. He reached over and took her hand, giving it a gentle squeeze. "Whatever it is, it can't be that bad, baby. Talk to me."

Instead of pulling away, Nina clasped his hand tightly and covered it with her other hand. "John, I do need to talk to you about something. I haven't been honest with you," she said quietly.

His voice warm and concerned, John repeated, "Talk to me, Nina."

"I'm dreading this, John. Going to Idlewild and being around your family, I'm just freaking out inside, but not for the reason you imagine. I really like your family; I think you know that by now. But people are going to start talking about all the pretty babies we're going to make and I just don't want to hear it. We aren't going to have any babies, pretty or otherwise. I don't want to have children, John. I should have told you this a long time ago, but I didn't. I wasn't trying to hide anything from you, at least not at first.

"To tell you the truth I never thought of us as a couple,"

Nina confessed. "Not because I didn't love you, but I didn't think there was a chance in this world you'd ever love me back." John's hand tightened on hers and she winced a little, which made him apologize. "It's okay, John. Later, when it seemed like this might actually work," she smiled crookedly at him, "I just couldn't say the words. I didn't want to lose you," she whispered. "I should have told you before this."

Nina was too overwrought to realize John had pulled off the road. He brought the SUV to a stop in the parking lot of a gas station and turned to face her. "Nina, stop. Stop right now, baby, and listen to me," he entreated her.

"I was relieved when we never discussed children. I should have been man enough to bring it up, but I was selfish and never said a word. I love you so much, Nina, I just hoped I'd be enough for you, even without babies." He paused and watched her face change from anguished to puzzled. "Yes, *querida,* without babies. I can't father a child. Nina, with the possibility that a child could inherit the liver disease that's a part of my genetic makeup, there's no way I'm going to have one. That's a decision I made after the transplant surgery. I should have talked to you about it but I was too selfish, too caught up in what I wanted more than anything in the world. I wanted you, just you. I just prayed that love would be enough even without children. I hope you can forgive me, *mi preciosa,* I promise you I'll never lie to you again."

Nina looked into John's eyes and saw nothing there but regret and love. "John, I can't believe we put ourselves through this torture for nothing. I should have told you," she said, wiping away a tear.

"I should have told *you,*" John countered. "What happened, baby? Why don't you want to have children?" he asked tenderly.

Nina sighed deeply and looked away from John. "I'm scared, John. I have no idea how to be a mother. I lost my mother so long ago she's like a pretty memory. And I had a lot of substitutes but aside from Marva, Patty Benrubi and Miss Velma, they weren't my idea of what a mother should be. I don't even know if I have what it takes to love a child the way it's supposed to be loved," she said flatly. "If I hadn't met you it wouldn't have been an issue because I wasn't ever planning on getting married or anything like that. But then . . ." her voice faded away and she looked at him for the first time since she started speaking.

John got out of the SUV and walked around to Nina's door, opening it and holding his arms out for her. He held her as tightly as he could, sharing her pain and trying to impart all the love he felt for her. It was the first time she'd expressed any sadness over the way she'd had to grow up and he marveled at the unfairness of it all. "It's okay, Nina. It's just going to be you and me, but it's okay. I love you more than my life and I'm going to make you happy for the rest of your life. I'm going to make it all up to you, baby, every bit of pain you ever went through. I'm going to take it all away," he vowed.

Nina smiled up at him. "All I want is for you to love me. You don't have to make up for anything, John, just love me." She leaned against him and then looked up with a mischievous expression. "You know, as much as your family likes making babies we're going to be outcasts if we don't have any children."

John laughed. "We'll be *babysitters,* that's what we'll be. Just think of it, Nina we can have our pick of nephews and nieces. Any time you get a hankering for a baby we can borrow one. Or two or three, as a matter of fact," he laughed.

"Are you sure I'm going to be enough for you, John? Every man wants to leave his mark on the world, to have a son to carry on his name. I can't give that to you," she reminded him.

"Nina, I don't ever want to have this conversation again. You are," he said as he caressed her face, "the only woman I've ever loved like this and you're the only woman I'm ever going to want. You excite me, entice me, you seduce me every time you look at me. I need you in my life, baby, I couldn't possibly live without you. You make me think, you make me laugh and you keep me on my toes. Winning your heart is the best thing I've ever done in my life, I'll never accomplish anything like this again. You're my greatest treasure, Nina, and you're more than enough for me, now and forever."

They continued to stand that way, wrapped in each other's arms, until Nina started to tremble from the cold. "Umm, baby? Can we continue this in a heated environment? My blood is still thin and it's *cold* out here," she said frankly. She was wearing a bright red peacoat and a scarf around her neck, but she was really getting chilled.

"My bad, baby," John apologized and put her back into the SUV. As he buckled his seat belt, John smiled over at her. "We'll be there in a little while and with any luck, the house will be all warmed up. Adam had Aunt Reba turn the heat on yesterday, so it should be ready for us."

Nina's relief was evident as she put her cashmere-lined leather gloves back on. "That sounds wonderful, John, absolutely wonderful."

In fact, the whole holiday was wonderful. Nina had more fun than she thought possible. Adam and Alicia were already at the house when they arrived and made them feel more than welcome. They showed John and Nina around the big place with obvious pride in Adam's design. The lower level of the house had a huge great room, an area that combined a well-equipped kitchen and an easy-to-live-in family room with a stone fireplace.

There was a big living room with another fireplace and a combination laundry room and pantry. There was also a space called a mudroom, a place where the family would get out of muddy and wet gear to prevent the house from being tracked up. And there was a study and two full bathrooms. Adam joked it was the key to harmony in a big family. "Always have enough bathrooms and you'll get along much better."

The upstairs had six bedrooms and three baths, one of which was in the master suite. There were big windows all around the house and on fine days it was sunny and warm. There were glistening hardwood floors throughout the house with beautiful big area rugs. The furnishings were simple, colorful and comfortable. It was the most inviting space Nina had ever seen and she told Alicia so. They were sitting on a sofa facing the big fireplace in the living room. The fire Adam lit was burning brightly and the two women were having a quick cup of tea before the rest of the family converged on Idlewild. Alicia thanked Nina for her compliment.

"Adam wanted a place where the whole family could be together on the holidays. I think this is one of his best designs. You can really see Adam in every room of this place," she said proudly. "The three cabins were a great addition too, and it's the only way we could be sure there's enough room for everyone. All the cabins have two bedrooms, a bath and a half and a sleep sofa. And every single bed in this house and all the cabins will be occupied in the next few days. That's a lot of people," she said thoughtfully.

"That's a lot of cooking," Nina responded. "We should probably go to the store and get the rest of the groceries."

Alicia agreed and said as soon as the men came back, they would go. Adam and John had gone out to get a Christmas tree while Nina and Alicia sorted through the assortment of Christmas decorations they'd brought from Detroit. While they worked, Nina looked over at Alicia and realized they were becoming friends. Their presence in each other's lives was inevitable, the men they loved were brothers and whether they chose it or not, Nina and Alicia were bound together. Nina had a lot of time to think about this as the other families arrived one after the other.

While Nina and the other women were fixing dinner, she looked around at Tina, Faye, Renee, Benita, Angelique and Alicia and realized this was her new family. These were the women she would share her life with, and whose lives would become a part of hers and John's. She was looking at her future and for the first time in her life, it looked warm and welcoming, not dark and lonely. She felt overcome by emotion and took refuge in chopping a huge amount of onions so her tears could flow freely and without question. She might have been crying, but these tears were from sheer joy, nothing else.

It was Christmas Eve and the big house was lit from top to bottom with holiday lights, firelight, candles, and the glowing faces of all the children. The Cochrans had developed the very sensible plan of pulling names for gifts. That way each person only had to procure one gift instead of hundreds. Renee explained further. "We also want to stress the fact that this is a religious holiday and not just a mad toy grab. It's very hard, considering the fact that you start seeing Christmas decorations in the stores in September, but we treat Christmas like it's Jesus's birthday." She brushed her shining black hair out of her eyes and gave Nina a sheepish grin. "Of course, we do it to keep from going bankrupt, too. Can you imagine having to buy something for every member of this horde?" She gave a theatrical shudder.

They were in the great room making cookies in assembly line fashion with the help of Renee's four little girls and their cousin Lillian. Lily Rose was playing with Bella and Kate in the great room under the supervision of the great aunts Daphne and Dahlia and Christmas music resonated through the house. The men were conspicuous by their absence, something Faye assured Nina wouldn't last. "Whatever they're doing they'll be checking in soon. The longest they can stay away without checking in is about forty-five minutes. Watch," she said, nodding meaningfully towards the doorway.

Sure enough, Andrew wandered in, ostensibly to get water, but all he did was nuzzle Renee on the neck and wander off again. Alan and Andre made an appearance, leaning over their respective wife's shoulders, sneaking a kiss and a cookie and leaving again. Adam didn't even bother to front, he just walked in, looked at Alicia for a long moment, kissed her on the lips and whispered something in her ear that made her smile and blush bright red. Nina was starting to feel like the odd man out and then she gasped as John's hands went around her waist. "What are you doing? I feel neglected," he said disarmingly.

"You need to quit," Nina murmured, but she was touched by John's open affection.

The doorbell sounded off in the distance and Adam's voice was heard calling to John, who went to see what he wanted. One of the aunts watched the loving look on Nina's face and chuckled. "That's the kind of look that makes babies, Nina. And you and John are sure going to make some pretty ones," the older woman said with a big smile.

Nina's stomach muscles constricted and her mouth went dry. She wiped her suddenly wet palms on her jeans and tried to think of something to say. John's sudden appearance in the doorway saved her. "*Chica,* come here, I want to show you something." He held out a hand to her and she took it gladly, walking into the warm, festively decorated living room. She was looking up at him quizzically as they entered the room. There was nothing new in here.

"What did you want to show me, John?" At first he didn't answer. He just stopped walking and moved behind her, putting his hands on her shoulders. She turned her head to look at him with a question in her eyes. He looked down at her with loving eyes and spoke in a quiet voice rich with affection. "There're a couple of people here to see you, Nina."

"To see me? I don't know anyone around here," she said, her confusion evident.

A strange voice said, "You know us, Shay."

Nina's head whipped around and she stared at the two men standing near the front door. They were tall, about six-foot-three, and slender with coffee brown skin and golden brown eyes. One man had a neatly trimmed full beard and black hair cut close to his scalp; the other had a shaved head with a perfectly shaped moustache and goatee. Nina's eyes grew enormous and she began to tremble all over. "Oh my God. Tony, is that you? Is that Victor?" Nina pressed both her hands to her mouth and the tears started flowing down her cheeks. She couldn't move a muscle, but the two men could and did.

In seconds, they had their arms around her and all three of them were sobbing and holding on to each other with a death grip. Nina was so overcome she almost fainted and the older of the two men, the one named Tony, led her over to the sofa to sit down. "C'mon, Shay, calm down, sweetie." He held her tightly and rocked her in his arms; kissing her forehead while the one named Victor held her hand.

When she finally calmed down enough to speak, she looked from one man to the other. "But how did this happen? Where did you come from and how did you find me?" she asked in a tear-filled voice.

"It's a long story, Shay, but we'd love to tell it to you," Tony said with a huge smile.

The living room suddenly seemed full of people as the women left the great room to see what the commotion was about. Nina's tears started again as she looked at her future sisters-in-law. "I have some people I want you to meet," she said to the group. "These are my brothers, Anthony and Victor."

Chapter 22

Eventually Nina was able to stop sobbing and begin to appreciate the miracle of being reunited with her brothers. Once the initial shock subsided, she was able, with the aid of a glass of water and a fortifying cup of tea, to introduce Victor and Tony Shannon to her fiancé and his family like a normal person. Everyone was gathered in the living room now, including little Marty and Malcolm who were the most subdued people in the room.

They had followed the noise into the living room where they found two strange men who were apparently upsetting their Aunt Nina. They bum-rushed the strangers, attacking their legs with gusto. Bennie and Clay reacted at once, snatching the boys up and demanding to know what they thought they were doing. Marty pointed at the men and said, "They hurt Aunt Nina and made her cry. I'm gonna get them for it," he said hotly.

Malcolm echoed his sentiments and turned reproachful eyes on John. "You should get them, they're not s'posed to hurt Aunt Nina."

"Son, I appreciate your chivalry but they're not hurting Nina, they love her. She's their sister," Clay told them.

Plainly skeptical, Marty wriggled out of his father's grasp and went to Nina. "Are you okay?" he asked anxiously. "Did they hurt you?"

"No, sweetie, they didn't. These really are my big brothers," she told him with a smile. "This is Victor," she said, putting her hand over his, "and this is Tony. They would never hurt me, Marty."

Malcolm joined them, looking from one man to the other with suspicion. "If they're your brothers, where have they been?"

Nina was seated between the two men and each of them had an arm around her, she was like the filling in a sandwich, but she didn't care. Leaning against Victor, she smiled at Tony with her heart in her eyes. "It's a long story, Marty. A very long story." Marty and Malcolm climbed on her lap without waiting for an invitation. "Okay, we like stories." To Nina's amusement they each kept a suspicious eye on one of her brothers, it seemed they didn't trust them in the least.

Despite Bennie's protests, Nina let them stay. It was crowded, but who cared at a time like this. "Okay, if you want a story, here goes," Victor said. He tried to direct his words to everyone, but his eyes were on Nina.

"After Mama died, when Donella came to get us, we didn't know we'd never see you again, Shay. She told us you were going to spend a couple of nights with Morgan and that you'd be coming to stay with us soon. She told us that over and over again, until a few days turned into a few weeks, then a few months, and by then it finally sank into our thick heads that she was lying," Victor said with a touch of anger.

Tony added, "Yeah, when we moved to Toronto with no forwarding address, that was kind of a giveaway. It took us a long time to figure out why she did it. She was a sick woman, Shay."

Nina blinked. "Why are you using the past tense, Tony?"

Victor tightened his arm around her. "She passed away last year, Shay," was all he said. Nina couldn't detect any kind of emotion in his voice; it was calm and matter-of-fact.

Little Marty was the opposite, as he demanded to know why her brothers kept calling her that strange name. "Her name is Nina," he said emphatically.

Victor laughed. "You may call her Nina but we always called her Shay. It's short for the name she was born with, Sharita."

"That's why it was so hard to find you, we were looking for Sharita Shannon and we couldn't find any trace of her," Tony added.

Nina looked sad for the first time. "That's because I haven't been Sharita for a long, long time. I changed my name legally about twelve years ago."

"Why did you change your name, Aunt Nina?" Marty asked innocently.

"It's another long story, baby," Nina said softly.

Bennie intervened then, holding her hands out to her sons. "We'll tell you all about it tomorrow, sweeties. Now it's time for you to go to bed. We have a big day tomorrow," she reminded them. She and Clay gathered up their sleepy children, as did Renee and Andrew. With help from Trey, Alan and Andre, they went across the road to the guest cottages to sleep, but not before hugging Nina tightly and telling her how happy they were she was reunited with her brothers.

Adam drove the aunts to their homes and Alicia went into the kitchen to make sure everything was put away and all was ready for the huge breakfast that was going to be prepared the next day. Soon there were only four people in the living room, Nina, John and Nina's brothers.

There was so much to be discussed and it wasn't going to all be talked about in one night, that was obvious. John couldn't stop staring at Nina, who was flushed with pure happiness. She finally met his gaze and he was almost undone by the love in her eyes. She left the sofa and crossed the room to sit on the arm of his chair, wrapping her arms around his neck for a hug. "John, I have my brothers back," she whispered. Suddenly she sat up straight and looked stricken. "I don't think I even introduced you," she gasped. "How could I be so thoughtless?"

John laughed gently and pulled her into his lap. "I think it's understandable, baby."

"Besides, he's the guy who found us, Nina. If it hadn't been for him, we might still be looking for you," said Victor. "We feel like we know him already."

Nina turned to face John, who was looking uncomfortably red across the cheekbones. "And just when were you going to let me in on this," she asked in an ominously quiet voice.

Sleep proved impossible for Nina. Although they still hadn't covered all the years they'd been apart, Victor and Tony made one thing clear: Donella was the villain in the story. Alone in the kitchen of the big house, Nina was making a coffee cake while she thought about the conversation they'd had the night before. "We were so torn up when we realized we weren't going to see you again, Shay. Sorry, *Nina,* I'm going to try to remember to call you Nina," Victor promised. "Donella was quite a piece of work. She hated Mama, and I mean real, true hatred. One big reason was she was convinced Mama had an affair with her husband and you were the result. That's why she didn't want you, sis."

Nina's eyes had gotten big and she didn't know what to say. Tony told some more of the story. "Oh, it gets worse. We kept trying to get in touch with Morgan and talk to you, we missed you so much, and there wasn't a lot we could do about it, being children ourselves. Finally after you'd been gone for about a year, she told us you were dead."

Nina shuddered the same way she had when she first heard the words. She couldn't imagine hating another human being enough to lie about her death. And to tell that story to children was, in her opinion, just sick.

John came into the kitchen and her face showed how glad she was to see him. She went into his arms gladly and kissed him.

"Merry Christmas, baby. You're my hero, I hope you know that," she whispered.

"I'm no hero, I just happened to be madly in love," he contradicted her.

"Yes, but you're still my hero. You brought my brothers to me and I love you even more because of it."

It was true, that was another thing that came out of the long Christmas Eve talk. Victor had explained, "For years and years we thought our little sister was dead and it had much more of an effect on us than Donella counted on. We had all kinds of problems in school, we were defiant and unruly at home, we were a mess. We felt like it was our fault you died, see, because we weren't there to protect you.

"Then Donella started acting crazier than usual, more possessive, more eccentric and paranoid. She thought everyone was out to get her and she kept talking about being punished for what she'd done. Eventually the whole story came out and it was not pretty. She was so obsessed with you; she was the one who got you taken away from Morgan. And Marva. If you'd been able to stay with either one of them, you'd have had a chance. But she wasn't having it. And she was also the one who got you taken away from that family who wanted to adopt you." Victor's anger was apparent, as his voice became flat and deep with emotion.

"See, she had this friend who was crazy about her because she was a big time singing star. The friend was one of those women who have to live vicariously through other people, you know the kind. Dumpy, plain, thick glasses, no life, you know? Anyway, ol' girl worked for social services and she worked her evil magic to get you manipulated through the system. Donella was totally obsessed with you, Shay. I mean Nina." Spent, Victor had stood up and started pacing around the room, leaving Tony to do the talking.

"Anyway, Shay, it all came out. The nuttier she got, the more she would talk and we finally realized you weren't dead; she'd just been feeding us a line. So we started looking for you. We hired detectives, we even moved to Chicago to see if we could pick up any hint of you. Everything came to a dead end because we had no idea you'd changed your name. It was like Sharita disappeared off the face of the earth."

Now it was Nina's turn to talk. She had been curled up next to John on the sofa of their guest cottage and she had to set the record straight. "I'd been living in California for about a year. I was working as a nurse's aide, which isn't glamorous work at all, by the way. You work hard for the money when you're an aide. But I liked it because I could also get sitter jobs where you're basically sitting with a patient in a nursing home or geriatric ward or something. I got to wear a uniform, which was great because I had very few clothes. And I had a place to sleep because most of these were night jobs. I was basically a booty-wiper and floor-mopper, but I kept those bootys clean and my floors always shone like glass. That's how I met Mrs. Whitney.

"She was this little old lady who'd run off every home health aide and sitter and maid her family hired. She was supposed to be really mean, but she just acted like that. She hated her family because they were all after her money. She could be a holy terror when she wanted to be. But I was recommended by this nursing home and I went to her house and she hired me on the spot because she liked me. I wasn't scared of her and she liked that. I stayed with her for four years, from the time I was almost eighteen until she died when I was twenty-one. She wasn't really sick or anything, she was just old. I used to cook for her, bathe her, help her get dressed, take her to the doctor, stuff like that. I'd do her hair and we'd watch old movies together. She loved *Charlie Chan* and *The Thin Man* movies."

Nina had started to cry a little, remembering her funny, feisty Mrs. Whitney. "She was the one who taught me to make preserves, John. She taught me a lot about life in general. I think I really made a difference in her life while we were together. And when she died she left me her topaz earrings and she also left me an inheritance. It wasn't a huge sum of money, but to me it was like a fortune." She laughed shamefacedly. "The first thing I did, after I got a place to live, was to get my teeth fixed. They were a mess after not going to the dentist since I was a kid. Then I invested it the way she taught me to and I had a nice little nest egg until," she looked guiltily at John, "well, I used it for something important.

"Anyway, I wanted a new life. I changed my name legally to Nina Whitney. The Whitney is for Mrs. Whitney, of course, but the Nina is for Nina Simone because she was tough, fearless and committed to civil rights."

"Yeah, well, that little change made it really hard to track you down, Shay. But luckily, you have a friend who noticed a resemblance between you and Mama. And this investigator saw the pictures in her office and knew what do with the information because he was working on a class action suit. The ongoing investigation we were doing to find Shay was somehow tied in with what he was doing and he realized someone was looking for you. And he brought the information to John who found us and brought us here. And the rest is history," he had ended with a grin.

"The rest is history, indeed," Nina smiled up at John. "If you hadn't been snooping around trying to get dirt on the horrible Oscar Giddens I might never have found them. You're overly protective, macho and interfering and I love you for it. For that and a million other things, I'll love you forever, John. And yes, you are my hero, my knight in shining armor, my Prince Charming." She stopped as the rumble of John's stomach told her he had more pressing things on his mind.

"Okay, okay. I'll get you something to eat before everyone gets up. But after that I'm going to spend the rest of the day telling you how wonderful you are. How's that sound?" She kissed him sweetly before turning back to the coffee cake.

"It sounds like a perfect day." John smiled and watched her slide the prepared pan into the oven.

Nina made good on her promise of breakfast. She quickly put together a delicious meal of grits, eggs over easy, smoked sausage and toast. While John was praising her kitchen skills she continued to work, making salmon croquettes for the family. He raised an eyebrow when he saw her rolling each one in seasoned cornmeal in preparation for cooking. "Hey, you were holding out on me. Why didn't I get those," he asked with mock indignation.

"You can have as many as you like when everyone sits down to eat," she said distractedly.

John sensed her shift in mood at once, and he asked her what she was thinking about. She smiled, a sad faraway expression. "I'm thinking about Mommy. I never knew how she died until last night. I was so little when she passed away I didn't understand what happened to her.

When I got older, I read different things about her being a drunk and dying of an overdose, that kind of thing. There were a lot of sensationalized reports about her. How she died destitute and how the IRS seized the house, oh there were awful things, John. I didn't have anyone to tell me otherwise so that's what I believed all those years," Nina said sadly. "But Victor told me the truth, that Mommy had a congenital heart problem and she just died in her sleep one night. All this time I thought my mother was an alcoholic and she was no such thing. She wasn't broke, either."

Tony and Victor had told her she had a trust fund. When they realized there was a good possibility Nina was still alive, they set up a trust for her so she would receive her share of their mother's estate. Nina had simply stared at them when they imparted the news. "I don't need money, I just need you," she told them. "I just want you back in my life forever."

Her brothers hugged her hard and Tony had said, "The two things aren't mutually exclusive, Shay. You can have the money and us, you don't have to choose."

"So many lies, so much hatred and deceit," Nina sighed. "I can't believe someone deliberately set out to destroy my life because she *thought* I was her husband's child. She didn't even know for sure, John, she just assumed it. She ruined my life and my brothers' lives too, even though that wasn't her intention. I think in her twisted way she loved them and was trying to make a family with them." Nina was shaking her head sadly as she washed her hands in the kitchen sink

John rose from the table and put his arms around her. He held her tightly and inhaled the sweet smell of her hair. "There's no question she was disturbed in a lot of ways, Nina. I think it's a testament to your early nurturing from your mother that you all managed to grow into stable, normal adults. You are all very fortunate, baby. After all you went through, to end up with your brothers back in your life. You have an amazing story, *chica.*" He kissed her, gently at first, then with increasing desire. "You're an amazing woman."

"I have an amazing man," she countered and the kissing was about to get really heated when the morning invasion began as Adam and Alicia came in the kitchen followed by Angelique, with Lily Rose.

All serious conversation stopped as Christmas Day began.

Chapter 23

While the women worked to get breakfast ready, the men cleaned the sidewalks of the snow that had fallen during the night. Nina kept stealing glances out of the many big windows in the great room; the snow enchanted her because she hadn't seen so much of it since she was a child. After a big happy breakfast of grits, hash browns, scrambled eggs, salmon croquettes, smoked sausage, coffee cake, biscuits and muffins, it was time to open presents. Nina had several presents for John, which she would give him later, in private. She was touched and surprised, though, when her brothers presented her with a gift. She opened the big square box slowly, trying not to mess up the paper on the beautifully wrapped gift.

Victor and Tony both groaned aloud. "Shay, please hurry up," they said in unison. Victor explained, "She used to do that when she was little. It would take her twenty minutes to open a package because she hated to mess up the wrapping. She always did things just so. Used to drive us nuts," he said fondly.

Nina just stuck her tongue out at the two men and kept on daintily removing the pretty paper. It was finally done and she opened the box to find a big photo album. Her hands started shaking even before she opened it. When she looked at the first page she started crying again, which caused little Marty to run to her side. The album was full of pictures of Nina as a little girl, pictures of her mother and her brothers; every picture Victor and Tony owned had been copied and laboriously arranged in chronological order. There were also pictures of her brothers over the years they'd been apart from her, something that was even more special to Nina. She sobbed happily and showed the album off to everyone. She was so thrilled about it she couldn't stop thanking Victor and Tony.

After the men cleaned up the kitchen so dinner preparations could start, there was a little downtime, time in which John and Nina were at last alone in the cottage. She put on a cotton shirt instead of the heavy red wool sweater she'd chosen because of its festive color. It was going to be too hot in the kitchen for a heavy sweater. John sat in a big overstuffed chair in the living room and Nina was curled up on his lap. Her head was on his shoulder so she could lose herself in the clean scent of his neck and she was holding his hand against her breasts. "I've never been happier in my life, John. I still can't believe all the trouble you went though for me, not to mention all the expense. This is the best present you could ever give me, you gave me my brothers back."

"You are entirely welcome, my love. It seems appropriate because you're the best present I'm ever going to get in my entire life. I can't wait until we're married, Nina. That's going to be the happiest day of my life," he said quietly.

They wanted nothing more than to spend the rest of the day wrapped in each other's arms but that seemed a bit impractical as well as rude, so Nina finished changing and they went back to the main house where Nina joined the cooks and was soon hip deep in making the cornbread dressing. With everyone working together the huge meal came together easily and it was a grand, festive affair. They dined on turkey, dressing, sweet potatoes, greens, standing rib roast, Yorkshire pudding, cranberry orange relish, macaroni and cheese, ham, potato salad, corn pudding, and salads, both tossed and spinach. Nina knew she was a member of the family for real when she had to stop Big Benny's repeated attempts to eat things he wasn't supposed to have. "Mr. Cochran, you know you're not supposed to have that," she said briskly as she intercepted a sweet potato casserole covered with a praline topping. She put a small baked sweet potato on his plate instead. "I made this just for you. Enjoy," she added and tried not to laugh at his consternation.

The men cleaned up the kitchen again after dinner and the women took it easy while the children played and the babies napped. Nina didn't even hear the doorbell; she was too engrossed in conversation with Bennie to pay it any attention. Angelique answered the door and turned around with a smile. "There's someone here for you, Nina."

Nina was in the middle of a sentence when she turned to face the door and what she saw made her heart soar. There was a tall, handsome middle-aged man with distinguished silver hair and a deep cleft in his chin. "Morgan," she said breathlessly, and then covered her mouth with her hand as Marva also walked through the door. Her hair was no longer long, curly and auburn, it was short, sleek and prematurely white, but it was still Marva, who, like Morgan, had tried to make a home for her. Nina tried to speak, but couldn't, she was hugging them both and crying again.

John watched her from the doorway, flanked by Tony and Victor. This was what he wanted for Nina, her happiness and everything she'd missed out on given back to her tenfold.

He was proud and pleased that he had some small part in giving her the deepest desire of her heart, but a tiny, selfish little corner of his psyche was just a little jealous that someone else had the power to bring her such joy.

Before he could mentally kick himself for being a self-absorbed jerk, Nina walked Morgan and Marva over to where he was standing. Putting an arm around each of their waists, she introduced them to John. "This is John," she said with such pride and adoration, John felt humbled. "This is my fiancé." She looked into his eyes and gave him the smile only he could get from her, a smile that equaled an eternity of love.

The momentary twinge of machismo vanished, leaving nothing in its place but the warming glow of Nina's love. John was indeed a lucky man.

A few days after Christmas, John wasn't feeling so lucky. Victor and Tony lived in Chicago and asked Nina to come home with them for a visit. They were so eager to get reacquainted with their little sister, it was impossible for her to say no. John had, in fact, encouraged her to go. He knew it was important for Nina to have a chance to rebuild the bonds that had been broken when the siblings were separated as children, so she went to spend some time with her brothers. John was prepared to miss her, but he wasn't ready for the huge hole her absence made in his heart.

The drive back to Ann Arbor without her was bad enough. He missed her scent, her conversation, even her infernal disco music. But it was much worse when he had to deal with the empty apartment. He found himself sleeping on her side of the bed, burying his head in her pillows to inhale the soft fragrance that was hers alone. They talked every day, but John was counting the hours until she would be back where she belonged, with him. The only thing her absence did was give him a chance to read some of her writing. She wanted him to read her college papers and journals, she'd told him, but he couldn't do it while she was around.

She'd tried to explain it to him once. "I really enjoy writing. I wanted to major in creative writing, but my instructor told me I'd never make it as a writer. He said I had no imagination and very little creativity," she'd admitted. "But I really love to write, isn't that ironic? That's how I ended up working for a publisher. When I got out of college I needed to find a job, of course, and even though I had a degree in education, my heart wasn't in teaching. I taught for one year and hated it," she said shamefacedly. "But I got a summer job temping at the publishing house and I loved it," she said, her face lighting up. "I could read all day, and it required me to be methodical and exacting. No imagination or creativity was involved at all. And they kept me on and I got to be better and better at every assignment and here I am, the perfect ghostwriter."

Now John took a great deal of comfort by sprawling across the bed every night reading Nina's writing. Whoever told her she couldn't write was full of it. Nina was an excellent writer, able to use a few perfectly chosen words to convey a world of meaning. Her work drew him in like a snake charmer's flute mesmerizing a cobra. It was like navigating the corridors of her heart and soul. And right now, it was all he had, besides their daily conversations. He didn't want to be selfish, but he wanted her back home in the worst possible way.

"Nina, all I'm saying is there's no rush. Getting married is a huge step for anybody, and you haven't even known this guy that long, now have you? I just think you should wait awhile, that's all. Just wait a little while," Tony said persuasively.

Nina was sitting in the dining room of her brother's brownstone, trying very hard to hold on to her temper. She'd been in Chicago for a week and this was the fourth time Tony had brought up the subject. Victor was no better, they were both determined to get her to postpone the wedding. It started out subtly enough with a hint here and there, but now they were like juggernauts, something Nina pointed out to her adoring brother.

"Anthony, you and Victor mean well," she said carefully, "but you've got to understand that I know my own mind. I know my own heart, too, and John is the right man for me." She and Tony were sitting at the same end of the table, facing each other and drinking big cups of cappuccino. She reached over and patted his hand affectionately. "I've been taking care of myself for a long time, big brother. You have to trust I'm doing the right thing."

Instead of returning the big smile she was giving him, Tony looked glum. "That's just it, Shay. You shouldn't have had to take care of yourself. You should have been at home with us. We should have all grown up together and you should have had a happy life, a regular childhood. We should have been a part of your life, Shay," he said angrily.

Nina sighed and put her cup down. She put her elbow on the table and rested her chin in her palm. This, too, was something she'd heard fairly often since she'd been with her brothers. If they weren't discouraging her marriage they were voicing their anger over their separation. She reached for Tony's hand with her free hand and held it tightly.

"I love you, Tony. I love you and Victor with all my heart and I wish things had been different, too. But the important thing is we found each other. Now we can get to know each other again and spend the rest of our lives together," she said earnestly.

"And that's exactly why you shouldn't get married right now," Victor said as he entered the dining room.

Nina groaned aloud and dropped her head. They really weren't going to give up.

Marva looked at Nina and she could see how troubled the younger woman was. And she could pretty much figure out why. "Nina, those brothers of yours are smothering you, aren't they?"

Nina gave Marva a rueful smile. "I can't hide anything from you, can I? I love them to death Marva, but I've got to go home. We can't make up for twenty-some-odd years in a week and I can't put my life on hold indefinitely. I'm trying to think of a way to tell them without hurting their feelings, but I haven't figured it out yet."

The women were seated in a popular restaurant in downtown Chicago, along with Patty Benrubi, who was Nina's first foster mother. They were waiting for Susan Benrubi-Hong, Patty's daughter, to come out of the ladies' room, a place she visited frequently as she was quite pregnant. Patty agreed with Marva.

"Honey, sometimes the best way is just to come out and say it. Don't try to think of the most polite way, just tell them it's time you were leaving and go. It's going to take a lot of adjusting on everyone's part before you get the family dynamic down pat, but so what? We're just glad to be a part of your life again. And your brothers are too, deliriously so. But the sooner you get married, the sooner they'll get used to the idea that their little Shay is all grown up now. I say get thee back to Ann Arbor, woman!"

Nina laughed as Patty put her arm around her shoulder and gave her a big hug. It had been the last thrill of the holiday when Patty and Hamed Benrubi had come to Idlewild. Dr. Benrubi and his wife had loved Nina like a daughter during the short time she was their foster child. They were touchingly glad to see her, and Patty told her how much they'd missed her when she was taken away from them.

"We should have fought harder, my darling. We shouldn't have let them get away with it," she said sadly. "We tried to get you back," she added. "We found out you really hadn't been adopted, but you'd been sent to the far ends of Illinois and the trail just stopped there. But we never stopped loving you. In fact, Susan's career is a direct result of what happened to you. She's a lawyer who specializes in children's advocacy," Patty had said proudly.

Both Susan Benrubi and the Benrubi's son Daniel had turned out well. Daniel had followed his father into medicine and was a pediatric surgeon. He was also married to a beautiful African-American woman who was in practice with him. Her name was Nekeia and she specialized in family medicine. The Benrubis were quite the melting pot these days as Susan was married to the very handsome Jimmie Hong, a restauranteur whose parents were both from Macao.

When Nina had come to Chicago she got to visit not only with her brothers, but also with everyone who'd been kind to her during those tumultuous years, Morgan, Marva, and the Benrubi family. Nina looked around the table and felt full, even though she hadn't eaten yet. There were Marva and Patty who'd been like mothers to her, and Susan, who'd been like her sister. Nina felt connected again; she felt whole in a way that almost equaled the way she felt about John, whom she missed dreadfully. Patty and Marva were right; it was time to go home. It was time to plan a wedding and start a new life.

* * *

John glanced at his watch. He had just dismissed his last class for the week and the thought of a long lonely weekend wasn't on his agenda. He opened the door of his apartment intending to pick up an overnight bag and leave again. If Nina didn't know when to come home, he knew how to go get her. To his utter amazement the apartment was lit with candles and there were fresh flowers on the coffee table and the dining room table, which was set for two. The scent of something incredibly appetizing floated out of the kitchen and he could hear Nina singing "Inseparable" in the kitchen. Stunned, John walked toward the source of the voice just as Nina was coming into the dining room.

"You're home," he said hoarsely.

"Can't fool you for a minute, can I?" Nina's brilliant smile was at odds with her flippant words. In seconds she was in John's arms, kissing him for all she was worth. He stared down at her and tried to speak sternly.

"I was about to come and get you," he told her.

"What took you so long? I've been ready to come home for two days," she murmured. "I missed you, *Papi.*"

"I missed you more. I love you, Nina. I'm afraid separate vacations are out of the question for us. I can't let you out of my sight again."

Nina smiled rapturously and rubbed her face against his chest. "Dinner won't be ready for a little while, so how about you show me instead of telling me?"

John gave her a wickedly sexy smile as he picked her up and carried her into the bedroom. "Absolutely, baby."

Chapter 24

Now it was just not possible to have a small wedding, not with so many people involved, especially since they all wanted to see Nina walk down the aisle to John. John admitted that's what he'd like, too. "I'm only doing this once and I want it to be not only beautiful and memorable but a lot of fun, like Adam and Alicia's wedding was. Let's go for it, *chica,*" he said persuasively.

"But John, all that money," she said hesitantly. "It's going to cost a lot of money to have that kind of wedding."

They were sitting in the living room of the apartment, at least Nina was sitting on the sofa and John was stretched out with his head in her lap and his eyes closed. He smiled to himself when he heard the genuine anxiety in Nina's voice. It was yet another thing to love about Nina, her practicality. She never spent a penny frivolously and could, in fact, stretch a dollar further than anyone he'd ever met. He loved the fact that she was trying to save his money and not spend it like some crazed chickenhead. But he also had to share something with her.

"Sweetie, did I ever tell you what my father did for a living?"

Nina raised her eyebrows and frowned. "You mean he wasn't a teacher?"

John smiled again. "Yes, he was definitely a teacher of

high school chemistry and physics, but he was also an inventor. He liked to create and he was always tinkering around with something. He came up with several modifications on the traditional exercise bike that led him to inventing and patenting a recumbent bike that is still used in gyms all over the world. And he invented a few other pieces of exercise equipment, too, as well as some ergonomically advanced equipment used in physical therapy. The bottom line is, he held a lot of patents and collected quite a few royalties, some of which are still being paid to his sole survivor. And I was an only child," he reminded her.

He waited for the full import of his statement to sink in, then laughed out loud at her reaction. He put his feet on the floor and brought his body up to a sitting position.

"Are you loaded?" she asked suspiciously.

He nodded as he pulled her into his arms. "Pretty much, baby. My dad made a lot of money, most of which he put into more investments and high-interest-bearing accounts. And he never told me about it until I was in college. He didn't want me growing up what he called spoiled and useless. He wanted to make sure I was grounded and sane and knew the value of hard work. Thanks to him and my mom, I was and still am. But if I choose not to work it's okay, we've got enough to care for our needs in a very elegant fashion. So go ahead and spend whatever you want on our wedding, it's fine. In fact I insist on it. And speaking of money," he intoned as he pulled Nina into his lap. "I know you spent your nest egg when you moved out here to be with me."

Nina's mouth fell open and she looked at John with dismay. "Who told you that?" she stammered, trying to hide her surprise.

"My publisher, who was your employer at the time. She blithely let the cat out of the bag when I called her to get your address in Oakland. Says she was impressed by the fact you were paying your own expenses when you came out here, and that you wouldn't get any pay until the contract was fulfilled." John stilled a wriggling Nina the best way he knew how, kissing her passionately until she relaxed in his arms. When he finally pulled away, John stroked her face with his long fingers and spoke to her in a voice full of the love he felt for her. "Nina, that was the most selfless, caring, loving thing anyone has ever done for me since my parents adopted me. But you know I can't let you do that. I'm giving you every dime of that money back, and don't even try to argue with me," he said firmly.

She did, of course, several times, which led to John kissing her some more in an effort to stem the protests she was making. "*Chica,* that's it, no more discussion. The money is going into your account and that's the end of it. There's no way in the world I could let you spend that kind of money on me," he said with finality.

"You really are the big macho man," Nina said fondly. She'd stopped struggling and trying to protest; now she was just looking at John with resigned affection. "You're going to be trying to be my *Papi* whether I like it or not, aren't you?"

"Yeah, I guess I am," he admitted without a hint of shame. "Are you gonna let me?"

She looked at his handsome face and gave him the smile that always made his heart skip a beat. "Yes, I guess I am," she said and kissed him again.

Chapter 25

The next months were more hectic than anything Nina could remember, but far more satisfying. The thought of attempting to plan a wedding was terrifying to her, but she had plenty of help. In addition to planning a wedding, she and John purchased a house and moved into it, which was in itself a massive undertaking. It was a big brick house built at the turn of the century in an area of Ann Arbor called Burns Park, which was near downtown and populated by big historic homes built at or before the turn of the century. Nina and John fell in love with it at first sight.

It was an imposing two-story structure with a cupola on top that would be a perfect study for Nina. There were five bedrooms, two baths and a study on the second floor and the first floor had a living room, dining room, butler's pantry, a maid's bedroom with its own lavatory, a big sunny kitchen and a shelf-lined library for John's study. There was also a small greenhouse adjoining the kitchen and a deep wrap-around porch that encompassed three quarters of the house. Very little had to be done to the house and Nina and John were able to move in after changing the paint in the master bedroom, the kitchen and the dining room. Even the floors needed nothing but a cursory buffing; the previous owners had revered the home's age and grace and had taken very good care of it.

Sometimes Nina would go from room to room in the house and just stare at everything. It was like being in a dream sometimes, a dream from which she never wanted to awaken. Then the phone would ring and it would be Victor, or Tony or Marva and her heart would fill up with so much joy she didn't think she could hold it all. For the first time, she truly understood how John felt upon finding out Big Benny was his natural father. Now she could comprehend his patient acceptance and gratitude to the man who'd given him life. She was finally able to open her heart to Benny and let his legendary charm pull her under its spell. She was even resigned to the idea that she'd be calling him Daddy, the way his other daughters-in-law did. *Might as well admit it, I'm one of them now,* she thought. But the thought didn't overwhelm her; it made her happy because she still had her own identity.

When Morgan and Marva came to Idlewild for Christmas, they were also bearing gifts. They had more pictures of Nina from childhood and Morgan even had family movies he'd had copied to DVDs. Hamed and Patty also had pictures of Nina and her favorite doll, which had gotten left behind when she was taken from the Benrubi family. "Susan kept this for you, sweetie. She prayed every night you'd come back to us."

Now that doll held pride of place on the chaise in Nina's new study. John had insisted she needed a place to write, although she kept trying to tell him she wasn't a writer, she was just a conduit. "And I'm a darned good one, too. There's nothing wrong with doing what I do, John."

"Nina, I read those stories you wrote in college. I've read the essays and the journal you kept for that class and that instructor was dead wrong. You do have imagination and your work is not technically perfect with no heart. You can really write, darling and I think you should pursue it. Starting with your own story, Nina. It would not only make a fascinating read, but a hell of a good screenplay. Trust me, *mi corazon*, you're the real thing."

Nina took his words to heart but she knew she wouldn't act on them until the wedding was over. If she hadn't had Big Benny's wife Martha helping her, as well as Patty Benrubi and Renee and Alicia Cochran, she was pretty sure she'd have drowned in tulle and silk flowers. But these women were not only organized and had wedding-savvy, they were indomitable and tireless. The kind of wedding they were planning usually took a year to pull off; they were going to do it in five months.

Patty's cheerful smile was like a beacon of comfort to Nina. She really believed Patty could do anything, especially after Patty presented her with Susan's wedding gown. It was beautiful—far more exquisite than Nina could have found in a store. What Patty said was true; once you had the dress, everything else fell into place. They didn't need to hire a photographer because Angelique's friend A.J. volunteered. Alan Jandrewski, known to friends and family as A.J., was the brilliant photographer who'd helped teach Angelique Deveraux Cochran the art of photography. Angelique helped by taking engagement pictures of John and Nina, as well as portraits of her with her brothers and with her surrogate parents. These pictures were displayed throughout the house in Burns Park alongside John's family pictures, and made Nina feel like a whole person for the first time in years.

As she looked at the women gathered in her living room to pick out bridesmaid's dresses and flowers, she felt like the wealthiest woman in the world, rich in love, not money. She sat next to Patty and sipped a glass of raspberry lemonade as she listened to the women debate the merits of various colors and fabric. They were united in their desire to have something that wasn't shiny, but they were flexible about everything else. Renee made a daring suggestion. "For once let's forget about the idea that the dress has to be something you can wear later. Let's just concentrate on making them the most beautiful dresses anyone ever saw," she said, and everyone agreed.

It was the same with the flowers, the venue for the reception, and the menu for the sit-down dinner. Everything just flowed together harmoniously, although only Alicia knew why Nina was so sublimely calm and happy during the highly detailed process of planning. It was because she and John had gotten married on New Year's Eve with only Alicia and Adam as witnesses. They'd gone to the home of a friend of Alicia's, a judge who was more than happy to perform the simple ceremony. Nina had worn a beautiful ivory wool suit and carried a small bouquet of pink roses and freesias bound with ivory ribbons. John looked dashing in a charcoal gray suit with a pristine white shirt and a silk tie given to him that morning by Nina. They repeated their vows while holding each other's hands and looking into each other's eyes with complete adoration.

Now Nina was relaxed and mellow and enjoying the days leading up to the big wedding instead of being a frazzled mess. Rushed they might be, but everything was in place, even the music. Nina had been touched when Bump assured her he was taking care of the music for the event, the same way he had for Adam and Alicia's wedding, and all the other Cochran and Deveraux nuptials. "The vows aren't official unless I play, baby. I'll be there with the band, so get your dancing shoes ready."

Nina almost wept when she remembered how she had once dismissed John's family as the sappiest people on earth. Now she saw them for what they were: warm, generous people who were lucky in love and wanted nothing less for their friends and family. That kind of love was like a contagious condition and Nina now seemed to have a terminal case. And she wouldn't have it any other way.

Alan and Andre shook hands firmly as they waited in the dressing room with the rest of the groomsmen. "Okay, you won the bet," Andre said solemnly. "I'll deliver your winnings in the morning."

Andrew and Donnie immediately picked up on both the word "bet" and Andre's glum expression. "Okay, what have you two been up to this time?" Andrew asked with amusement.

Alan was happy to explain. "We had a little wager going on how long it would take John to land Nina and I won. A year's supply of golf balls," he reported with great satisfaction.

Donnie groaned. "Aww, you two still making those lame bets? Why don't you ever put some money on the line?"

Both men looked horrified at the very thought of actually risking their hard-earned cash. They loved to bet on any and everything but only for things like golf balls, green fees, golf tees and the like. Donnie shook his head in despair. "My brothers the high rollers," he said with resignation.

"John, you really need to sit down, man. I haven't seen a groom this jumpy since Marcus and Vera got married." Clay's deep voice was full of amusement. There was nothing a happily married man liked more than seeing a bachelor about to cross the line into matrimony. John was in a category all by himself, though. He was possibly the happiest groom in the history of weddings.

"I'm not jumpy, Clay, I'm just . . . just . . ." John rubbed his chin as he tried to think of the appropriate word. His face relaxed into the smile that was never far from his face these days. "I'm just happy, man. Really, really happy."

Adam laughed. "You're light-headed, that's what you are. Getting those braids let the air get to your brain and it's making you dizzy. Trust me, I know the feeling," he said with a grin. It was true, if anyone understood what it felt like to suddenly not have the long ponytail you'd worn for years it was Adam, who'd cut his off the previous year.

John ran his hand over his braids and smiled. On a long rainy weekend Nina had braided his hair for him while he re-read her work. He read much of it aloud, to her initial chagrin. He had to prove to her how talented she was and while her hands were twined in his hair seemed as good a time as any. He loved the look and feel of his new style and so did Nina. His hair now hung in long, thin twists that made him look exotically sexy. He'd tried to tease her about it once, saying he'd gotten a haircut.

She was in the kitchen of their new home making him a lovely dinner for an early spring evening; roast chicken with herbs under the skin for flavor, tiny potatoes in butter and parsley, spinach salad and his favorite dessert, *dulce le leche* ice cream with her homemade brownies. She was dancing around the kitchen singing "Goin' to the Chapel of Love" and looked utterly carefree until she heard John's voice coming from the dining room. "Nina, I'm going to get my hair cut for the wedding, how does that sound?" That was when John found out Nina could speak Spanish.

"Man, she cussed me for old and new," John told his brothers. "I had no idea she could understand a word of Spanish let alone speak it. I think that's the only reason she stopped yelling at me that day, I looked so stupid standing there with my mouth open."

Nina had indeed ended her tirade and angry as she was, she still smiled at the look on John's face. "Close your mouth, *querida.* I probably should have mentioned I'm bilingual."

"But . . . how?" John stammered.

"Our housekeeper from the time I was a baby was Dominican. She spoke to us in Spanish all the time and when I first started talking I used as many Spanish words as English. Besides, I've been living in California for years, how could I not know at least a little Spanish?" she asked reasonably. "I should have told you I could speak Spanish a long time ago, but it's so handy to understand what's being said when no one knows you can."

John had given her what he hoped was a stern look and asked if there was anything else she wanted to tell him.

"Not a thing, darling," she answered in perfect Mandarin Chinese.

The men all laughed heartily at the story. John laughed along with them, saying that Nina was the perfect woman for him. "And in"—he glanced at his watch—"ten minutes I'm going to make her my wife. What could possibly make this moment any better?" he asked with his arms spread wide.

Victor scratched his nose with his forefinger. "Um, just guessing here, but maybe some pants," he said in a deadpan voice.

Tony agreed, adding, "And some shoes, man. Shay's kinda particular about shoes."

John looked down and realized he was indeed half dressed. "I thought it was kind of chilly in here. My bad."

The church was decked in flowers, big arrangements of spring blossoms in various shades of pink with abundant greenery. The candles were lit and Patty and Marva were seated in the mother-of-the-bride places. The voice of Ceylon Deveraux cascaded over the family and friends gathered to witness the vows. She was singing "Ave Maria" and it was like a balm to the soul. After the bridesmaids, Renee, Tina, Faye, Angelique, Benita and Paris, were in place, as well as the junior bridesmaids and flower girls, Nina's matrons of honor, Susan Benrubi-Hong and Alicia Cochran, took their places. Then it was time for Nina to be escorted down the aisle.

First Big Al walked with her, since he was her last father figure. He handed her over to a visibly moved Dr. Hamed Benrubi, who walked her to Morgan. Morgan kissed her on the cheek as he entrusted her to Victor and Tony who took her the rest of the way to John, who didn't bother to try to hide the lone tear trickling down his cheek. Nina shed a few tears of her own when the minister asked, "Who giveth this woman?" and her brothers, the Benrubis, Big Al, Miss Velma, Morgan and Marva all stood up and said "We do."

Nina tried hard to control her shaking hands but the emotions were too powerful. She looked up at John with tears sparkling in her eyes and whispered, "I love you." John flouted tradition by bending down to kiss her forehead and caress her cheek. "And I love you, Miss Parker, for always."

By the time they were pronounced man and wife there wasn't a dry eye in the house.

Epilogue

In her entire life Nina never imagined it was possible to be as happy as she was now. She had the love of a lifetime in John. He made her believe all things were possible, like winning the class action suit against Oscar Giddens. Thanks to Alan and Andre Cochran, Giddens had to make good on all his promises and everyone in the Oakland neighborhood was able to purchase his or her home and get out from under his venal thumb. Nina was able to purchase her darling little dollhouse and sold it back to Giddens at a profit since his mother really did want to live in the house. When Miss Velma came to Michigan for the wedding she reported that as luck would have it, Mr. Giddens's mother was a sweet lady, nothing like her son.

"We go walking together in the morning and we watch Oprah in the afternoons," Miss Velma told Nina. "She hasn't made one single change to your house, either, she just fell in love with it the way it is."

Miss Velma also filled Nina in on some other things that had happened as a result of the class action suit. "Everyone was so happy about what that fiancé of yours did to help us get started with the lawsuit, they renamed the playground Whitney Park after you, sugar. That's so we'll always remember you. You did a lot for that neighborhood even before the lawsuit, Nina. You helped bring it to life."

Miss Velma had looked around Nina and John's new home and surveyed the host of family and friends gathered for an informal dinner in the days before the wedding. "I'm so happy for you, sugar. This is what I always wanted for you. I knew that man would bring you the happiness you deserve if you'd just let him love you. And I was right, wasn't I?"

"Yes, Miss Velma, you surely were. I have so much now," Nina had spread her hands wide as she looked around her at her new life. "More than I ever dreamed."

Every day was full of joy and excitement now. Nina was so content and happy she'd even agreed to be interviewed on Paris's talk show. Paris was allowed to film the preparations for the wedding as well as participate in it, although her participation was out of friendship. When Nina thought about how much notoriety Paris could have gained by exploiting her, the realization that she didn't do it out of respect and affection for her was truly touching. Paris didn't overplay her hand, either, she treated Nina's wedding with the reverence it deserved. After the wedding, while the camera equipment was packed up in preparation to go to the reception, Paris and the other bridesmaids were fussing over the bride.

"Nina, I still can't get over that dress, girl," Paris told her. It was truly gorgeous, made of matte silk satin in a dazzling creamy white; it was strapless with a dropped bustier bodice and a cartridge-pleated full shirt with a ten-foot detachable train. The dress was bordered in re-embroidered Alencon lace and the bodice was made entirely of the lace with crystal beading that made it shimmer in the dimmed lighting of the church. Nina looked so exquisite it was unreal, like a bridal Barbie doll. There was a sheer bolero jacket worn in the church for modesty; it was removed for the reception. Nina's hair was blown straight and pulled up and off her face with a fall attached so expertly no one would guess it wasn't her hair. She wore Susan's diamond tiara which she'd worn at her own wedding as had four other generations of Benrubi women. Nina also wore the pearl pendant with the diamond cap setting and the matching pearl and diamond drop earrings John had given her that morning.

Nina thanked Paris for the compliment and returned it. They were in the anteroom of the church, about to leave for the reception. "You look fantastic as well, Paris. That color looks beautiful on you and so does the dress. Titus doesn't seem to know what hit him," she teased.

Paris turned pink with pleasure. She was glad when the wedding party was dispatched to the limousines that would take them to the reception because it gave her a chance to escape the intense scrutiny of Titus's sexy eyes. Once they reached the posh hotel where the reception was being held, though, she could feel Titus staring at her again. The pink color returned to her face along with a heated response to his nearness. Paris's body continued to react during the reception because of the way Titus was looking at her, like he wanted to take a bite of her perfumed flesh and devour it. *If he doesn't stop I'm going to get up and leave,* she thought. She wouldn't have done any such thing, not really, but the heat was spreading from her face to other body parts and she was more than uncomfortable.

She tried to pay attention to Nina and John dancing to "*Amigos Par Siempre,*" sung by Marcus and Vera Deveraux. It was the newlywed's first dance and it looked beautifully romantic. She focused on John's relatives from Puerto Rico, an attractive and friendly lot. Nina had told her of Cousin Lola's attempt to snare John. When they were in the anteroom of the church Nina had whispered to Paris she was stunned by the woman's transformation.

"Paris, I'm telling you, she was a Latin hoochie-mama on the make and now look at her! She's all covered up from her neck to her knees. And I think she and Alejandro have finally seen the light because they act like there's going to be another wedding in the very near future. Amazing," Nina marveled.

It was true; Lola was wearing a chic but modest silk shantung suit in aqua. Her hair was cut into a becoming bob and John's friend Alejandro never took his eyes off her nor did he leave her side. *I think Nina's right; it looks like there's true love on the horizon here,* Paris thought as she continued to scan the room from her vantage point at the head table. She suddenly felt self-conscious, as though someone was staring at her. She held her breath as she dared to look at the other end of the table. Sure enough, Titus's hot eyes were burning her up, even from that distance. Paris forced herself to remain composed while John and Nina finished their first dance.

After it ended, Paris tried to escape his intense scrutiny by going to the ladies' room, even though Nina was now singing "I Believe in You and Me" to John. It was terribly rude of Paris but there was something about the way Titus was staring at her that was driving her mad with unfulfilled desire. Unfortunately for her, Titus anticipated her move and was waiting for her outside the ballroom. He held out his hand and she was helpless, she took it with no hesitation and let him lead her into an atrium filled with fragrantly exotic plants.

He didn't hesitate; he pulled her into his arms and kissed her with a hunger that echoed her own; she was captured by his sensuality and had no desire to escape. She could have kissed him forever; his lips were like the essence of life to her at that moment. Suddenly she was jerked out of his arms and a rough voice demanded to know what was going on.

Paris didn't even have to look around; the source of the voice was all too familiar to her. She groaned and dropped her head, covering her face with her hands. Then she lowered her hands, straightened her shoulders, and looked to each side before sighing heavily. "Titus, have you met my brothers? Lucien, Wade, Julian and Philippe, this is Titus Argonne."

She looked around at the unsmiling, brutally handsome faces of her tall and untamed brothers and sighed. It was going to be a very long night.

To My Readers

I can't tell you how much your support has meant to me. Your words of encouragement and expressions of appreciation are what keep me going. I hope you enjoyed John and Nina's story. She was one of my favorite heroines to write about because she was such an unusual character.

In answer to your many cards, letters and e-mails, Paris and Titus are next! I promise those two will find their way to each other in spring of 2006. Of course, Titus might have to battle his way through her big brothers, but I think he's up to the task.

Look for their story, *The Closer I Get to You*, in the spring of 2006. Until then, thanks again and again for your support and enthusiastic response. Stop by my website, www.melanieschuster.com and say hello.

Stay blessed and be healthy!

Melanie
I Chronicles 4:10
MelanieAuthor@aol.com
P.O. Box 5176
Saginaw, Michigan 48603

About the Author

Melanie Woods Schuster currently lives in Saginaw, Michigan where she works in sales for the largest telecommunications company in the state. She attended Ohio University. Her occupations indicate her interests in life; Melanie has worked as a costume designer, a makeup artist, an admissions counselor at a private college, and in marketing. She is also an artist, a calligrapher, and she makes jewelry and designs clothing. Writing has always been her true passion, however, and she looks forward to creating more compelling stories of love and passion in the years to come.

MORE SIZZLING ROMANCE BY
Kayla Perrin

BOOK YOUR PLACE ON OUR WEBSITE AND MAKE THE ARABESQUE ROMANCE CONNECTION!

We've created a customized website just for our very special Arabesque readers, where you can get the inside scoop on everything that's going on with Arabesque romance novels.

When you come online, you'll have the exciting opportunity to:

- View covers of upcoming books
- Learn about our future publishing schedule (listed by publication month and author)
- Find out when your favorite authors will be visiting a city near you
- Search for and order backlist books
- Check out author bios and background information
- Send e-mail to your favorite authors
- Join us in weekly chats with authors, readers and other guests
- Get writing guidelines
- AND MUCH MORE!

Visit our website at
http://www.arabesquebooks.com